I0723921

EMOTIONS

THE COMPLETE DUOLOGY

VIOLA TEMPEST

Emotions
The Complete Duology

© Copyright 2023 Viola Tempest

All rights reserved. No part of this publication may be reproduced,
distributed, or transmitted in any form or by any means, including
photocopying, recording, or other electronic or mechanical methods, without
the prior written permission of the publisher, except in the case of brief
quotations embodied in critical reviews and certain other non-commercial
uses permitted by copyright law.

Any references to historical events, real people, or real places are used
fictitiously. Names, characters, and places are products of the author's
imagination.

Cover Design by CReya-tive

CONTENTS

PARALYZED EMOTIONS

EMOTIONAL DEVIANTS

EMOTIONS

THE COMPLETE DUOLOGY

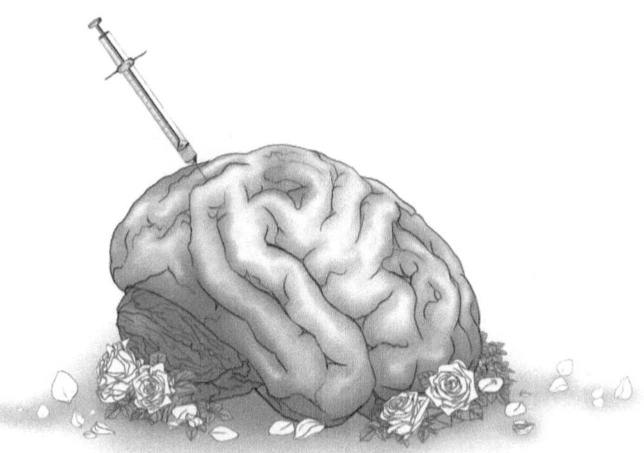

VIOLA TEMPEST

PARALYZED EMOTIONS

EMOTIONS BOOK ONE

PARALYZED EMOTIONS

EMOTIONS BOOK ONE

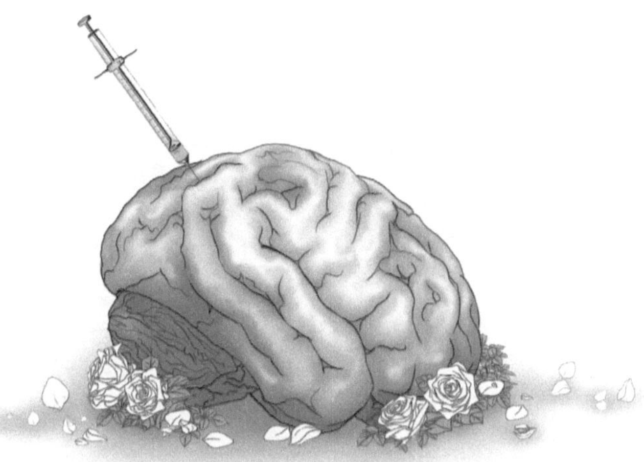

VIOLA TEMPEST

PROLOGUE

Hi, my name is Constance Fay. Two years ago, I was captured and forced into Bellevue Psychiatric Hospital against my will. But I was made to believe it had been my choice.

Here is my story.

The thing about Bellevue, is that nothing is what it seems, at least, not on the inside.

I was admitted into the hospital for one reason, but soon enough, I started doubting what that reason had been. I was fed lies and was left broken and confused. My skin was violated against my will, and the feeling of needles piercing through me continue to haunt me to this day.

I was used like a lab rat, abused, lied to, and it felt like torture, even worse than any nightmare I ever had. I used to feel so much that, at times, I wouldn't even be able to think straight, and nightmares would cloud my judgement. Pills after pills were fed into my system, and I didn't even know what I was taking. I felt afraid most of the time, and darkness took over constantly. I didn't know what was real and what was a nightmare.

Maybe it was all a nightmare.

I did meet someone, though. Someone who would change everything, someone who taught me how to laugh again, and reminded me what it was like to be alive. We spent our days together, helping each other heal and remember. Trying to figure out what was real and what was not, sifting together through our memories to try and figure out the truth. The truth about ourselves. The truths about the hospital and it's director, Dr. Theodore Faulkner.

Our torturer.

But all that is forgotten now. Thinking about it is almost like looking at a movie through a dirty glass. I can remember everything that happened. I remember the stingy pain of needles being plunged into my skin, the black ink spilling down the walls, the nightmares, the pills being shoved down my throat. I remember the last time I saw him. The last time I saw Kai. I remember blood, so much blood. But the dread is gone.

When I think about it, about every single memory of my time at the hospital and what came after, the drama that came before and led me there... I feel nothing. I'm happy.

So stupidly, irrationally happy. Everything's fine. So, I look back in my journals, endless documents of those days.

On all the pain and dread. I let it all sink in; I let it get into my skin. But it doesn't. I'm happy, so I place my father's gun against my forehead while I read.

Everything's fine. Just fine. Perfectly fine.

CHAPTER
ONE

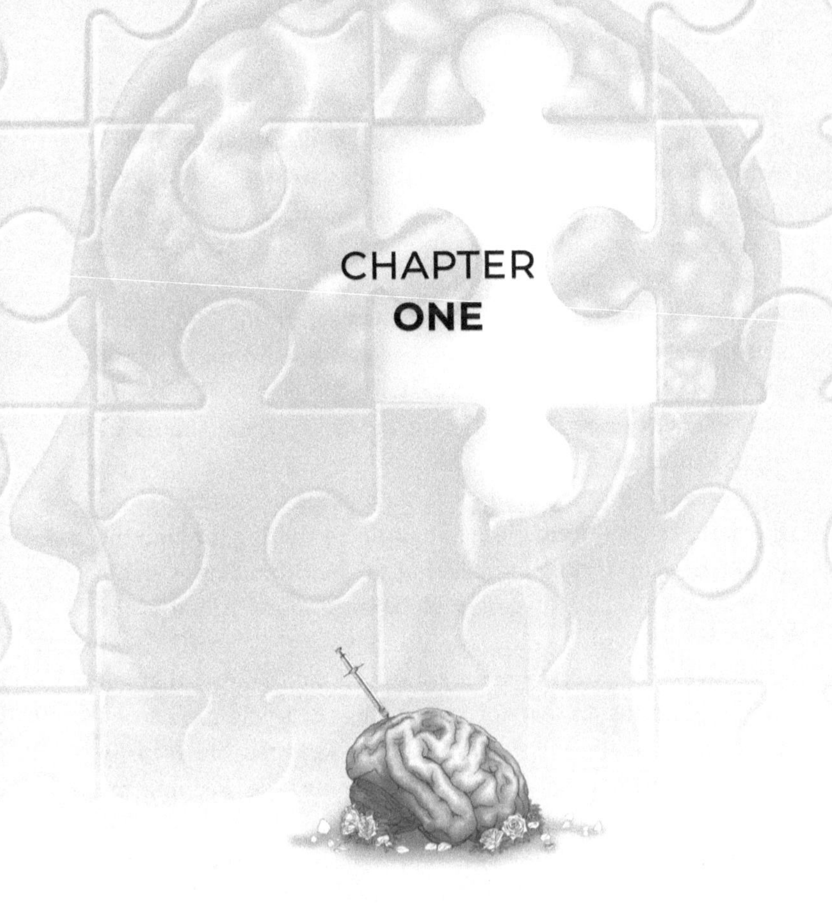

The night was dark; the crows were cawing in the far distance. A quiet whimpering disturbed the eerie silence that fell heavy on the bleak and solitary hospital room inside the adult ward of Bellevue Psychiatric Hospital. Inside, lied a young woman, me, my appearance sickly thin and pale. My frail body was curled up on a small metal bed frame, my breaths flowing heavily from my mouth.

I didn't know what was going on, or why I was so frightened, but my mind was stuck in an empty dream, floating in a pool of black, aimlessly. It was a thick black oozing liquid that took over everything. A heavy darkness that surrounded me, pressing into my body, stealing the air out of my lungs. And inside that darkness, a pair of glowing yellow eyes watched me. Waiting, watching, piercing me.

Needles were stuck into my arms, stabbing me over and over. A knife, a small bottle of pills, a bottle of something else. A blanket, restrained in my arms, screaming. So much screaming. The beeping of machines all around me, a sterile and eerie room, the walls black with the oozing liquid, but that seemed wrong. They should be white. There should be lights shining into my eyes.

And suddenly, a casual smile tried to get to me through all the darkness, a sincere piece of happiness ripping through the blackness with teeth and nails, but the black mass took it, ate it. It took him, and I was left alone once more. Alone in the emptiness of it all.

However, it wasn't the darkness and the shadows that left me whimpering in fear for hours on end; I was used to all that. They usually went away when I wrapped the security blanket I had kept since childhood around me, keeping me safe.

No, it was what lurked beyond the darkness that kept my sweat and tears pouring, draining my essence until I became the void that lurked around me. Every emotion that I couldn't feel bombarded me, and no matter how hard I screamed, it all just wouldn't stop. I desperately wanted to be free from it all. I was willing to try anything.

I continued to toss and turn, my blanket falling over onto the cold cement floor. I then shivered from the sudden chill blowing into my room. The shiver quickly turned into violent shakes, forcing me awake. Three in the morning was never the best time for me. What was I even doing? I didn't belong here.

I tried to keep myself warm, wrapping my slender arms around my emaciated body. I sat up and felt my oversized white jacket slipping off one side of my shoulder. As I scanned the room for anything unfamiliar, my heart began to beat quicker in my chest.

However, as expected, there wasn't much to be seen. Nothing but a chair and a doorless closet, filled with the same monochrome colored clothing I had been wearing for the past several months. Hell, this cell of a room barely had a window to shine the moonlight in, only a thin sliver of glass pressed against the thick walls. And the light above me? Nothing but dimness as it flicked on once every twelve hours. Sometimes I wondered if a prison cell would've been more spacious.

My head was pounding, and my bladder felt ready to explode. Walking over to the bathroom every night proved to be a nightmare. None of the inmates, I mean patients, were allowed the privilege of their own private bathrooms, forcing us to travel down several halls just to empty ourselves out. But making that trek during the nighttime proved to be much worse than during the day. When the lights were out, the crazies came out too, turning my trip to the bathroom into a nightmare on death row.

As I stood up from my bed, my legs almost crumbled beneath the weight of my body. The room spun like crazy around me as I tried to steady myself from falling by grasping onto the metal post. Even in motion, the chill continued to pierce against me. Why won't it leave me alone? I turned toward the sliver of the window and hissed as the cold bit into my skin. I tugged at the jacket, pulling it over my shoulders again, just to watch it slip off.

God damn.

My stomach twisted and turned as I proceeded toward the wooden door. However, the pain was so unbearable, like sharp knives stabbing into my wounds. I doubled over with a groan, trying not to throw up, blood or bile, God only knew what. It felt like days since I last ate anything; not like anything was going to come up, anyway.

I picked myself up, but time after time when I tried to stand up, my stomach cramped, causing even more pain than before. I tried taking a few deep breaths again, hoping that the pain was just due to nerves.

After a few deep breaths slowly through my nostrils, and trying not to focus on the agonizing pain, I finally straightened my body up, ready to try again. I took no more than two steps before the pain forced me to hunch over yet again as I tumbled down and dragged my feet across the cold flood. It felt like I hadn't moved in months, my joints and muscles so weak I didn't even know how I was still standing.

Several agonizing moments later, I finally reached the wooden door and pressed my forehead up against it, letting out a loud groan. My body was still shivering. I couldn't understand why everything was so fucking cold. For a moment, I thought about crawling back over to the metal frame and grabbing my blanket off the ground, but I knew I didn't have the strength to make it. The added weight would just hold me in my place.

Reaching my right hand up along the door, I frantically searched along the board for a handle. No luck. Nothing but splinters and glass. After several more tries, I gave up and slid back away from the door, staring at the object with my own eyes. No wonder I couldn't find a handle; there was no handle to grab onto, nothing resembling an actual door other than the few hinges along the side of the frame. I remembered a handle; why wasn't it there?

"Hello?" I called out hesitantly, hitting my hand against the door with every ounce of energy I could muster up.

The sound of my palm slapping against the metal echoed through the room, and an unbearable ringing started in my ears. I squeezed my eyes shut, focusing on anything but the pain, and continued knocking with the little strength I had left.

Then I saw it, a shadow, the creepy shadow in my dreams.

I shifted my body back in tension and fear. I heard scraping against the other side of the door, a panel sliding over to the left before bright yellow eyes came into my vision. My eyes burned from the intensity of the creature's eyes, and I flinched back even more, stumbling over the jacket that had completely fallen off my shoulders.

"Hello?" I asked again but with little confidence.

Despite the haunting shadow, at least that confirmed that I wasn't alone, I wasn't sure if this bright-eyed creature was any better than solitude, but maybe my imagination was just running amuck. Either way, I had to find out what was going on. I didn't belong here, yet, here I was, with no answers or hint of a way out.

"Hello? Can you help me? Why am I here?" I called out once again, expecting another response of silence, when I heard a deep voice call out.

"Back up, darling," the voice of a man called out, his voice squeezing into the room through the small constructed window.

I frowned, ignoring his warning and only stepped closer to the door. I could hear chiseling and scraping on the other side, and was curious as to what was going on. I reached over to the spot where the sound was coming from, just to quickly pull my hand back into my stomach and wince.

"What the hell? You scraped me!" I shouted in pain as red marks formed along my fingertips. "Tell me what's going on, right now!"

"I warned you to back up," his voice was deeper this time, and sounded like he was trying not to laugh.

"I want answers," I responded.

It was a wonder to me why I was trying to be defiant. It probably would have been easier to get answers if I listened to him, but my head was too heavy to even attempt to think straight.

He let out an annoyed sigh and then disappeared.

Confused, I pressed my forehead against the door and tried to look out past the window into the hallway, but all I could see was a door right across from mine and the walls on either side of it.

"Please!" I called out into the hall.

I jerked my head back and nearly stumbled to the ground. The sudden movement caused my stomach to cramp again, but it didn't hold a candle to the fear that shook the rest of my body. A stick with a metal-pointed end was sticking through the slot, and the bright-eyed man wielding it laughed again. I held up my hands and lowered my head as a sign of obedience.

He was a monster, laughing like a maniac with his twisted teeth and scary eyes. He was a nightmare that came to reality to haunt me.

A second later, as if on a timer, the door unlocked and slid open. I watched as two white shoes came into my line of vision, and I slowly traveled up the length of the man's body and settled on his face, successfully taking him all in.

His eyes weren't as bright as I thought they were, and his shadow was nothing out of the ordinary like the one in my nightmares. He wasn't very tall, and his face looked pinched. Like his mother squished his cheeks together too much as a child, and it stayed like that for the rest of his life.

He was still holding the stick, jabbing the pointed end into his own hand to look menacing. Or maybe he was just holding it. It would have worked if he weren't wearing rainbow scrubs. Finally, he let out a sigh and dropped the stick to his side, tapping the tip of it against the ground.

"Good morning, Ms. Fay," he said in a falsely sweet smile as he took a large step toward my direction, the sound of his step trembling against the Earth.

I stepped back, wanting to keep a good distance between us. Given the dimensions of the room though, I figured that would be nearly impossible to do. My eyes darted to the stick he still held in his hand and wondered what he would have done if I continued to rebel.

"Ms. Fay, do you know where you are?" he asked, looking around the room. Disappointment crossed his face when he noticed that the blanket was on the ground. "Tsk, you know that you have to keep this room clean. It is not yours."

I was about to tell him off, order him to give me some answers, and let me out of here, but all that came out was, "What do you mean this isn't my room?"

He gave me a tired look before bending down to pick the blanket off the ground. I almost lost it when he brought it up to his nose and sniffed it before placing it back down onto the bed.

"You're just a guest here," he spoke with such sincerity. "You wouldn't stay at a friend's house and just leave all your belongings scattered across their floor, now, would you?"

Suddenly, I saw it again. The bright glow deep inside his eyes sprouted up once again, a glow so bright that it blinded me, a sharp pain zipping across my head as I stumbled back and scraped my skeletal knees against the sharp frame of the bed.

The man rushed forward, grabbing hold of my shoulders and steadying me. "Are you okay?" he asked.

My body froze. His hands felt so cold, like a block of ice, and up close, his eyes looked even more menacing. I struggled to look him in the eyes. My body was shaking faster than ever, but I didn't want to risk making a move that would potentially get me killed.

My heart pounded faster as I saw him reach inside his body, my instincts telling me a knife was on the other side. If he was willing to stab me before, what's to stop him from doing it again?

"Whoa, whoa! What are you doing? What is that? Are you trying to kill me?" I shouted as I tried to twist my body away from him, stopping when I heard the sound of a simple click.

A simple flashlight.

"Calm down, Ms. Fay. It's just a flashlight. I just need to make sure your vitals are stable."

For someone who was just accused of attempted murder, he sounded awfully calm. He grabbed the back of my head to keep me from jerking as he flashed the blinding light straight into my eye.

"Nothing too out of the ordinary," he said as he clicked the light off. "How are you feeling today?" He checked my pulse with two fingers against my wrist while he waited for an answer.

So much had happened in such a short period of time that I couldn't tell the difference between my fear and my confusion. I climbed up and slumped my limp body back against the wall and closed my eyes. Everything was piling up in my head so quickly that I couldn't focus on what to say next. It was beginning to be too much, and all I wanted to do was lie in bed underneath the blanket until it sorted itself out again.

"Ms. Fay. Ms. Fay, wake up! You're dozing off again," I heard a voice whisper deep inside my head again as my body was jostled.

I opened up my eyes slowly and saw the bright-yellow eyes once again, my pale skin turning a shade of green in response. I covered my mouth and breathed through my nose quickly to dispel the feeling of vomiting right then and there.

"Stop, please stop," I begged against my hand.

I looked up at him, and he quickly withdrew his hand from my shoulder. "I'm feeling sick to my stomach," I muttered, letting my hand fall onto my lap. I stared down at the lines on my palm for a moment before looking up again. "Why am I here? Where am I?"

He clasped his hands behind his back, his voice suddenly soft. "You are at Bellevue Psychiatric Hospital. You were brought in a few months ago after you threatened to set your parents' house on fire with them and yourself in it, well, according to your file, anyway. I've only just been assigned to your care. Your family didn't feel safe with you around, so they sent you here. You don't remember?"

I frowned in disbelief. That didn't make much sense. Why would I be at my parents' house? I was twenty-seven. Was I staying over? The last time I had been with my parents was for Christmas. Was it around Christmas?

"That doesn't make any sense," I told him. "Why can't I remember that?"

"It was a traumatic event for everyone involved, and your brain must have blocked it out from your working memory," he told me. "It happens all the time with patients who experience trauma." He checked my eyes again before standing straight. "Stay here. I'll be right back."

Before I could get another word out, the door was locked again, and the strange man was gone. I blinked a few times and shivered again. I grabbed the blanket that was now balled up on my bed and wrapped it around my shoulders.

Left alone in my room, my head started spinning, and I thought I could hear voices whispering to me.

"Bellevue is a dark, dangerous place," they told me.

"You should get out of here; you'll never be the same ever again."

I pressed my hands against my ears, trying to shush the voices in my head. I didn't know much about Bellevue Hospital, but I vaguely remembered the stories. I remembered people whispering about this place, about weird experiments being done in the dark basement, about people leaving not the same way they entered.

But how could I know what was real and what was not? Had I really heard any of that, or was it just my mind conjuring up stories because I was scared? More than scared, I was terrified. I couldn't remember where I'd been the last three months of my life, if what the mysterious man with yellow glowing eyes had said was right.

In that precise moment, I could barely remember the night before, or even the dream I just had a few minutes prior. So, how could I know if anything my mind was whispering to me was even real?

"You know what's real; you just need to push past the fog," a male voice whispered inside my head.

No, no, no. I couldn't do that. There was too much pain behind that curtain of fog; that fog was what was keeping me sane. But, was I even sane? I wanted to scream out loud; the burning in my lungs was getting unbearable.

What was real? What was not? I wanted out. I needed to get out of this horrible cell. The walls were pressing in on me, and the voices wouldn't shut up.

Just as my eyes were getting too heavy to keep open, as the walls were finally closing in on me, killing me, the door unlocked again. I lifted my head and watched as the same man came in with a glass of water and some pills. I looked down at the small white pills and gulped. I had never been a fan of taking medication. It felt wrong going down my throat no matter how I took them.

"I don't want them," I told him quietly.

"I'm not asking. I'm telling," he told me. "Take the pills. They'll help with the headaches and the nausea. Swallow them, and I'll take you out to the yard."

"The yard?" I asked innocently.

The pills rattled inside the cup as he shook his head. "With the other patients. Non-violent, of course."

"I don't want to—"

"You have to. Take the pills so we can get going." He sighed.

It was clear that he had enough of me already.

"I'm not taking them! I'm not taking anything you're giving me! You're trying to kill me!" I yelled all of a sudden, all the fear and anger I was feeling exploding out of me as I knocked the cup out of his hand.

"Ms. Fay, that was very rude," the man said in a calm tone, almost too calm. He moved over to the floor and picked up the pills, his eyes never leaving me. "Please, take them. Trust me, you'll love the yard. You haven't been out there in a long time; the sun and fresh air will be good for you."

I cowered back against the wall, looking at him with huge scared eyes. "You're not lying to me? I can really go outside?" I asked in a small, shattered voice.

"You have my word," he said solemnly.

I swallowed hard and snagged the pills he had picked up, and the water as well, as he stretched his hands out closer to my face. The pills rolled around the bottom of the cup, and I let out a shaky breath. I closed my eyes before tossing the pills into my mouth and chasing them down with the entire cup of water.

The pills forced their way down my throat, scrapping the inside of my throat on their way in, and I focused on the man's chest. The feeling made me gag, and I had to do everything in my power not to send them back up. It was causing tears to form in my eyes.

The man sighed and popped his hip out to the side.

"I hate when you're dramatic," he mumbled almost too low for me to hear, snatching the small cup away from me.

Did he really say that? Or was it all inside my mind? He waited until the pained expression left my face before helping me to my feet.

"Alright, come on."

My body was still shaking as I leaned more into him than I would have liked to, but I didn't care. I couldn't care. It slowly got easier to walk though as the medication started to take effect.

As we approached the gates, I could hear loud screams and what sounded like a trashy reality show. I glanced up at the man.

"Do I have to?" I asked, not sure how I was going to like this.

I felt anxious and uneasy about seeing people; I felt like I'd been alone for so long.

He gave me a smug look before helping me stand straight again and opening the door.

"You don't have a choice, Princess. Go out. You'll like it."

CHAPTER
TWO

I looked around the yard when I stepped out, and I scrunched up my nose as I was assaulted by the smell of at least fifty people crammed into one tiny gated yard. At least, it wasn't as cold as my room was. The sun was warm against my skin, and that was a relief. It felt like a blessing to have the warmth tickling my skin, and I closed my eyes against the brightness for a second, taking in the pleasant sensation.

Everyone crammed in that weeded yard looked just as miserable as the next. There were some people tearing the skin off their bodies, others pulling out strands of hair. However, as I looked at the other patients, I realized that most of them looked painfully normal. There were a few who were facing walls or muttering to themselves, but a lot of them just looked like regular people, just like me.

But something in my head told me that they weren't normal. I wasn't normal either apparently, but I didn't feel like they probably did. I turned back to the man and swallowed hard.

"I don't belong here," I said quietly so the others wouldn't hear.

The man raised his eyebrow. "You threatened to burn a house down. I'm afraid you do belong here," he told me.

He pushed me gently into the yard with a wink before walking away and locking the gate behind him.

I stumbled forward, feeling eyes turn to look at me. I closed my eyes and took a deep breath to calm myself down. It was probably just my paranoia. As soon as they caught a quick glimpse of me, everyone who had first turned looked away. It still felt like everyone was staring at me though, and it made my stomach twist.

It took a few seconds for me to regain my composure, and I started to walk toward the chair that was pressed against the far wall that faced the outside world I so much struggled to remember, a world I couldn't remember ever living in.

My memory was getting the best of me. I couldn't remember being stuck in this hospital for more than a couple months, so why couldn't I remember life anywhere else but here? I could picture the faces of my family, my parents, and a few facts about my life, but I couldn't remember the exact moment I was admitted into the hospital, or why, how I had gotten here.

I settled into the chair as I saw other patients do the same, all wishing they didn't belong here. I looked over to my left and saw a pair arguing, most of the sounds high-pitched and animated. Sometimes I wondered, was I crazy before coming here, or did all of this drive me there, a constructed stage to bring seemingly normal people together just to brand them as insane?

I did remember something that seemed to be from when I first got here, maybe the first few weeks. A burly woman, or at least I hoped was a woman, had tried to start a fight with me to assert her dominance. But I wasn't about that life, that drama. I didn't come here to get pushed around like a prisoner. I'd respond much better to those who were civilized and treated me like a decent human being.

Then again, the yellow-eyed man did tell me that I had threatened to burn down my parents' home. I didn't think I was even capable of something like that, but apparently, I was. Did I actually start the fire, though? Would that make me a violent patient, a criminal, instead of someone who acted impulsively and lost control in that very moment?

The questions clouding my brain were starting to hurt my head again, so I turned my focus to the people around me, instead. There were honestly too many of them for the size of this dinky yard we were in. It was barely larger than the size of the cold room I had been sleeping in.

It became hard to keep track of who was who too, but some of their faces were vaguely familiar. There was a woman who looked oddly similar to me, dressed in the same oversized white jacket that I was wearing. The bottom was torn and frayed like mine from when I kept picking the exposed threads out and putting them in a pile.

There was also a guy to my right who kept watching and imitating a nurse. The nurse wasn't doing anything, except maybe talking with the other nurses. She had a silly smile plastered on her face, completely ignorant of the weird people doing weird things in front of her. She seemed so immune to it all, but maybe that's how it was after a sane person was exposed to the crazy for such a long time.

The guy would watch the nurse and then use a crayon to write something down as quickly as he could. Whenever the nurse looked over, he'd put the piece of paper under his leg and look away like he wasn't doing anything. The nurse would always give a knowing smile before shaking her head and going back to her conversation with the other nurses.

It was so odd.

There was an older man in the farthest corner from me. He was sitting at a tiny table with two chairs, in front of a chess board. He'd think for a while, move one of the white pieces, and then he'd jump chairs, going to the other side of the table and thinking for a long time before moving a black piece. He kept repeating the same pattern, thinking, moving, and then changing from one side of the board to the other. He'd run his fingers through his ashen hair every once in a while, and then bite his lip. His lips would then move slowly, as if he was talking to himself, and the sight made me so nervous I had to look the other way.

A few feet away from me, there was a girl sitting on the floor. She couldn't be more than eighteen years old. There were no kids in this hospital, so that's why I knew her age, but in all honesty, she was so frail and small that she seemed to be barely fourteen. She had a stack of dry leaves from the trees as well as little sticks, and she spread them out all over the floor. They were classified by shape, color, and size, a perfect arrangement of dead nature. It was oddly satisfying to watch her measure the leaves against each other, over and over again.

I kept looking around, trying to find little details about the people around me. There was one guy that seemed completely out of it. He was talking to himself, settling down closest to the outside world. He was sitting on the grass, his legs folded over each other, with his feet resting over his knees.

I tried to strain my hearing to see if I could pick up on

his words, but the arguing couple next to me was getting louder and louder. I kept watching him though, trying to figure out what he was on about. It took me a while, but I finally realized he wasn't talking to himself, but rather talking to the tree on the other side of the fence. He was gesturing with his hands as he was telling it a story, or that's what I thought.

I sighed, happy that I wasn't like any of them. If I were, then I would rather not be seen by anyone. I would be happy living away in the little room they had me trapped in. It would be less embarrassing that way.

"People watching, huh?" a handsome man asked as he fell into the spot next to me.

I jumped and looked over at him. I wasn't used to feeling so jumpy, and I wasn't sure if my heart could take another scare, especially not after the events from the morning. I looked at the man before me for a moment before turning my head away from his radiant smile.

"I'm not here to talk."

The man frowned and shifted on his seat. He looked out to everyone around us. The frown didn't last long, and he was smiling again.

"Oh, come on. You have to talk to me. I'm the most interesting person here," he teased. He nudged me and quickly leaned back at the disgusted look on my face. "I'm only playing. I'm probably the most boring person you'll ever meet."

"Then why are you even talking to me?" I sighed, wiping a hand across my arm where he'd touched me.

He clearly didn't get the hint.

He shrugged innocently and held out a hand. "I'm Kai Hastings."

I stared at his hand before looking up at him. I gave him a loose handshake before pulling my hand back into my lap.

"Constance Fay."

"I know," he said with a wide grin.

My frown matched the size of his grin. "What do you mean? How do you know?" I asked.

I didn't like someone new just knowing who I was. It was different when it was a nurse, a doctor, or the creepy man with bright yellow eyes who seemed to know so much about my existence here. He probably had seen my file a million times in the few months that I had been here.

But this was a man I just met. I couldn't remember ever seeing him in the hallways before, not like I had many memories of them, anyway. He was someone who shouldn't know anything about me. As far as I knew, the only place I'd spent time in since I got here was in my room.

There was no way that he could know me. Was there? Had I been in this yard before? Why couldn't I remember that? I felt like I had been in this same chair before, like I was having some sort of déjà vu.

Kai shrugged his shoulders and leaned back against the chair beside me. He pushed himself up before falling onto his foot after he tucked it underneath himself.

"I just know things," he told me. He tapped a finger against his temple as he winked. "It's a superpower of mine."

"Oh, great, another crazy one," I murmured.

I turned away and caught sight of a woman trying to flirt with a nurse to get a double dosing of her daily meds.

"I've got a secret for you," Kai told me despite my blatant attempts at ignoring him.

He poked my arm when I didn't look over. His finger pressed almost directly against the bone, and the smile disappeared quickly from his face.

When I turned, he quickly turned it back to his megawatt smile. He didn't want me to see him concerned or upset. It wasn't the right time.

"Stop touching me," I growled, pushing his finger away.

"But I've got a secret," he insisted.

"I don't care."

"Yes, you do."

"No, I don't."

"I know that you do. Do you want to know why?"

I groaned and pulled my knees to my chest to hide my face away.

"Please, leave me alone," I practically begged.

A nurse walked over to us with a frown on her face.

"Is everything alright over here?" she asked, looking between the two of us.

"Yes," Kai said before words could exit my mouth. "We're just talking. You know how it is. Sometimes people bicker. Don't worry about it."

I opened my mouth to speak, but the words fell back down my throat as the nurse started walking away. I turned slowly to face Kai.

"We're not bickering. I want you to go away, and you're refusing to leave."

"I only want to talk, Constance," he told me. He softened his smile and lowered his head a little to look more welcoming. "I promise… that's all I want to do."

I let out a heavy sigh before turning to fully face him.

"Fine." I gave in.

"Fine?" he asked, his smile widening again.

"Yes! But I don't want to hear about any secrets you have. I don't need some crazy guy whispering conspiracy theories in my ear."

I'd overheard one of the crazies arguing about the government hiding the fact that there were lizard people living among us and posing as politicians to take over the Earth. I didn't need any further craziness like that.

"That's fine with me," he told me. He wiggled a bit as he got more comfortable in his seat. He looked around the room, biting his lip before nodding. "Okay, who do you think has been here the longest?"

"I think I'm going to have to go with the man talking to

the tree," I responded, giving in as I knew he wasn't going down without a fight.

Surprisingly, we continued talking for the rest of the day. I didn't want to admit that I enjoyed his company, but I did. He seemed more normal than the people surrounding us, though, some of them didn't seem to be too far gone, which was good.

I was simply happy to have someone to talk to, even if for a little bit. As I curled up in my stiff, cold bed that night, I figured I could survive my short stay here.

At least, I hoped it was short.

CHAPTER
THREE

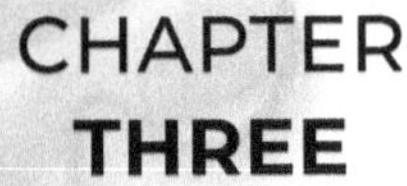

The next morning, I found myself in the same spot as the day before. I was one of the first ones in the yard and couldn't be less thrilled. Despite the length of time, it was difficult to see how people could remain so occupied with absolutely nothing to do other than pick at our own fingernails. It also felt a lot smaller than the day before. With all these people, I found it easier to toss and turn in my own bed.

I struggled to relax and remain in my own thoughts with so many people trying to have conversations around me all at once, screaming at each other. I wanted so desperately to ask one of the nurses to let me go back inside to spare my mind from this trash around me. But after getting rejected and ignored so many times, it just seemed like wasted breath to try again at this point.

I was chewing on my nail as I continued to stare at the bickering couple before me. My eyes were glued to the woman on the left like a screw, the one who I thought resembled me. She was a very odd-looking woman, her hair tied in six different hairstyles, and her clothing torn only on one side. When she saw me staring, she came over to me and stood a few inches away, looking down at me.

"You look like I used to when I was younger," she said, and then started to chew on her nail.

I looked up at her, and then looked back down. I didn't want to talk to her; I wasn't in the mood to make any friends here, and God damn, if I find out I have a relative here.

"What's your name?" she asked me. "I'm Cadence; you can call me Cady if you want. I don't remember if we've met before."

"Constance," I said in a low voice, feeling too rude not to reply to a direct question. "And you can call me Connie if you like it better."

"Great. We are friends now."

With that, Cadence walked away and stood by the outside fence, her eyes lost in the distance as she seemed to stare into nothing. She seemed smarter than the rest of the patients somehow, like she was hiding something that no one else knew about.

Kai walked into the yard not too long after that and spotted me. He grinned and bounced over to me before falling into the seat next to mine. He laughed as I bounced slightly from the startle that he gave me. I almost felt like I was having a heart attack, if the pills I had been forcibly taking didn't already push down any emotions I had left inside my body. He propped his elbow up on the back of his chair and turned his eyes to the same couple before me.

"You know," he started, successfully scaring me out of the trance the quarrel had on me. "My aunt used to behave like this all the time, always bickering and never accepting defeat, even though she knew she no longer had any ground to stand on."

I held a hand to my chest with my eyes shut as I took in steady breaths. My eyes opened only when he stopped talking, and he turned to look at me.

"You have got to stop scaring me," I told him.

I didn't want to be related to anyone in here... except maybe Kai.

"Sorry, it's a problem of mine. I'm just too quiet. I always snuck up on my parents as a kid without trying, and my older brother told me it's what gave my dad the heart attack that killed him," he told me.

I held a hand up between us and shook my head. "I just got so much information about your family in such a short amount of time. I think we need to talk about both incidents separately, and then I should be able to digest it."

Kai laughed quietly and nodded. "Alright, alright," he told me, trying not to laugh more. "My Aunt Shelby was my dad's older sister. She was an adorable little lady, but she was also crazy, old, and cranky. She was that typical lady in the neighborhood who knew everything that was going on with everybody else, even if she had no business in any of them. She loved the gossip as much as she loved her bickering. It didn't really matter what she believed in; she'd always go against whatever point we were trying to make. If I said salads were healthy, she'd find something against them and tell me I couldn't only live on salad if that was all I ever ate. Eventually, I'd give in and end up seeing that they weren't really that healthy, right?" Kai kept talking and talking, his eyes never leaving me as he told me story after story about her aunt's silly arguments against everything and everybody.

He moved onto talking about his father after that, telling me about how he'd died of a heart attack all of a sudden. It had taken a really hard toll on his family, and his mother had to struggle to keep the family afloat while working two part-time jobs at the same time. He talked about her with longing admiration, and I could tell that, despite their differences, they'd had a great and loving relationship.

————

As the day went on, I found myself hanging onto every story Kai had told. He had a lot of them, too. It was like I was living inside a story book. It made the day go by much faster, and I barely noticed if we had already had our morning pills and lunch or not. All the hours of the day seemed to fuse together, and I lost track of it, not really knowing which part of the day I was stuck in.

When we were settled on the chairs again, probably after lunch, I decided to take on the story telling. There was something that had been bothering me since I woke up the day before.

"I don't feel right being here," I told him quietly. I glanced at him before sitting up straighter. "Not in a 'I'm not crazy' kind of way, but more with the fact that this place just seems off."

"It *is* a mental hospital, after all; it tends to give the off vibe," he reminded me. He turned and crossed his legs on the chair. He rested his elbows on his knees, and then his chin on his hands. "But please, tell me more."

"Well… after I showered this morning, I saw something on my stomach that doesn't fit in with any part of my life or what I remember or what was told to me," I whispered. After making sure that no one was looking at us, I raised my shirt and showed him the scar that crossed over my stomach. "A few days ago, I didn't have this scar. I was clean. Fine. But after... after... seeing the man with the bright yellow eyes, this scar just started to mysteriously appear out of thin air."

Kai looked at the scar, and then looked up at me. It looked like he wanted to touch it, but he respectfully kept his eager hands to himself.

"The man with bright yellow eyes? Is he a patient here? I don't remember seeing him around, and I know a lot of people here," he said, tilting his head to the side.

"Yes! He came into my room a few days ago, told me he was a nurse, and that I threatened to burn down my parents' house with everyone still in it," I whispered. My eyes got wide, and I sat up quickly, putting my hands up. "I didn't though. At least, I don't think I did. It couldn't have been me. I couldn't honestly ever hurt my parents or commit such a crime. I just... I can't remember anything else."

Kai frowned and glanced around quickly. "Can I tell you my secret now?" he asked, moving closer to me. "I promise that it might help shine some light on the dark parts of your memory."

I groaned and shook my head. "No, I don't want to hear your secret," I mumbled.

It was easy to forget where we were when we were just talking about normal family things. I didn't want to be reminded about why we were both here. I didn't want to know why Kai was here. I was happy to wait in blissful igno-rance until I was allowed out. If he started acting crazy, then I would have to wait out the rest of my days in the hospital alone.

Kai let his shoulders sag, and he nodded.

"Okay, fine," he whispered softly. "I won't say it, yet. But I want you to remember that I know something you might need to know."

I sighed but nodded.

"I'll keep that in mind," I told him. "I think I might try to take a nap. The food might be the worst, but it makes me tired." I shifted on the chair and let my head fall back before closing my eyes.

Kai laughed quietly and looked around us.

"Good luck," he told me. "I doubt you'll be able to sleep here."

"I can sleep anywhere," I assured him. "Just make sure none of the weirdos come near me."

"I will be your ever-faithful knight," he told me with a smile.

He rested his head on his hand as he propped his elbow against the back of the chair.

He watched as my breathing evened out, and my clenched hands loosened enough to show that I was finally relaxed. It must hurt to see me as lost as I was, and all he could do was hope that I would listen to him one day.

CHAPTER
FOUR

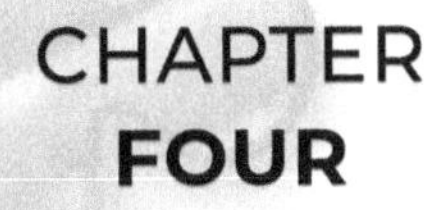

I had spent the week after that with that mindset. I didn't bring up feelings in the conversations with Kai again. I didn't want to ruin the experience I was having. I could barely remember the last time I had an actual good time.

Before my dark days, or the days I couldn't remember at all, I remembered spending Christmas at home. It was one of the last memories I had from everything that had happened before the hospital. One of the few that had come back to me only just recently. I just finished my semester at grad school and was ready to take the much-needed time off. I had been struggling a bit at school; my grades weren't as good as they used to be for some reason, but I couldn't remember exactly why.

I had fun then. It wasn't anything much, though. Just opening a few presents, having a few drinks, and spending time with family I rarely ever saw. But then I'd left and went back to my apartment, the one I shared with my best friend. I didn't really want to think about it, but for some reason, the memory kept poking at my brain.

I had walked into the apartment, all the holiday joy still lingering inside of me, and I opened the door to find… to find my best friend on the couch with my boyfriend, Kyle. I remembered my utter disbelief as I looked at them curled up together, so confident with one another. Leg over leg, and arms tangled in hair. A mass of limbs interlocked together. I think I yelled. Maybe I yelled.

Or I cried. I'm not really sure.

It took him a long time to get me to calm down, and after a few days of coming and going, of begging and apologizing, of presents and flowers and chocolate and so many 'It was a mistake,' I caved in. We ended up back together, pretending, or trying to pretend, that nothing had happened.

My friend moved out. My boyfriend moved in.

It was what was meant to happen, or that's what I told myself. I had spoken with one of my other friends about it, and she had insisted I was stupid for going back to him. But we've been together for almost five years, and I wasn't going to throw all that away over one silly mistake. I wasn't willing to forget about every single good moment we've had together because he had cheated on me once.

Or I hoped it was only once. I never talked to my roommate again; I didn't want to hear her excuses. She had tried to blame it all on my boyfriend, and that wasn't fair.

Kyle and I talked about it, set our differences aside, and he explained to me why he had felt so distant from me lately.

He'd said I was changing, but that he still loved me and wanted to stay with me. That he wanted us to work it all out. So, we did. He apologized over and over, we made peace, and we moved on… It was what was best for all of us.

All the fun I had while away was balled up and tossed into the back of my mind after I entered the apartment. Hidden away from me like all the rest. And the pain from the realization was blurry. It was how I knew how to function. It made me feel safe. All the happy memories were protected from my own self-deprecating mind.

But when I was there, talking with Kai about his life and hearing all his wild stories, I was happy. Well, almost happy. It was the closest I was going to get. I didn't think that I would ever be genuinely happy ever again.

As I was lying on the grass and listening to him speak, I couldn't help but imagine pictures that went along with the stories. I hadn't even realized that he stopped talking, and that I was just making up the rest of it in my head. It wasn't until he touched my arm that I did. I opened my eyes and looked at him.

"What? Is it time for therapy?" I asked.

He laughed at me and shook his head, "such a daydreamer, you are."

There were two types of therapy that every patient was expected to go to during their stay at Bellevue. Group therapy was every Tuesday and Thursday. On Mondays, Wednesdays, and Fridays, it was individual therapy.

It was a tedious and monotonous routine. Almost every day was the same, and if it wasn't for those specific activities we had once in a while, life could have just blended into one long day. The light turned on in the morning, and someone came over to make sure I was up. I'd be escorted to the bathroom, where I would use the facilities, get a shower if it was a Monday, Wednesday, or Friday, and then be escorted outside to the yard for an hour or two. Time wasn't something I was completely aware of inside that place.

After the time was up, we'd go back inside for our morning pills, or sometimes, they'd bring them over to us. Most of us were stubborn like that. We spent almost all morning out in the yard until it was time to head back inside to have the bland and boring lunch.

Lunch consisted mostly of purees and other shapeless meals that had absolutely no flavor to them. They changed color, but they all seemed to be the same crap. If I ate it all, I'd be allowed pudding, a measly four ounces.

The afternoons blended in between therapy sessions and group activities when we sometimes got to play silly games or even watch TV all together, and then dinner would be served back in our rooms, with more pills to make sure we slept through the night.

Little did those pills do to help me with the nightmares that haunted me every time I closed my eyes, though. Those yellow bright eyes kept coming at me night after night, together with images of needles piercing my skin, knives hanging from invisible hooks on the walls, and pills rolling down my tongue.

Therapy wasn't my favorite time of the day.

I had only gone to the group therapy sessions lately, and I didn't even dare to speak there. It would mean admitting defeat, which I wasn't ready for. I didn't need to be there, which meant I didn't need to participate in their group activities.

Well, except taking pills three times a day, which I couldn't avoid. I asked what mine were for, and I was told to ask my therapist. My therapist was the one who was supposed to be having one-on-one therapy sessions with me. But for reasons I couldn't fully understand, my sessions had stopped a few weeks ago. Or had it been months?

Apparently, I hadn't been cooperating, and after I attacked

my therapist by throwing something at him, they'd decided to have me in reclusion for a while. Was that why I had been locked in my room for so long? I didn't seem to be able to get a grasp on my own thoughts. It was like having a lot of information mixed up together inside my brain.

There were things I knew, but there were so many more I wasn't sure were right. I knew all this. I knew I had been in my room for weeks, knew I had been in the hospital for at least three months, but I couldn't be sure if any of that was really true.

Nothing was certain anymore. I couldn't trust my brain, and I couldn't trust what anybody was telling me, either.

And going back to the pills I was taking, I didn't believe that any doctor had actually prescribed me the medicine. I think the nurses were shoving generic pills down my throat, even if they didn't know what they were for. The thought of hiding them under my tongue had crossed my mind, but I convinced myself that someone would find out soon enough, and I would get in trouble. The image of the nurse with the stick had caused me enough worry about the kind of things they did to patients who stepped out of line, that I didn't want to experience it myself.

I blinked a few times as I realized that Kai was still speaking to me, but I had spaced out and heard none of it. I shook my head and pulled my hair out of my face.

"I'm sorry. I didn't catch a single word you said," I admitted.

Kai took a deep breath before letting it out slowly.

"I need you to really concentrate on what I'm telling you," he said each word as slowly and clearly as he could and nodded his head.

I looked him in the eyes and nodded my head along with him.

"I'm listening," I told him just as slowly.

"That nurse that you saw when you first woke up was

lying," he told me quietly. He grabbed me by the shoulders and squeezed them, hoping that it would keep my attention on him. "You've been here for almost a year. When you first got here, you were sent off, your memory erased. I can't keep this secret from you any longer."

I stared at him for a long while before letting out a hysterical laugh and shaking my head. "God. I can't take you seriously," I told him. "You always have these wild stories that you tell. I don't know if half of them are even true."

"Everything I have ever told you is the truth," he said seriously. "You can always rely on that. I wouldn't lie about something like this, anyway. They're trying to feed a fake memory into your head so you'll become more compliant. You can't let them do that. Do you understand?"

I rolled my eyes and shrugged his hands off. "Give it a rest," I murmured.

"I know you don't really remember what happened, but you need to try. They came to your room. At least two or three nurses. They dragged you out of the room, and you fought against them. I heard you actually knocked one of them in the jaw before they could restrain you. They took you to one of the labs in the basement. A dingy room with no windows. One that smells stale and feels like you're inside a prison, even more than your room. They injected something in your arm and kept you under observation for days. But something went wrong. It messed with your head, and your memories got all jumbled because of it." Kai was talking while looking at me intently, and I could see images popping in my head as he did.

I pictured three large male nurses coming into my room. My fist collided against one of the guy's jaws. The nurse with the bright yellow eyes grabbed me hard from the shoulders. A dimly lit room with no windows that smelled like a doctor's office and hadn't been inhabited for months. A syringe poking into my arm. No, that was a memory from my dreams. Needles piercing my skin over and over while surrounded by darkness. It was not real; it was all a dream. A nightmare.

"None of that is real," I said weakly.

Kai groaned and dug his fingernails into his palms. "Why don't you believe me?"

"I can't believe anyone who's in the loony bin," I admitted.

I dropped my feet onto the floor and leaned my head back.

"Especially the people who work here, the doctors, the nurses," Kai replied, his tone still serious. "They're the most delusional ones out of all of us. They think they're better than us just because they don't suffer from any kind of mental illness or are better at hiding it. They think they hold power over us."

"Do you hear yourself right now?" I asked, rolling my head to the side to look at him. His face was red, and his eyes were starting to shift around as if they couldn't settle on one thing. "Why are you here?" I asked.

Kai sat back, and his eyebrows shot up.

"What?" he asked.

"You heard me. Why are you here? What did you do to get sent here?" I asked again, leaning more toward him. I tilted my head to the side.

"Why does that matter?" He frowned and looked away.

I found out later that it wasn't that he was ashamed, but that he didn't want to tell me as it would've caused me to dismiss him even more.

I smirked. "You're one of the crazy ones, aren't you? The real crazy ones. Do you hear voices in your head? Are they telling you that the nurses are out to get us?"

Kai squeezed his eyes shut. "Stop," he told me in a whisper.

If he kept his eyes shut long enough, his mind would start closing off everything else before he got too worked up.

"I'm only asking you a question, Kai." I laughed. I moved closer. "Why won't you answer it? You tell me everything about your life. Why not this?" I felt like I was the one sounding crazy now.

"I don't want you to think I'm lying," he admitted.

It was clear that he had been in this type of situation plenty of times before.

I shrugged my shoulders. "I'm going to think that, anyway. Might as well tell me the whole truth."

He put his hands in his hair and tugged on the short strands. It helped only a little to keep him focused.

"I have PTSD," he finally told me. "I take medication, and it keeps my head clear of everything. I'm only here because… I lashed out once. It was the wrong place, wrong time. But I take my meds now, so you can believe everything I say. My head is clear. As clear as it's ever been."

I stared at him. I looked over his face quickly before going to his hands in his hair as they tugged.

"I don't," I told him. "How can I believe you?"

Kai stopped suddenly and let his hands drop to his sides. Then he remembered something.

"I knew your name," he told me.

"What?" I frowned.

"I knew your name. When I first came over to talk to you, I knew your name, and you asked me how I knew it. I lied to you then, but that was only because you honestly didn't know who I was. We've spoken before," he told me quickly. "In fact, I was one of the first ones you spoke to when you first got admitted. You sat in that same spot and people-watched before you walked over to talk to me. You told me that you wanted to go home, but you knew that it was best for you to be here until you were better."

I was quiet for a while. It was hard to believe anything he said anymore.

"I still can't believe a word you say," I admitted, taking my hands to the side of my head, trying to get the voices to quiet down.

I was so confused; I didn't know what to think anymore.

"Connie, please, listen to me. You need to make an effort to remember. You first came in here willingly. They brought you over after an incident, but it's not what they told you. It was something else. And after you came here, they convinced you to stay for a few days. You signed yourself in, said it'd be better for you, but after that, things changed. They… they did things to you, played with your mind, messed up your memories, and that is why you are here now, confused. I think you might also have some form of PTSD or something. What you went through, it was too much, so you're forgetting about it because you're not ready to deal with it. But I'm telling you, you're strong, and you can do this; you can deal with anything that happened."

He was talking so fast, in hushed whispers and looking around, as if he was scared that one of the nurses would hear what he was saying. I didn't know what to believe anymore. Everybody had a different story to tell about me.

But there was one thing I was sure about, if even just that.

"I wouldn't ever want to be here," I told him. I looked up at him, and my dark eyes seemed to have glossed over. "Why would I tell you that it was better for me to be here?"

Kai's shoulders fell. He pinched the bridge of his nose as he tried to organize his thoughts. After a moment, he tapped his finger against his nose and lifted his head.

"If you don't believe me, then just ask the director of the hospital, Dr. Theodore Faulkner. He'll definitely tell you the truth. He's not allowed to lie about this if you ask him straight up."

———

That night, I struggled to fall asleep. It was strange, since all day, I was mostly exhausted. My energy had come right after Kai told me to talk to the director. It wasn't something I wanted to think of, but it had been on my mind nonstop.

What was I going to do, go up to a nurse and demand to see the director of the entire hospital? Things like that didn't work in the real world. The nurses would probably shut me down or give me more medication to shut me up. I had seen what some of the other patients were taking and how it affected them.

In all honesty, I didn't know who to believe. What the nurse told me didn't settle well in how I believed myself to be, and what Kai told me couldn't be true because then, I was missing far more from my life than I first believed.

All I wanted were answers. Ones that were one hundred percent true. Ones that couldn't be overthought so much that they became just another fantasy inside my head.

CHAPTER
FIVE

Hours after shutting my eyes, I finally fell asleep. My body was stiff as a board as I lied in bed until a dream finally pulled me under.

The darkness had made its way back into my room, into my dreams, and it was taking over the whole place. I felt like there was more than just the shadow of a creature coming out of the wall, it's yellow eyes never leaving me. It was staring me down, watching me as I moved. It was a threat, or a warning. It was there to show me something, but I couldn't figure out what that something was. The twin yellow lights got brighter and brighter, and then it was gone. It had taken over the whole room, which was all coated in a yellowish tint, and inside of it: words.

"Stop!" I screamed against the words.

Each one of them kept growing and growing, and I screamed until my voice had disappeared. Even then, I didn't stop trying. My mouth hung open with every attempt.

The words broke against me, and relief rushed over me, but the black ink spilled out from them and started to fill the door like a rising tide. It climbed up my skin and reached my mouth, forcing itself down my throat until I was drowning.

I opened my eyes again, hoping that I was back in my room at home, but there was nothing but darkness surrounding me. No light. No hope. Just miles and miles of darkness.

A sharp pain tore through my stomach, and I clutched at it, trying to protect myself from whatever was happening. It didn't stop each shot of pain that went through me.

I was silently screaming in agony with my eyes wide and my fingers digging into my arms. Dark red liquid began pouring out around me. I tried to get away from it, but no matter where I went, it was there, and only spreading further.

I felt every part of my body getting heavier and let my head drop toward the ground as I struggled to hold myself up on all fours. The sight of the words *Help Me* carved into my stomach made me sick.

My eyes rolled back, and I fell to the side. Everything went black.

I woke up from the dream with tears streaming down my face. My hope for waking up in my own bed was a hopeless cause as soon as I saw the dim light that seemed to always shine on my face. I didn't move to wipe away the tears, but instead, my hands moved to my stomach, where I traced the scars that were left there. My fingers dug into the marred flesh, and it made me cry out in pain.

My cries poured through the thin cracks of the door and traveled up the hall to the nurses' station. As soon as one of them realized what it was, they rushed to my room and forced open the door. I curled up on my side, with my knees pulled up tight against my chest, as I kept pulling at my stomach. Each line of the scar had been reopened in the dream, and I wanted to feel that pain again if it only meant I could feel something.

Two other nurses rushed in after the first nurse had called for help. They wrenched my hands away from my abdomen from where they were trying so desperately to pull the mended flesh apart. I didn't struggle against their rough hands as they held me down against the bed. I looked at each of them, trying to find the words I needed to say.

The man with the yellow eyes was there, staring at me without saying a single word. His eyes were glassy and bright, and I felt like he was trying to tell me something, but I couldn't figure out what it was. He seemed to always be there lately. Wherever I looked, he was staring back at me, trying to talk without words, trying to get something out of me.

What did he want?

I quickly shook my head as I saw a needle produced seamlessly out of nowhere.

"No," I finally croaked. "I'm not... I don't want that. Please. I just want to speak to the director... I can't remember his name, but I want to speak to him."

"Hold her down," the nurse with the needle said. "This will be quick; you need to calm down."

"No!" I screamed at the top of my lungs. "I want to speak to the director. I'll calm down if you take me to him. You can't inject me!"

I kicked and thrashed, trying to free myself from the nurses' grasp. Their fingers were digging into my flesh, hurting me, pinning me, and I couldn't stop thinking about needles in other circumstances. I had a feeling some of the things Kai had said were true, but no, it couldn't be. It couldn't be.

"Let go of me. You can't do this! You can't!"

The nurses looked amongst each other. Some silent conversations were shared, and I felt like I had a chance. I let my body relax, looking up at the nurse with the needle.

"I promise I'll behave; just, please," I pleaded. "Take me to see the director."

"Maybe you should listen to her," the man with the bright yellow eyes said.

The nurse with the needle paused her approach and looked at the others before letting out a sigh. "Get her out of bed and cleaned up. I'll talk to Dr. Faulkner. If she shows signs of trying to hurt herself again, sedate her. Don't hesitate," she stated.

I was pulled from my bed and up into a standing position. I wavered slightly as I stood there, my eyes glazed over from the dream. There was no more waiting. I needed answers.

The nurses moved me around as they changed me out of my sweat drenched clothes. I knew I was being difficult for not cooperating, but I didn't have the energy to even try.

When I was finally changed, they led me out of the room, half dragging me. I looked around the halls as they walked. I tripped over my feet a few times, and the nurses leading me down the hall cursed every time they had to catch me and set me back onto my feet.

"Can't you walk for yourself?" one of the nurses asked angrily, gripping my arm.

"I'm trying," I mumbled. "I really am."

He rolled his eyes and tugged me to a stop once they reached the office door. He grunted and looked down as I fell into his side. He pushed me into the other nurse before knocking hard on the door.

An ancient man, with the name *Dr. Faulkner* on his lab

coat, opened the door and smiled at the nurse, the wrinkles around his mouth becoming more prominent.

"Please, leave her with me. I can handle this," he told them.

"She's a bit out of it," the nurse explained.

The director laughed. "I can see that," he assured them. He took me gently by the arm and pulled me away from the nurse holding me up. He looked at the two nurses again. "What? You know I'm a doctor, right? I do know how to care for my patients. Go. I'm going to talk with the patient in private."

I stared at Dr. Faulkner's hand, noticing how soft it felt. When he gently pulled me into a seat across from his and pulled his hand away, I started to look around his office.

Everything was mostly made of dark wood, and books lined the shelves around them. I wanted to get up and read them, but I knew that I was there for a reason.

But what reason?

"Ms. Fay," Dr. Faulkner said.

His gentle voice drew me back to the conversation, and I blinked at him.

"A nurse told me that you woke up from a nightmare trying to hurt yourself. Are you feeling alright?" he asked. "Are you hurt? Do you feel compelled to hurt yourself or others right now?"

I narrowed my eyes before looking down at myself, half expecting to see blood staining the front of my shirt. I ran my hand along my arm before pushing up the sleeve.

"I'm fine. I'm just a little raw from when the nurses grabbed me," I told him, showing the red rings that were wrapped around my arms.

Dr. Faulkner nodded slightly. "I will have a word with them and see what actions I need to take so that doesn't happen again," he assured me. He grabbed a notebook and a pen, and started to twirl the latter with his fingers. "Why did you wish to speak with me?"

I watched as the pen spun and then stopped, spun and then stopped, spun and then stopped, before looking up at him. If I focused hard enough, maybe I could remember what I wanted to say.

"I...," I started, but shook my head.

I tugged at my hair as I leaned forward. Why couldn't I remember? What was wrong with me? A wall was blocking me from all relevant thoughts, and there was no way of getting around it. I kept hitting against it, hoping that it would break.

"Depression usually does that," he told me calmly.

My head snapped up, and I frowned. "What?"

"Depression usually does that," he repeated. He stopped spinning his pen and used the tip of it to tap against the brain sculpture on his desk. "It makes it harder to remember things. You see, when you're suffering from depression, your brain can't process things as quickly as it should, so it can't retain a lot of the information that is given to you. It also makes it harder to concentrate and think."

"I'm not depressed," I told him.

Dr. Faulkner grabbed a file and showed me the file name. It was mine. He opened it, and then showed me the police report, which was on the first page. "You were brought here after you had an extreme episode and an overdose," he explained.

"That's not what the nurse told me," I informed him. "He told me I threatened to kill myself and my parents..."

"Yes, well, he was instructed to do that," he told me. "You were given an experimental drug that backfired. It made the symptoms of depression worse for you, and it seemed to have wiped quite a bit of time out of your memory. During your time on the medication, it was like you were in a coma. We had to give you a feeding tube because we couldn't wake you up long enough to eat. But don't worry, we're already working out the kinks and will be making a new one soon enough."

"What do you mean, I was given an experimental drug?" I asked, my hands shaking as I rested them on top of the desk.

"Yes, we work on experimental medicine in this facility, and you knew this when you signed up for the program. Here," he said, showing me a few papers with my signature on them.

They showed that I had agreed to try on experimental procedures, and that all decisions regarding my health were now to be made by the hospital.

"That can't... I would never..."

But it was my writing. It was my signature; it wasn't forged, and I knew that much. I pushed my brain, trying to remember, trying to get the memories that were lost to come back to me.

"Oh, yes, you did. You wanted us to fix you. You wanted to forget all about those petty dramas in your head, all those toxic memories of your past, and you were more than willing for us to do anything necessary for it. You wanted to be normal, that's what you said. You wanted the voices in your head telling you that you weren't good enough to stop. You wanted to be happy. And that's what we are working on. The trial we did on you might have been a failure, but it taught us a lot about the things we needed to improve. We have treated several patients ever since, and we are happy to say that the drug is doing much better than it did before. Less memory loss, a few issues here and there but...," Dr. Faulkner shook his hand dismissively in the air. "It's almost ready, and once it is, we will inject you once more and be done with all these unwanted and invasive memories."

I shook my head. "No... I don't want any more drugs. I want to go home," I told him. I hung my hands between my knees and leaned toward his desk. "I've got a life back there. Please."

Dr. Faulkner gave me an apologetic look and shook his head. "You can't go home just yet," he told me. "The court found you a danger to yourself and to others so they sent you here. This is supposed to be a time of healing. That's why we gave you the drug."

"You put me in a coma," I deadpanned. I squeezed my eyes shut as I fell onto the back of the chair. "I'm not a danger. I would never hurt myself."

"I have plenty of evidence here, and accounts from what happened earlier, to state otherwise," he told me. He held the folder up and offered a smile. "Take a look yourself."

I took the folder from him and started to look through it. With each page I flipped, my body began to sag more. It was like reading a story about myself, but one that was too real to be true. I kept reading over the police report on what happened that night.

I stopped moving, as all the memories of the events came back all at once. I closed my eyes and tried to grab onto each one of them.

CHAPTER
SIX

I couldn't remember the last time I had gotten a break. It felt like every day I forced myself to go through had added a brick into a bag I carried on my back. Whenever I did give myself a break, or at least when I didn't do anything, that bag sat square on my chest and pulled me deeper and deeper into a void I couldn't see.

It was a lot easier when I first started my graduate degree in physics. I was so excited that my dream school had finally accepted me. Everything seemed so new even though I had done a ton of schooling already. The professors treated me like I was an actual adult and challenged me. There were so many possibilities, so many doors that were just waiting to be opened.

I knew it was cliché, but it was my dream to become a physicist, and it was finally coming true. Everything I had ever wanted.

However, midway through my education, something shifted inside of me. It wasn't anything I could name, though. It felt like someone had picked up a piece of me and put it in the wrong spot.

The classes I found so easy before became a burden for me to even think about, and doing anything that was related to school made me shut down for hours. I would stare at a single page, draw aimlessly across my notes, or just simply give up and go to sleep.

When I wasn't doing schoolwork, I wasn't doing much else. My days consisted of going to work when I could and playing video games while forgetting to eat, or just simply not being hungry, to sleeping all day. It took all of my energy just to get up and go to class, and sometimes, I didn't even bother. Why would I? Even if I showed up, my professors would still give me zeros for the missed assignments.

The strangest part of all was that I honestly used to love going to class and doing homework. I used to love challenging myself. Then someone had to go and move that piece and change everything.

My grades started to slip, and professors who saw me as a star student stopped me after class and tried to speak with me. Even my favorite professor pulled me to the side one day.

"I noticed that you're not really producing the same quality work you did last year," he started, leaning against the table at the front of the room. He studied the bags under my eyes and how disheveled I looked. "Is everything alright?"

I simply shrugged. "Yeah," I told him. I shifted the bag on my shoulder. "Just tired, I guess."

He smiled and put a hand on my arm. "You know what it sounds like you need? A vacation. Last summer, I went on a solo trip to Peru…"

A balloon started to fill with air inside my chest, and it pressed against my lungs, making it harder to breathe. I closed my eyes, trying to focus on what he was saying, but it became more difficult with each passing second.

"And when I was at the beach, I felt so relaxed. It was the perfect getaway for me to…"

He kept talking, and I kept trying to catch his words in the air, but they felt ethereal; I just couldn't grasp them. My eyes were barely open, but unseeing. The whole room looked like a blur, and I nodded whenever he did a pause thinking, that way, it might look like I knew what he was talking about.

"Yeah," I managed to say once throughout his speech.

"So, as I said, I think you could do with a break, okay? Don't exert yourself," he finished.

Seeing it as my cue, I nodded rapidly and ran off as quickly as I could before the air completely failed me.

I managed to get as far as the nearest bathroom, where I rushed into a stall and sat down, holding my head between my hands as I breathed raggedly, tears streaking down my face. Why was I even crying? I knew he was just trying to help me, but it seemed like no one understood. They had no idea what I was going through, and I just wanted them all to stop trying to fix me when I knew they couldn't.

My boyfriend also started to notice that something was off around the same time as my professors did. He first noticed something was off when he found me still asleep on a Saturday afternoon. It wasn't like me to sleep in so late; I was usually up and moving by 6am. It'd been some time since we broke up and gotten back together, and even though things were still a little rocky, we were certainly doing better.

At first, I thought I just slept in because I had pulled an all-nighter binge watching my favorite show, but when he asked me about it later on, I just shrugged and said that I couldn't fall asleep. It kept happening more and more after that. Kyle was worried for me at first, but eventually, he started to get annoyed. I stopped contributing to the relationship, stopped putting in the effort I did before to show him that I loved him. I just didn't care about it or him anymore, I couldn't.

Nothing was worth it, not even him, so why would I even try? I was aware that there were things I was supposed to do, like doing dishes, laundry, cleaning up around our apartment, and cooking dinner. But I just couldn't be bothered. I always told myself I'd do it the day after, and instead, turned the TV on and lied on the couch, refusing to move for hours as the images I pretended to care about flashed on the screen.

He confronted me one day after he found my dirty clothes all over the bathroom floor yet again.

"Constance," he snapped, marching into the bedroom. He held up the soiled clothes before tossing them to the corner, where there was a pile of them already. "What the hell's going on with you?'

I looked up at him innocently. "What do you mean?" I asked quietly.

"I mean, what's happening? Did aliens come and replace you with some slob or something?" he asked. He looked around the room, his nose scrunched up. "You were never like this before."

I sighed and closed my eyes. "I'll take care of it later," I told him. "I've just been drowning in homework lately. I'll do it tomorrow, okay?"

"You said the same thing yesterday, babe! Are you trying to piss me off? Are you trying to do all this on purpose so I'll break up with you?"

I gawked at him. Was I?

"No, it's not that, sorry, I just… I have a headache. I'll do it tomorrow, okay?"

I gave him the puppy eyes, hoping he'd leave me alone with the headache excuse. Did I want to break up with him? The thought had surely circled my mind. I wasn't sure he was the problem, but the fact that there was another human in the apartment with me sometimes annoyed me. It was like, whenever he got home, I'd had to pretend that things were good, that I'd been busy, that I've been doing something instead of eating and watching trashy reality shows.

He'll get home, and I'd be sitting on the couch, and he'd asked me what I did all day. I'd lie and tell him I'd had classes and only just got home and wanted to chill for a few minutes before getting dinner started, but reality was, I had been in bed all day, unable to get up. I'd then find an excuse to convince him to order takeout, so that way, I wouldn't have to cook or worry about dishes.

So, yes, I had certainly thought about breaking up with him, not because I didn't love him, but because I couldn't deal with his accusing stare every time he found me watching TV or just lying in bed.

Despite the worry and the anger I was causing, none of it seemed to get through to me. I just stayed inside my head and forced everything else out. It was safer that way.

My school started to send me notifications through emails and letters on the status of my grades. Each letter had gotten more and more threatening as they were sent out. The first one asked me to speak with the graduate advisor, and then they started to tell me that my grades needed to improve or actions would be taken against me, aka, I would get kicked out of school.

Anytime I saw my school emailing me, or whenever I received a letter from them, I would either put it in the trash or toss it onto my desk, or the table, or the passenger seat of my car, and would forget about it. I had every intention of looking at the letters later, but it was as if I'd set them down in a different dimension and never thought of them again.

My change in demeanor had also caused me to get annoyed with myself. Most days, as I lied in bed, I got angry for not being able to get up and do the things that needed to be done. All the dirty clothes, books, random items I should have thrown away, were all scattered across my room and disgusted me. I wanted so desperately to clean it all up, but something was stopping me, a pull I couldn't explain.

I was filled with relief when the semester finally ended. I didn't have to worry about anything for almost a month, and once I was back in school, I would start over fresh. That was the way it had to be.

I went home for Christmas and had a great time with my family. I ventured out a bit more and let myself have a little fun. I thought things were finally turning around for me. Then I went back to my apartment on campus and found myself back in the same cycle as before. It had been a year since the disastrous return home from the previous Christmas, and the memory of it was bugging me.

When I emailed my advisor to set up my classes, I finally received the horrible news that I had been kicked out of graduate school for my poor grades. That did not help with my mood.

At first, I was outraged. How dare they do that to me? I had poured everything I had into school, and now, it was all gone. All those years of dedication and sacrifices I had been through, all for nothing. Then I felt a sudden dread that I would never be able to get my dream job, and that no other school would accept me after they learned that I had been kicked out of one already.

My thoughts began to spiral out of control, and I couldn't grasp onto anything solid to keep me grounded. Everything was a "what if," and there were no answers to give.

It all zeroed down to the fact that I was worthless. If I

couldn't do something as simple as go to school, then what was the point? Why did anything I do even matter?

————

After a week of wallowing in the dark hole I'd dug myself into, I had enough. I couldn't handle another moment of the angry, self-pitying thoughts that swirled around my head, trying to battle against each other on who would be the one to do me in first.

I grabbed a bottle of Prozac from the cabinet, my boyfriend's prescription that I didn't care whether he needed, and dragged myself into the kitchen.

The cold air did little to help me cool off as I searched for a drink to wash everything down. My fingers wrapped around the neck of the strawberry vodka, and I tugged it free from the fridge before I sat at the counter. I opened it and started to chug straight from the bottle.

It didn't take long before I felt the effects of the alcohol. I had always been a lightweight, and it hit me like a ton of bricks. I looked over the counter with a heavy head and spotted a knife in the kitchen sink. Just another thing I never got around to. I grabbed it before sinking to the floor. I looked between the three things I had, the vodka, the pills, and the knife, and closed my eyes. It was what I had to do. I couldn't chicken out. I had to just do it.

In one swift motion, I popped off the top to the Prozac and tossed the remaining pills into my mouth, chasing it quickly with the vodka.

After I forced them down, I looked at the knife and spun it slowly in my hands. I wanted to send a message. That's what people did. Right?

I started to carve into my stomach, my eyes drooping to a close as I struggled to stay awake. I could feel the pull of the knife every time I started a new line for a letter, but there was no pain.

I was completely and utterly numb.

Then the knife slipped from my hand, and my head dropped forward as the pills started to do what I wanted them to. Blood pooled around me, and as my unresponsive body fell to the side, it knocked over the strawberry vodka.

I was surprised when I woke up in a hospital bed. I looked around the room and tried to sit up, but my stomach was on fire. I squeezed my eyes shut and then opened them again, hoping that I wouldn't be there, but of course, that wasn't how it worked.

What I had done was all just a blur in my memory, but the emotions behind it were still there. I was terrified of them. I wanted them gone, and I couldn't think of any way to do that besides ending my life.

I tried to sit up again, but pain shot through every part of my body, starting from my abdomen. A loud cry escaped me, and a nurse came to the door quickly.

"I need something for the pain," I told the nurse once she was close enough. I grabbed her hand and squeezed it. "Please, it's too much. I can't take it anymore."

The nurse gave me an apologetic smile. "I'm sorry," she whispered. "The doctor and the police told us not to give you anything so that you remain lucid. Let me have a look though to make sure everything is still intact." She lifted up the blanket to inspect the bandage.

I could only see a giant bandage covering my stomach, and I wondered what I had done to warrant something like that. I closed my eyes as I tried to remember, but everything went fuzzy after I grabbed the bottle of pills from the medicine cabinet.

"What happened?" I decided to ask.

The nurse gave me another smile. "You overdosed and cut your stomach," she explained. "If you wait just a little longer, the doctor will be here shortly to speak with you. He'll have more answers for you."

Not too long after the nurse left, the doctor came in. I opened my eyes and tried to sit up, but stopped myself when I remembered that I'd cut my stomach.

"I'm trying to figure out what happened. I don't remember anything."

"I'm here to answer some of your questions, Ms. Fay. If you let me. I'm Dr. Faulkner, and I'll be taking over your case."

"My case? What do you mean?"

"Well, Ms. Fay," the doctor said with a tight smile. "Your boyfriend found you after you overdosed on Prozac and cut your own stomach. We're keeping you here for a seventy-two-hour watch. After that, you may be released if we deem you stable. You will receive good care here. I have been appointed as your psychiatrist to continue your care after you go home. Of course, this is all up to you. You are an adult. You can stay here for longer if you feel like that might be better."

I leaned back and thought over the options. I had nothing waiting for me at home. School had abandoned me, and I was pretty sure Kyle did, too. I had no desire to go back to that life. But on the other hand, I didn't want to stay in a hospital. The stale air was making me nauseous, and I had never liked the white-walled buildings.

"I don't know," I said shyly.

"You don't need to decide right now, but I'll be back after the seventy-two hours are over, and we can talk about it then. You can go home to your boyfriend; he was pretty worried when he brought you in."

No, I didn't want to go back to him. I didn't want to go back to the apartment and all the memories. The pills, the vodka, the blood. The letters from the university were still scattered all over the place, and that hideous couch I had found him on with my best friend a year ago was still part of the furniture. No, I couldn't do that.

"I want to stay," I said in a small broken voice, and I saw the doctor's lips curve up into a smile that made my stomach churn.

"That's good, Constance, very good," he said as he looked at my file with gleaming eyes. "I'll send over a nurse with the papers in a few minutes so you can sign yourself in."

Little did I know then, that signing myself in would become the worst decision of my life.

At the time, I hoped that I had done the right thing by staying at the hospital. It was all so strange to me still. I was transferred to the psychiatric ward the next day, and my first day there, I sat in a sad chair in the yard, curled up in the corner, trying not to talk to anyone. Not like there were eager conversationists waiting in line for my company. I just wanted to get the days over with.

It didn't take long though for the whole lone wolf plan to shatter. Kai sat next to me, and we started talking. I could remember it now; he had been there on my very first day. But he looked different in my memories. There was something about his clothing, about the way he looked back then… But I couldn't pinpoint what it was. He'd looked different, he'd looked… normal.

Before the seventy-two hours at the mental facility were up, I began to panic. I didn't want to be there anymore. I wanted to go home and just forget about everything that I had done. I wanted to forget; I wanted to go back to being normal. I wanted to go back a few years in time, take it all back. Take it all away.

Dr. Faulkner sat me down after one of the on-call doctors had expressed his concern about me and the other patients who had to listen to my complaints. Apparently, he was worried that I was a bad trigger for the other suicidal patients.

By that point, the meds had turned my mind into a fog. I had forgotten all about the pills, all about the university, and the cheating, and the couch, and the knife and… and… and… I had forgotten about everything that hurt. I was becoming numb again.

"I heard you want to go home," Dr. Faulkner said as he looked at me from across his desk. He shook his head before grabbing my folder. "Unfortunately, you cannot do that. Your lawyer cut you a deal with the judge, and instead of spending time in prison, you get to spend ten wonderful weeks with us."

I couldn't remember getting a lawyer or even needing one, really. The police never spoke to me. Not even once. They spoke only to the doctors, and the doctors relayed the messages to me. He had told me about the fire I had threatened to burn, but I couldn't get my mind around the concept. Thinking had become so hard.

"I… I don't understand. I thought I signed myself in," I told him after a moment. I pushed a hand through my hair. "Why can't I go home? I want to go home. I need to go back to school. I'm missing out on classes."

Two nurses came in behind me, and at Dr. Faulkner's nod, one of them injected something into my neck. They easily lifted me from the chair into a wheelchair and took me from the room, half asleep, half conscious.

The last thing I could remember was being wheeled into a laboratory setting. After that, it was all dark until I woke up again, which I now know was almost six months later.

They had drugged me. They had injected drugs into my bloodstream, fucked everything up inside, messed with my brain, with my body, my soul. They had erased my memories and fucked up my mind even worse. I couldn't tell reality from imagination anymore. They had savaged my body, my mind, my being, my all.

CHAPTER
SEVEN

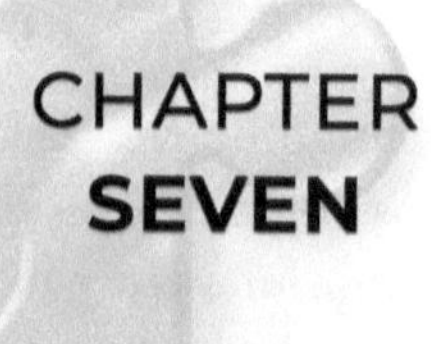

After reading all the files I had been given, I looked back up at the doctor. I couldn't believe what had happened to me. Carefully, I pressed a hand to my stomach and felt the raised skin underneath my jacket. I had really done all of that to myself.

"No, it can't be," I whispered in disbelief.

My memory had come and gone so many times in the last year, it was hard to be sure what was real and what was not anymore. I was overly confused and scared. How could I have done something like that to myself? But I could remember feeling empty and numb, wanting it all to end.

Dr. Faulkner nodded slightly before reaching across and snatching the file from me.

"You have about eight weeks left with us. We want to get you in the best position you can be in before you return back to normal society. But don't worry, the days will start to blend together, and you won't even care how long it's been."

I didn't believe that. Not even a little bit. I gave him a small nod though and moved to stand up.

"Thank you for answering my questions," I told him.

"Oh, hold on, Ms. Fay," he told me, holding up a finger. He wagged it back and forth before pointing to the chair. "I'm not done speaking with you. I've got something I need to tell you."

I frowned and glanced at the door. "I thought we already covered everything."

"No," he said, his voice becoming quite serious. "You have caused two disturbances in my hospital, and if you cause a third, I will have to take punitive action. I do not want to send another one of my patients elsewhere, especially a prison. You will be on your best behavior for the rest of your stay here, so I suggest you get yourself settled in."

"Of course, sir," I said quietly. "I'll keep that in mind."

"I do hope so," he hummed. He waved his hand, dismissing me. "You're free to go back and join the others. Your individual therapy will be starting again tomorrow at 8am. Do not be late."

I stood from the chair and gave him a small nod. I turned and left the room, my legs still a bit wobbly, but for a different reason now. More than just one threat had been made in the conversation, and none of them eased any of my worries.

As I walked back to my room, I started to think of how I was going to survive the next eight weeks. I would have to play by the rules as best as I could and adhere to the everyday schedule.

The only thing I thought would be a problem was the medication they were giving me. I had not gotten the chance to ask what they were or how they had affected me. If I wanted to survive and not get lost in the days, I would have to figure out how to stop taking the pills.

A nurse found me as I was walking to my room and walked me the rest of the way. No patients were supposed to be walking alone. I wondered briefly if all the rules were made up on the spot to give the nurses total power over the patients at any time and for any ridiculous reason.

I quickly shut that thought down. It was too close to what Kai had been hinting at in our conversations.

The nurses thought they were better than us just because they were wearing colorful rainbow scrubs, and we were wearing plain oversized white jackets.

I passed out on my bed when I arrived back to my room, and managed to fall asleep while creating a list in my head of all the things I wanted to talk to Kai about. I felt like he was onto something.

———

Dr. Faulkner watched my leave and waited a moment before standing up and gathering a few folders. As he started out of his office, he began to think about all the progress they were making in such a short amount of time. He had been working on this project for a long time; it was his life's mission, and he couldn't be prouder of how far they had gotten. He couldn't believe how lucky they were to have such willing participants for their studies.

That thought caused him to laugh out loud as he got into the elevator. A few other doctors looked at him, but as soon as they saw that it was the head of the hospital, they kept their mouths shut.

For years, they had been working on a serum that was supposed to cure all types of mental illnesses with just a single shot. It was supposed to act like a vaccine of all sorts. All patients had to do was get a shot once, and they would be set for life. The shot was meant to rewire the brain in a way that would make any kind of abnormality turn on itself and rewire back into what the standard genome believed to be normal.

The project was like a child to Dr. Faulkner, and he wanted to see it through to the end. He needed it to be finished, needed it to be done and be distributed to the whole world. He was going to make sure no one ever again suffered more than needed due to these illnesses, and he didn't care how many test subjects he needed to go through to obtain the perfect formula. His mind was his own kind of messed up. He could see no reason to stop, as he only had his goal in mind.

Dr. Faulkner's son had suffered from bipolar disorder, and it was a struggle to watch him deal with it throughout the years. They had diagnosed him early in his childhood, and Faulkner had been confident that he was the most suited person to deal with his son's illness.

His mother had fled a few years after the diagnosis, claiming that she couldn't deal with the kid's outbursts. But Faulkner stayed by his son's side, every step of the way. It hadn't been easy, but they somehow managed. Being a full-time father and a medical professional was hard, but he did his best.

His son had suffered from bullying all through middle school, and it had only gotten worse once he entered high school. No medication was good enough to keep him stable, and he usually picked fights with the wrong people. It was during one of his manic phases when he was still too young, that he'd managed to pick a fight with someone twice his size.

It wasn't the first time he had gotten in trouble because of his condition, but it was certainly the worst. One tragic night, Dr. Faulkner rushed over to see his son when he was called into the hospital by the paramedics. Unfortunately, he had been too late. There was nothing he could do to save him. He sat by his side and watched as his son's vitals flickered on the screens. He died the next morning, as Faulkner watched the numbers spike up and down, up and down, and lower, lower, until they all hit zero.

It was this death that had given him the idea that there should be a cure for all mental illnesses. It was the desperation brought by his death, and the emptiness he had felt after his son was gone, that motivated him to make a change. Faulkner had been left alone, with no wife, no child, no one but himself. And that left a void inside of him that he needed to fill with a purpose, with something worth living for.

It'd been unfair for his son to die because of the illness, so he decided to dedicate the rest of his life to finding a cure. To live for that sole reason.

He started to work on the serum as the head scientist a few months after his son died. First, he'd found bacteria that repaired damaged tissue. It'd been found in a few rare animals and insects a couple years prior, and other scientists tried to use it in their own experiments, but they didn't know how to control it, how to make it work for them. That was what he was still trying to do. Control it.

The hospital had brought in hundreds of patients every single month, some of which would be long forgotten in no time at all. People with no families, no friends, no one who would miss them, no one who checked on them. It gave them a farm of test subjects. All they had to do was treat them, sedate them, and then use them as their guinea pigs. If everything was done by the books with the patient's authorization, then no one would be able to harm them. It was all legal. Just perfect.

Two years later, Dr. Faulkner hired two new researchers after things started to pick up at the hospital, and they found that if they mixed the serum with some of the main components of most mental illness drugs on the market, they would be able to protect it and allow it to travel through the body without the immune system attacking it.

One day, barely a few weeks after admitting me to the hospital, he reached the research lab and hurried to where he knew the two lead researchers would be. As he imagined, they were both hunched over something, working diligently.

"Morning, boys," he called, patting them on the back. "I've got a few recommendations for you to take a look at. You can see who the next lab rat will be."

One of the scientists, Joseph Sterling, grinned as he turned around.

"Perfect," he said as he snagged the folders. He looked through a few of the names before looking back up at him again. "After the last person you sent, I think we'll definitely be able to make greater progress with this new version of the serum."

"Oh? And why is that?" Dr. Faulkner asked, leaning over slightly to look at what they were working on.

"With the way she reacted to the drug, it helped us figure out how it works on the brain. Also, the antibodies we put in to help ward off possible infections had ended up attacking the new tissue and the bacteria that was building the new tissue, so we know that we have to take that out," Joseph told him.

He rooted through the mess on his lab table before pulling out the scans. He looked over at the other researcher with a smile before nodding.

I was lying on a metal table a short distance away, my brain foggy as I was barely conscious after everything that had been done to me. They'd injected me with something that clearly messed me up, and there were things I couldn't process at the moment. But I knew where I was, and I knew the three people talking in front of me.

Joseph's partner leaned forward and started to explain. "As you can see, the usual problem areas in the brain of someone who suffers from depression start to heal themselves in a matter of hours, really. I wish we could have seen the MRI for the entire time, then we'd really be able to see the growth. But then the whole thing lit up like a Christmas tree, and that's when we noticed the memory loss starting to occur. The serum had been eating at some of the healthy parts of her brain, causing a lot of damage. It doesn't seem to be stopping, so we're working on a second serum to counteract the effects. She's been half conscious ever since, and we're scared that with the amount of damage, we might need to induce a coma."

"And that helps us how, again?" Dr. Faulkner asked.

"Like I said, it helps us figure out what went wrong with the serum," the researcher explained. The voice was so familiar; it tugged at something in my chest. "Now that we know we can pinpoint the problem, we recreate it without the Christmas lights... if that makes any sense."

This second researcher sounded annoyed, or maybe angry. He didn't sound happy like the first, and it made me even more nervous and afraid.

Dr. Faulkner nodded slowly and looked around at all the other researchers working.

"Well, keep up the good work. I want the next batch of experiments done as soon as we can. I want to set up a conference call with pharmaceutical companies as soon as possible so I can get us more funding. I also want to get a patent on it so we can make some of our money back."

"Yes, sir," Joseph told him with a quick nod. He picked up the top folder and flipped through it quickly. "We're hoping to have the final serum created soon, and then we can set up a few weeks for the trial run on one of these guys. I really have high hopes for this one."

Dr. Faulkner grinned. "I'm glad you think so. It's good to have confidence," he smiled. "For now, I'll let you two get back to work. I don't want to distract you any more than I already have. If you need anything else, just let me know."

"Yes, sir," they both chorused before focusing back on their work.

Dr. Faulkner hummed softly as he walked out of the lab and onto the elevator.

Joseph turned to the other head researcher and sighed.

"He never really gives us a lot of time, does he?" he murmured.

He turned back to the microscope and looked into it.

"I mean, he *has* been working on this for almost a decade before we took over," his partner reminded him, a smile forever plastered on his lips.

He combed his hair back and leaned against the metal table. He looked across the notes he had strewn about and shook his head. And then he glanced at me, his smile dropping an inch.

He'd been so sure that they had perfected the serum weeks ago, but only made it too dangerous for anyone to use, he'd said so himself. Whatever happened to me showed them what they had done wrong and what they needed to change to create a serum that would work. I was just a side effect, a mistake, a lab rat.

"We took it over for a reason, though," Joseph finally murmured. He pushed away from the microscope and looked at him. "He could do it, and so can we. He can't be rushing us. One wrong move, and everything could be destroyed. Any small mistake can set us back months. You know how it works. He knows that too, and still expects us to be done in weeks. Imagine if we wrote up that report and had a spelling error in it that changed the entire thing. What then? Start all over when all it needed was a simple tweak?"

The other researcher sighed. "You're preaching to the choir," he told him.

He looked at the reports again, and all the brain scans they managed to get.

The serum had started building up the appropriate receptors in my brain, and even started coating it with something that picked up on the scan. It reached about halfway before everything started to malfunction, and the serum actually started to eat away at what it had just built up, along with what was there before. I imagined I could feel the little things inside my brain, eating away.

But they were able to catch it in time, and that was when everything started to get even worse for me. The researcher wasn't proud of what had happened, but he was happy it'd happened in a controlled setting. He'd smile at me with his million-watt smile before leaving the lab for the day, and that was my last memory before everything went completely black for months.

CHAPTER
EIGHT

I went into the yard later that day to talk to Kai. Speaking with Faulkner sent shivers up my spine, and I really needed some reassurance that I was going to be fine, or at least a distraction, if nothing else. But he wasn't there. He didn't show up for any of the scheduled activities, either. It started to make me worry, but I did my best to hide it. The last thing I wanted was for anyone around me to know that I cared for anyone there, especially if they had close relations with Dr. Faulkner. It could easily be used against me.

But when another day passed, and then another, without

Kai showing up, it got harder to hide my nail biting and how I was always looking at the gate of the yard whenever it opened.

"You're worried for your friend," Cady said as she stood casually next to me on the second day.

"I don't know what you're talking about."

"You do; you're not stupid like the rest. You're smart. They just messed you up. Hooked needles to your arms, didn't they? They gave you pills that fucked you up even worse. They want you to be a doll. But you're a warrior."

Her tone was soft, and she spoke while looking away into the distance, never at me. Her lips barely moved, and I wondered, for a moment, if she was really talking to me or not. Maybe she was just talking to herself. But then she said his name.

"Kai is strong, too. They fucked him up, but he's not like us. Remember that, he's not like us."

After saying those cryptic words, she walked away, leaving me alone, wondering.

———

On the third day, I was ready to give up on trying to find him when I arrived, but then I spotted him sitting in our corner at one of the chess tables. He looked like he was moving the pieces around and playing a one-sided game. The old man who usually played alone was sitting at the table next to him, also playing by himself.

My heart started pounding as I quickly made my way through the people who were already scattered around the yard. I stopped short of him though when I heard him speaking to the chair opposite him.

"I told you not to move that piece," he said with a grin. "I'll beat you in three moves tops. Just you wait."

Carefully, I took the seat across from him, but it didn't

seem like he even noticed. His eyes were gleaming as they looked over the pieces on the board. They weren't his normal glazed over eyes. They looked clearer than they had ever before.

"Kai," I said quietly, trying to get his attention without scaring him.

He glanced up at me and smiled, and for a brief moment, I thought he saw me. The thought was gone though when his hand darted for a piece and moved it.

"I guess it will be just one more move then," he said aloud.

I let my shoulders drop, and I looked over the pieces before moving one on my side. I jumped at the same time Kai did. Our eyes met, and I didn't move another muscle.

Slowly he relaxed, and the old goofy smile came to his face.

"Well, good morning, Ms. Fay," he laughed quietly. "It's nice to finally see you again."

"Where have you been?" I asked, sitting back on my seat.

I motioned toward him to make a move on the board.

Kai chuckled quietly and raised an eyebrow. "I've been sick," he told me with a shrug of his shoulder. He glanced to his right, and his eyes bounced up and down like they were eyeing someone, but there was no one in his direct line of sight. He then turned back to me. "You've abandoned the chair. So kind of you."

"Don't get used to it," I told him as I looked him over. There were dark circles under his eyes and prick marks all along his arm. It even looked like there was dried up vomit stains on his shirt. "Did you not change or shower the entire time you were sick?"

He rolled his eyes as he finally moved one of his pieces. "These were the only clean set of clothes I had. I couldn't just come out here naked," he told me as he leaned back in his seat. "There was a guy here once who did that. I thought he was a nudist while everyone else thought that being naked was a part of his mental illness. I've done my fair share of reading on mental illnesses, and trust me, I didn't find the desire to be naked as a side effect of any of them."

"You've studied a lot on mental illnesses?" I asked.

I was quite impressed. I moved my piece before starting to tap against the plastic table.

"When I was younger, I wanted to be a therapist, essentially," he laughed. His eyes shifted to the right again for a brief second. "I don't know. Now that I think about it, it's stupid. I know what so many of them are like; it's ridiculous."

Suddenly, I remembered him. Or I almost did. Smiling down at me as I lied on the metal table, half dead.

"What made you stop studying?" I asked, knowing deep down that his answer was going to be a lie.

Not because he wanted to lie to me, but because I could tell his memories had been tampered with. He didn't remember who he used to be; they had erased the guy I knew and gave me back this other version of him. The smile was still there, but he was so far gone.

"Well, I was diagnosed late in life with PTSD, and… they kicked me out of school, just a few months short of getting my masters," he told me. "I went to live with my mother, told her that I hated taking the meds, and so I stopped taking them, and then I was sent here. That's what happened to that dream."

I frowned deeply and looked away. "That's sort of what happened to me," I told him. Have they stolen my story and fed it to him? Or did they tell us all the same story? It was harder and harder to tell what was true and what was not. "That's why I ended up here. I had a mental breakdown after I found out I got kicked out for failing, and then tried to kill myself with liquor, pills, and a knife."

The piece he was holding dropped from his fingers, and

he looked at me with disbelief. "You remember?" he asked. "Like, honestly, truly, remember?"

"No, I'm just pulling your leg," I said flatly. When he just blinked at me, I kicked him lightly under the table. "Of course, I remember. Dr. Faulkner told me everything."

I started to tell him about how I was only supposed to be at the hospital for three days, and how it somehow turned into months without me knowing. Then the experiment that was done on me without my consent. I didn't mention that I thought he had been there, wearing rainbow scrubs and smiling down at me while he thought I was unconscious.

"I went through a lot of the same things," he whispered to me. He glanced around to make sure no one could hear us. "My mother dropped me off and said that I was going to stay for a month so I could get back on my schedule of taking my meds without having to deal with any other stressors, and it's been almost a year. They keep telling me that my mom doesn't want to sign me out."

"Why don't you just sign yourself out?" I asked.

"I can't," he sighed. He glanced toward the rest of the yard, his fingers drumming quickly against the table. "Since my mom signed me in here, she's the only one who can sign me out. Plus, everyone thinks I'm too sick to be able to think clearly and make rational decisions. I don't know why she wouldn't want me out of here. I'm taking my medication every day. I've been doing amazingly. I probably wouldn't even have to live with her if I didn't want to."

"Maybe she just thinks it's best for you in here," I suggested.

Kai shook his head slowly. "No, no, that can't be it," he whispered.

I sighed but nodded. He wouldn't believe me even if I told him. After all, I hadn't believed him when he told me the truth about myself. I had to wait, come up with a plan to make it all better. I needed him to remember.

"Well, let's finish this game, and then maybe we can people-watch some more," I told him. I moved one of my pieces with a grin. "I think I'll beat you in two moves."

Kai grinned. "If you were smart, you would have been able to see that you would be able to beat me in one move but now… I've got your queen."

———

From there, it became easier to be friends with Kai. Having almost everything about ourselves out in the open helped me get closer to him, and I felt more at ease when he was around. It was kind of strange for me. It's like neither of us knew the truth about ourselves, but we knew the truth about each other, and that, weirdly enough, kept us closer together.

Every day, we would find each other in the yard, and then take our morning pills before sitting down at the chessboard. It turned out that both of us were pretty good at chess. Or we both really sucked but couldn't tell.

Then we would go off to breakfast together, where I ate mostly just fruit and yogurt, but it made me feel a little better than I had before. It was also better than the sugary cereal Kai always asked for.

After breakfast, we would go back out into the yard and start all over again. We would hang out until group therapy. Group therapies were usually split by gender and category of mental illness, so there were usually a ton going on at once.

When therapy was over, we would reconvene for lunch. I liked the ice cream provided at the end of almost every meal, but we had to actually eat something in order to get the ice cream. I would eat most of my plate, which wasn't very full, and then throw away whatever I didn't eat when the nurses weren't looking. Kai wasn't a big fan of the ice cream but would still take it anyway, just so he could give it to me. He always did small things like that. Like allowing me to win at chess, even though he was better. Or finding little trinkets around the hospital that he could give me.

Some of the patients also got pills again at the end of the lunch hour, and I was one of them.

It was a cold afternoon when I was in the queue for my lunch meds, and I noticed that Cady was in line in front of me. She grabbed the plastic cup, shoved the pills in her mouth, and then downed some water. As she turned around and saw me, she lifted her tongue, showing me that the pills were still there. She pretended to cough, and I saw her tug on the sleeve of her jacket, hiding the pills now in her hand. After taking my own pills, I looked for her again in the yard.

Cady looked at me and winked as she sat on the floor next to the girl who always lined up sticks and leaves, and playing with one of the sticks, she dug a little deep hole in the grass and shoved the pills in.

I started paying more attention to her after that, and I saw her doing the same stunt lunch after lunch. She'd crush the pills against the concrete on the sidewalk and then blow the dust, throw them over the fence to the outside world when no one was looking, or hide them inside the crooks and nooks of the plants in the yard. Every time she did it and got away with it, she looked at me and winked.

———

One afternoon as Kai and I were playing chess, he nodded toward one of the newer patients.

"What do you think about him?" he asked, his eyes quickly darting over the large form of the guy. It was a new game we've started playing.

I looked over and studied him for a moment before turning back to the board. It was my turn, and I was certain he was just trying to distract me.

"I think he looks completely harmless," I told him as I picked up one of my pieces and moved it along the board.

"Hm, that's not what I asked," he told me. He wrinkled his nose at the pieces on the board and wished that he'd never asked me to play with him. "Do you think he belongs here?"

"And I answered it," I told him, crossing my arms over my chest. I looked at him again. "He's big, has lots of muscle, but looks completely harmless. You have to remember, to get stuck in here, you have to be a danger to others. He doesn't belong here."

That was my answer for most of the people we evaluated together. There was just one person who I believed should be there, and it was Frances, the man who thought he had a glass eye but didn't. They weren't sure why he thought he had a glass eye, but the doctors had to keep a bandage over it to stop him from trying to take it out.

Another one of our favorite topics was exploring all the crazy possibilities as to what the hospital was actually doing to its patients. It ranged from fairly plausible answers to whoever came up with the most creative response.

We entertained the idea for the entire day and tried to come up with who was doing what job to hold the entire operation together.

"I think he's the whole head of the operation," Kai told me as we talked about one of the nurses. He pointed to his head. "He's tiny, but he's got lots of brains."

"Okay, I need more of an explanation than that," I told him.

I looked at the nurse and listened as Kai explained his reasoning step by step.

It was a small escape from my depressive episodes, but it was still an escape. I felt a little more normal every time we spoke. I genuinely laughed, ate, and had a good time.

I was certain it had to be the medication they were giving me. No human could have that effect on people. But I did give him a small bit of credit for putting the smile on my face, even after the medicine kicked in and did a lot of the magic. He was the one keeping me sane, and I liked to think he thought of me the same way.

I'm not sure when the idea started festering in our brains, but after watching all the patients and the nurses for a while, our game started to shift. We weren't looking over at the patients and playing anymore, suddenly, we were plotting.

We've both known for a long time that there was something wrong with the place, but we avoided talking about what we knew to each other. It was like one of those secrets that everybody knew but avoided talking about, the elephant in the room. I'm not sure what triggered it, but one day, Kai turned the game to us.

"What do you think of that one?" he asked, pointing at me.

"What are you talking about? That's not how the game goes," I complained.

"Well, it is now. What do you think? Why are you here?"

"I've already told you," I said with a huff. "I tried to burn my house down, or maybe tried to kill myself. Who knows what the hell is true anymore?"

"I do," he said softly, his smile dropping all of a sudden. He reached a hand over, touching my fingers lightly with his fingertips. "I know you, Connie, and you'd never hurt anyone. You hurt yourself because you thought that was the only way out, but it's not. And you don't belong here."

"Neither do you," I replied without thinking.

"No, I do. I wasn't taking my meds. I needed to be controlled," he said dryly.

"Kai," I said his name with as much strength as I could muster. "Do you remember when you told me a secret?" I asked. Kai nodded. "Well, I need to tell you one, too... I know who you really are."

"What are you talking about?"

"Kai… You are not a patient here. You used to work here," I stated with as much audacity as I could.

It was suddenly clear to me. I remembered Cady's words as she told me Kai didn't belong, that he wasn't one of us. She knew the truth, too; she was the reason I was so certain that this wasn't one of the lies fed to me by my messed-up brain.

Kai looked at me with his eyes wide opened, and then burst out laughing like a maniac.

"Come on, your move," he chuckled.

CHAPTER
NINE

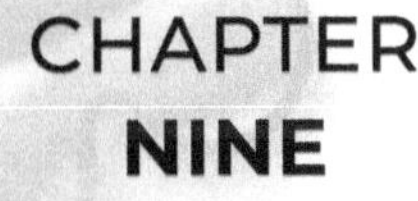

I t took me a few days to get my point across to Kai. He wouldn't believe what I was saying at the start, but as my memories became clearer, he started to remember. We worked together through figuring out what was true and what wasn't.

"So, let's go over it again," Kai said a week later. We started talking about our memories daily, trying to figure out exactly what had happened. "You're saying that I was the one who injected you with this serum?"

"Yes, I think so. I remember lying on a table, half asleep,

half awake, and you were there, talking with Dr. Faulkner and another researcher. I think his name was… Joe… or Jake… something with a J."

Kai scratched the back of his neck, his eyes lost in the distance for a while.

"Joseph," he mumbled.

"What?"

"Joseph, that was his name. Is. Joseph and I used to work together!" he exclaimed the words a bit too loud and covered his mouth with a hand.

We've been trying to remember his name for so long.

We looked around the yard, scared that we had gotten one of the nurse's attention, but after pretending we were both lost in thought for a while, mumbling to ourselves, we felt safe to talk again.

"I think I remember now," Kai said. "We thought we had come up with a serum that would help, that we could use to cure all mental illnesses, but when we tried the drug on you, it backfired."

"Dr. Faulkner said that's why I lost my memories. That's how I ended up in a coma."

"Yes, and no. Faulkner wanted to wait and see if the drug would keep going on its course, but I thought it was going to kill you… We argued…" Kai looked up to the sky, blinking repeatedly as he thought about what happened.

He looked the same way I did whenever I tried to figure out what was true and what was not. "I remember seeing you there, unconscious on the table. You'd wake up every once in a while and mumble a few words… I couldn't do that. That's not what I'd signed up for. I worked day and night with Joseph to get another serum ready, one that would reverse the effect of what we first gave you." Kai took a shaky breath in and leaned in closer as he lowered his voice. "But when we gave you that second dose, your brain seemed to almost shut down. We could see in the scan how your memory was being tampered with. We weren't sure how bad the effects of the drugs were going to be, but we had to try; it was the only way to save you."

"My memories…," I said. "I'm not sure I can trust either of them, the real ones or the made-up ones. I feel like I don't know what's real and what was a dream," I finished.

I've been struggling so much trying to figure out what was reality. I knew my therapist was right, and some of my memory loss could be linked to traumatic experiences that I didn't want to remember, but my whole life seemed like a traumatic experience now.

Kai touched a finger to the back of my hand, looking me in the eyes.

"I'm sorry," he said softly.

"I have already forgiven you."

I had. I knew Kai only wanted to do what he believed was right, and he had been my only friend since I arrived at this mental institution. His smile was the reason I was still here, the only reason I kept some level of sanity. I remembered his smile while I was on that metal table, only half conscious, the drugs messing up my brain, and I knew that was the reason I had managed to pull through. I wanted to see that smile again.

At that very moment, Kai smiled at me.

"We should get out of here," he said.

"Out of here? What do you mean?"

"I mean, out. I know what Faulkner wants. He wants to mass produce this vaccine and sell it to the whole world. And I'm not going to let him do it. He's testing people against their will! What he's doing, it's illegal, and he needs to be stopped. We need to go to the authorities; we need to do something. And we need to do it fast. I'm sure the serum should be almost ready by now; we weren't far from getting it right."

"And... your solution is breaking out of here?" I tugged at my hair and leaned closer to him.

"Yes," he flashed me a grin, and I felt my heart melting.

"We can do it; we can get out during lunch. We'll need to be fast so they don't notice we're gone. We're allowed to roam to the bathrooms freely during that time, so we can meet in the hallway, and I know my way around here. We can make it out. I know we can. I've been thinking about this for days now."

Breaking out of the hospital? It was a crazy idea, but I wanted so badly to be out, to reconnect with society. I wanted to go back to my apartment, to see the world again. I wanted to walk around the streets and be able to wear clothes that were my own. And most of all, I didn't want to die like a lab rat. It had been too close of a call, and I didn't want to test my luck again.

"Okay," I said softly.

"Really?" Kai's eyes opened up wide.

I nodded, and Kai held my hand in his, squeezing it lightly. It made all my nerves tingle with sparkles, and I wanted to let him know how much that meant to me. But I couldn't; all words were stuck in my throat.

"Three days from now, lunch time," Kai whispered to me before we went our separate ways that night.

———

I couldn't sleep that night. Of course, I couldn't.

I knew the nightmares would haunt me, and I was too scared I would wake up a nurse with my screams, and they would sedate me. I was too scared something would go wrong, and I wouldn't be allowed out the next day, or the one after.

I was paranoid and almost didn't sleep for the next three days. I'd spent the nights just lying on my metal framed bed, lying on my back, and digging my nails into my palms to keep myself awake as much as possible.

I thought about this place, and all the things Kai had told me in the past week. Kai rebelled against the hospital after what they had done to me, and seeing me in such a bad state provoked his first outburst of anger.

Turns out, he trashed one of the labs while arguing with Faulkner, and that was why he had been diagnosed with PTSD. I was sure it was just another one of the hospital's excuses to experiment on people. They wanted to silence Kai, and what better way than to drug him?

How many needles had they injected in his arms? How much had they tampered with his brain the same way they had done with mine? He'd come back full of marks and bruises on his arms after telling me the truth about myself, how I hadn't tried to burn my house down, and now, I knew why they had done it. They didn't want me to remember.

We needed out.

We needed to tell the world what was happening.

———

Lunch came around too quickly that day. We spent the morning mostly in silence, pretended to take our meds, but instead, hid them under our tongues and crushed them among the dirt outside once we were back in the yard. Cady, once more, had proved to be a silent ally somehow. We've been doing that for the past three days in an attempt to have our minds clearer, and I certainly felt different. Like my mind wasn't as foggy, as if telling what was real and what was not was somehow easier.

I even stopped seeing the man with the yellow eyes, and I wasn't sure if it was because he had been assigned to a different post, or if he'd never been there to begin with. Was he even real, or just one of the imagined creatures generated by my brain?

By lunch, my hands were trembling. I went to the dining room but headed straight out as soon as I got there. I walked around the hall, my hands trembling the whole time.

As a hand grabbed me from the wrist, I jumped in the air, and the hand covered my mouth as I screamed.

"Shush, it's just me," Kai whispered against my ear as he shoved me behind a corner. We looked to both sides of the halls, finding the space empty.

"I told you; you need to stop scaring me!" I whisper-yelled.

"I'm sorry," he said softly, his hand still wrapped against my wrist.

It felt warm and comforting, and I didn't want him to let go.

"Okay, let's walk casually, and if anybody crosses our path, you stay quiet. I'll do the talking, okay?"

I nodded, and we came out of the corner and started walking side by side. We were so close that Kai's arm was brushing against mine. Once we reached the end of that hall, we'd be at a crossroad where, if we went right, we'd end up in the wing that was destined for staff only. If we went left, we'd be back where we started. I had never gone past the staff door, but I knew Kai had, and he'd told me he'd find us a way to get through.

"Stand against the wall, and pretend to check your nails," Kai said, stifling a laugh.

I did as he told me, my heart hammering against my ribs, and sweat clinging to my clothes. He went to the door and looked at the pad on the side with all its numbers.

"Do you know the code?" I asked in a whisper while I still looked down at my nails.

"Who do you think I am? Of course, I do. I've been watching this door for days trying to figure out what the code is," he winked at me, and I covered my mouth to hide the smile spreading on my lips, and the way my heart had just jumped on my chest at his smile.

Kai punched a few numbers, and the door beeped once, twice, but didn't open. A small light flashed red, and the sweat on my forehead doubled.

"Fuck," Kai mumbled under his breath, looking to the sides again.

The hall was still empty, but we knew we wouldn't be that lucky for much longer. Kai cursed again and punched some more numbers.

The pad beeped once.

We heard steps coming closer, and then loud noises coming from the cafeteria. The steps turned the other way and began to speed up as they headed toward the noise. It seemed like someone had started a commotion in the cafeteria, and I wondered in the back of my head if Cady was real or a guardian angel looking after me. I was so sure, deep down, that it was her.

A fraction of a second had passed, the pad beeped again.

The door opened with a low buzzing sound. Kai jumped in the air, grabbed my hand, and led me down the hall, slowly closing the door behind us after we went through. We could hear voices up ahead, a few doors to the front, and Kai murmured in my ear.

"That'd be the staff room where they usually have lunch. We have to be as quiet as mice."

We tiptoed until we were close to the door, and then Kai kneeled on the floor, looking through the small gap of the closed door.

"Okay, we need to crouch so they won't see us through the glass on the door," he said. "Just make sure not to make any noise, and be as fast as you can."

Kai crawled his way across the door in a few strides, and when he signaled, I followed. I was almost giggling when I got to the other side, and we both took our shoes off, holding them in our hands as we tiptoed our way to the big exit sign at the end of the hall as fast as we could.

I knew the door led to a staff parking lot as Kai had told me, and he said it'd be easy enough to sneak through to the other side of the fence and avoid security at the gates. I had to hope he knew what he was talking about. I had no other choice.

We were close, so close to freedom, so close to the real world. We were getting out; we were going to be free.

"Are you ready?" Kai asked me as we reached the door, and he put his hand on the doorknob.

"I am." I put my hand on top of his, and together, we opened the door to the outside world.

CHAPTER
TEN

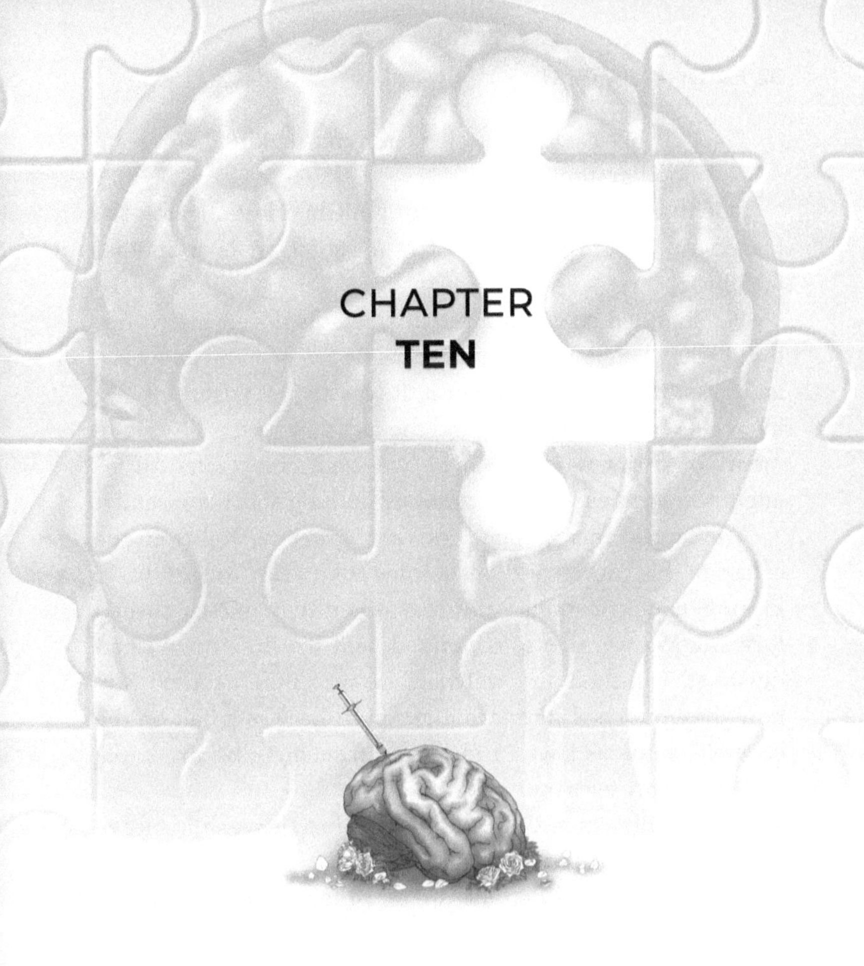

The light from the sun blinded me for a second, and when my sight adjusted to the image in front of me, my heart dropped to the floor.

"Isn't this Hastings and Fay? What in hell are you two doing here?"

There were three male nurses standing outside, cigarettes in between their fingers, and all eyes were focused on us. The largest one of them had been the one to speak. I knew him from the night of my breakdown. He'd been the one to leave the bruises on my wrists.

"No!" I yelled, moving a step back and shaking like a leaf. Kai stood in front of me.

"Gentlemen," he said politely. "I'm Chief Investigator, Kai Hastings, and I'm taking Ms. Fay for some trials at another facility."

He sounded so confident that I even believed his words. But it wasn't enough. Everybody inside the hospital knew Kai and his story; we were sure of it. It was all just wishful thinking, believing in fairy tales, and the fact that such a silly statement could get us out. Maybe we were crazy after all, as attempting this escape was certainly nothing short of insanity.

The largest man jumped forward, grabbing Kai from the collar of his jacket and restraining him. Kai fought back, kicking and screaming, and the other two nurses rushed forward. We were defeated, ended, and the little hope I had mustered vanished as I watched the way they handled Kai, how they punched him in the gut until he was a ball on the concrete, same as I was a few feet away, hugging my knees and crying my eyes out.

"Leave him alone," I mumbled. "Just leave him, leave him."

A pair of hands lifted me up, and I felt the familiar pinch of a needle in my neck.

I saw another syringe heading toward Kai, and he was still kicking and screaming as the needle pierced the skin on his neck.

The edges of the world blurred, but I kept my gaze on Kai. On the way back in, the two nurses lifted him up, looping his arms around their necks. They walked him in front of me, and someone guided me behind as I was barely able to walk, a hand under my elbow as I dangled like a zombie, half dragging my feet behind me.

"Dr. Faulkner won't be happy about this," one of the nurses said. "How did they get this far? It was a close call."

"Should we take them straight to his office?"

"No, I heard he was downstairs in the lab. Let's just take them there. We gave them enough sedatives for them to be compliant for at least the next hour."

They took us to an elevator. We went down. And down. The red numbers were blurry.

I heard Faulkner's voice before I finally saw him. He sounded angry, yelling commands around. I felt the cold metal underneath me. Leather straps bounding my legs and my arms. I blinked.

Dr. Faulkner and Joseph were talking. I knew it was him; I'd recognize his deep and menacing voice anywhere.

Joseph was grinning widely.

"Not only did I find the right chemical balance for the drug to work and found the thing that was holding us back, but now, I have the right patient to use it on," he laughed, and my stomach churned. No. Not again. "It's been a long time since I've seen either of them in this lab. Maybe this is meant to be."

Joseph flipped through the folder as he got closer.

"Kai," he said with a smile before setting it down. He glanced up at him and saw the restraints on his arms. "Oh, were you being naughty?"

"Why are you doing this to me?" Kai asked, looking around the room quickly. His voice was broken, barely more than a whisper. He tugged on the restraints and cried. "Please. I just want to get out of here. Can you please help me get out? I don't want to be here anymore. You know I shouldn't be here. Help Connie… She doesn't deserve this. Haven't you done enough damage?"

"Don't worry, Kai," Joseph said with a soft smile. He pulled out the folder between us and opened it to show him what was inside. "You're going to be injected with Siero. I finally managed to get everything right. I know it will work just fine this time, and who better than you to receive the first shot? It seems fated."

Kai shook his head quickly. "No. I don't want it," he told him. He shook his head again. "I know what the vaccine is. I remember everything!"

He found my eyes across the room, and I felt the tears running down my cheeks.

Joseph sighed and motioned for the nurse and his assistant, Lorenzo, to come in.

"You are going to be connected to this scanner for the entire duration of the trial. If you are deemed healthy and sane, you will be allowed to go back to your normal life in no time. We'll keep you here for a while, of course, to monitor you, but you'll be a free man in no time, trust me."

Lorenzo wheeled in the portable scanner and stood behind Kai. As he tried to put it on, Kai thrashed about.

"Mind giving me a hand?" he asked Joseph through his teeth.

Joseph sighed and got up, holding Kai still. "If you remain calm, this will go a lot smoother," he told the man. "I know you're probably being told differently inside your head, but it's the truth. Stop resisting."

Lorenzo finally managed to get the scanner onto his head and strapped it around his chin. "We're going to run this for a few minutes, and then we're going to inject you with the serum. All you have to do is sit still."

Kai closed his eyes and rocked, shaking his head.

"How long do we have to wait?" Joseph asked.

"Five minutes to get the first scan, and then after that, we can stick him," Lorenzo explained.

After about five minutes, the nurse stuck the needle in his arm, quickly pushing the plunger. I watched as Kai jerked but then froze, his hand squeezing into a fist.

"Done," she whispered.

"Good," Joseph murmured, watching the scans. "Leave."

Kai strained his head to the side and gritted his teeth tightly.

"I don't wanna," he murmured. "I want to go home."

"You'll be able to soon, Kai," Lorenzo told him. He leaned against the table and watched Kai's head drop to the side. "How is it looking?"

Joseph grinned and showed him. "The parts of his brain that were affected are shrinking already," he told him with a laugh. He walked over to Kai and put his hand on his shoulder. "I think we've done it. Now, it's just a matter of waiting."

Lorenzo grinned and watched Kai sit motionless. He let out a sigh and pushed away from the table.

"Let's get him to the room, and we can wait for him to wake up there."

They wheeled him and the scanner out of the room.

"I'll come back for Ms. Fay in a minute," Lorenzo said as they left. "She seems almost out of it, shouldn't remember a thing in the morning with the amount of sedatives and drugs we've given her."

———

Dr. Faulkner couldn't hide the grin on his face as he looked over the results Joseph had brought to him. He looked at the scans, and then looked at him.

"And you are sure it will hold?" he asked.

He needed to be sure. If they had another one backfire, then he wasn't sure what he would do.

"Yes. Absolutely," Joseph told him with a wide grin. He motioned for him to follow. "We wanted something that would scan his brain the entire time he's with us, so we connected him to monitors that watch his brain function." He stopped in front of a large window that looked into a small room, where Kai Hastings was sitting and reading a book.

"Nothing looks different," Dr. Faulkner told him. "He's just reading a book. That's not anything new to someone with PTSD. They do it all the time."

Joseph gave him a flat look before turning to the monitors that a few people were sitting at.

"These are all focusing on his brain function, and mapping out how his brain handles certain situations. He is one hundred percent cured. He's been off his meds for almost two full weeks now, and I'm certain that this is his brain if it were healthy. Nothing is there to impede it or cause any hallucinations. One hundred percent pure."

Dr. Faulkner nodded before watching as Kai just sat there and read the book he was given, and then he looked down at the results handed to him.

"This is perfect. I'm glad you got this far already. I'm going to talk with a few pharmaceutical companies today and see who wants to invest in this," he told him. He put a hand on Joseph's shoulder and squeezed. "You've done great work. Just remember that your name will go down in history."

Joseph smiled. "I sure hope so," he told him with a laugh.

Dr. Faulkner quickly walked back down the hall and to the elevator. On his way up, he studied the results again. He couldn't believe that they had finally done it. It all seemed surreal.

Once he reached his office, he sat down at his desk and logged into a video chat with seven other people. He grinned at all of them before pulling up his presentation so they all could see it.

"I know you're all wondering what miracle drug I'm trying to sell you today," he started with a grin. "Well, I'll tell you. I've had a team of scientists working on a serum that will cure all mental illnesses forever." He went on to explain all the inner workings of Siero, showing all the research they've done.

"Wait, wait," one of the men on the screen said, stopping him before he could go any further. "You're asking us for money when you don't even have a test subject who has reacted positively to this?"

"Oh, we have a test subject that's just that," he assured them. "I just received the results from the lab moments ago, so that's why they're not in the presentation." He pulled the files out and started to show them. "This patient has been in this facility for almost a year now. He suffers from PTSD and has been taking heavy medication to control it since he was diagnosed with it when he was just twenty. We took him off all of his medication, and then injected him with the new serum, and his brain has been functioning like... well, like yours and mine would." He put down the papers before leaning forward. "I'm not looking for you to believe me right now. I'm just looking for you to have a little faith. With your investment, we can get more equipment, better researchers, and we can get this serum tested out and finished within the month."

There was silence on the other end of the call as they all started thinking.

Dr. Faulkner couldn't wait for their response while continuing to stare at them.

"Call me back with your answer, and I will discuss it in further detail with you all individually, if you like. Now, if you'll excuse me, I have to get back to work. I have a hospital to run."

CHAPTER
ELEVEN

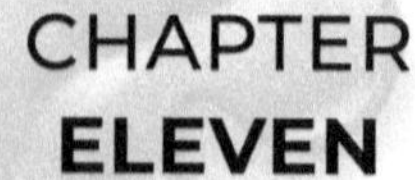

The morning after our attempted escape, I walked into the yard, and I was surprised to see that Kai wasn't there. I hadn't known him for that long, but it seemed out of character for him to not show up.

Did they do something to him?

The last thing I could remember was walking out through the emergency door and finding a group of nurses outside who'd been smoking in the parking lot. After that, I woke up in my room, not sure of what day it was or where I was. It'd taken me a while to even remember the day before, and when I asked the nurses where Kai was, they pointedly ignored me.

Time flew, and the first week without him was enough to bring all the good things I had built up down. Every day, I slipped further and further back into the dark corner I had found myself in for the past two years, and I didn't want that. Not again. With Kai gone, it felt like things were sort of duller. I had no one to talk to and no one to sit with during meals. It was odd.

I wanted normalcy again.

It got so bad that the doctors even upped my medication dosage, which made me feel more energetic, but I still didn't want to do anything. There was nothing there for me to do by myself.

Cady had come to see me during the first few days, a sad smile on her face.

"I see you didn't make it out," she had said.

I never replied, so she eventually moved away, distancing herself from me. I'd seen her through the corner of my vision a few times, lingering around, but if she had approached me again, I didn't register it.

As I was sitting with my one-on-one therapist one morning, he stared at me, and I stared at his desk. The first half of our hour meeting was silent, and he knew that I would go like that for the rest of the hour, but he couldn't have that for the sixth day in a row. It was his job to get me talking.

"Are you going to tell me what's wrong?" he asked me, tapping the end of his pen against the edge of his notebook.

"No," I told him. I looked down at my hands before I started to pick at the skin around my nails. "Nothing's wrong."

"Are you eating?" he asked. "The nurses tell me that you're not eating."

"They took my silverware away," I murmured. "Don't like eating with my hands."

"Is there a reason they took it away?"

I looked up at him with an evil look in my eye.

"I'm fairly sure it's because you think I'm going to hurt myself. I'm not going to, by the way. I don't like hurting myself. I only do it if it helps."

He shook his head. "It never helps," he told me. "It only gives you a different kind of pain to focus on. Tell me what's going on."

I glared at him before turning to face the wall on my left. On the shelf, was a small statue of a president. It looked like Theodore Roosevelt from where I was sitting. For the rest of the session, I studied the statue. I didn't look over a single detail. When the clock in the room finally chimed, I wasted no time in standing up and heading to the door.

"Ms. Fay," the therapist warned me.

"I'm not talking," I told him. "And our time is up."

I left the room, leaving the door open behind me.

———

Two weeks had passed, and there was still no sign of my friend. I still wasn't doing well. I was beginning to think that he had died. The hospital had gotten to him and killed him. It wasn't a logical thought, but it was the only one that I could come up with.

I walked into the yard after spending another silent hour with my therapist, and I went straight for the set of chairs. Most people tended to stay away from them, as they knew that was where Kai and I usually sat.

I nearly tripped over a set of feet as I shuffled toward my seat and was about to shout at whoever it was, but I stopped dead in my tracks.

"Kai Hastings," I breathed, my eyes widening.

Kai smiled up at me and waved.

"Hi," he laughed. "Long time no see."

I quickly sat next to him.

"You can sure say that again. Where have you been?" I asked.

He shook his head.

"I can't tell you that," he told me, keeping the smile plastered on his face. "But I can tell you that I feel absolutely fantastic. I'm like a new man."

"What do you mean you can't tell me? We tell each other everything, remember?" I said quietly. I tugged on his arm. "Come on, I've been so worried about you."

"I'm sorry, Constance," he told me in a soft voice. He patted my hand before pulling it away from his arm. "I can't tell you."

I frowned and narrowed my eyes at him.

"Something's wrong about you," I murmured.

He gave me a sympathetic look.

"Nothing's wrong with me," he promised.

We both fell silent. I couldn't stop thinking about what had happened to my friend. Was it the new drug that Dr. Faulkner's been working on? Had they injected Kai? I felt like I should remember something, like there was something important I was forgetting about. The vaccine had gone wrong before. What if it hurt Kai? I didn't want to think about any of that.

I looked over at him and saw that he was watching TV. I let out a sigh and shook my head.

"Well, since you're fine, I might as well tell you about the weeks I've spent without you here," I murmured. "I... well, I haven't been doing great at all. I can't sleep because of the medication they put me on, and I'm not even allowed silverware anymore. I've been sitting in this room for hours with no one to talk to. We had plans. We needed to get out, and now, it seems like... Seems like you don't care about any of that anymore. You have to understand by now that I've actually missed you," I admitted.

"I've missed you, too," he told me. He put a gentle hand on my shoulder and gave me a smile. "I just know that everything will get better soon. Don't worry. We're just fine here."

I was trying really hard not to let Kai's new way of thinking affect me, but all I could see was the stupid fake smile that was constantly plastered on his face. I wanted to wipe it off and draw the old one back on.

———

On our way out to the yard one day after lunch, I finally had enough. I waited until the nurses weren't paying attention and grabbed Kai by the sleeve before pulling him to the side. His eyes were wide as I tugged him around the corner and shoved him against the wall.

"Constance, please calm down," he told me. "We're going to get in trouble if they see us out here like this. Come on, let's go with the others into the yard. I want to play some chess."

I shook my head.

"Nope," I laughed. I glanced around before putting my hands on my hips and staring up at him. "You're going to answer my questions. Understand?"

His shoulders dropped, and he let out a frustrated sigh. It was the first sign of any other kind of emotion besides happiness. Though it didn't last long, and the smile was back in its place.

"Answer what questions?"

"What did they do to you? Did they do an experiment on you?' I asked quickly.

I searched his face for anything that would give the answer away, but the stupid smile was too distracting.

"I already told you that I can't answer any questions like that," he laughed. "Look, I think you just need some sleep, a little tea with dinner, and then you'll be right as rain tomorrow."

I shook my head again, my eyes never leaving him as anger brewed behind them.

"I'm not going to do that. It won't work. I'm going to keep asking you this question until you tell me the truth."

"You need to calm down," he told me. He tapped a finger against my head. "You need to clear your mind and try to think normally… like me. I'm sure you will be able to soon."

I watched him walk out to the yard, dumbfounded. Think normally… what did that even mean? That really hit the nail in the coffin, though. They had definitely done something to him.

I just hoped that it didn't hurt him like it hurt me.

I walked into the yard and took my seat next to Kai.

A whole month had passed, and I was sure I was going to kill Kai. Every day, he got worse and kept pushing the idea onto me that I had to be normal like him.

"You're not normal, though," I told him one day, shaking my head. "You're so far from normal, it's not even funny. I've heard the stories that you told, and that's you. The abnormal you. The real you. The guy I became friends with. This…" I motioned a hand over him before shaking my head. "This is not normal. You're too… I don't know. New. Like someone wiped your brain or something."

"That's impossible," he told me.

He turned away from the TV to look at me.

"No, it's not," I sighed. I started to pull on the loose threads at the bottom of my sleeve. "I had months of my life missing. I'm sure whatever they injected you with will do the same to me at some point."

He shook his head.

"No, it won't. I'm almost certain of it," he assured me. "I

don't know why you can't embrace this new me. I'm happy and healthy."

"You were happy before, weren't you?" I asked. I pushed my hair out of my face before letting out a frustrated groan. "I was happy before. I had a friend who could help me get through my time here."

"I'm still here," he told me.

I shook my head. "Not in the same way. I'm happy that you're... healthy, but I didn't see anything wrong with you before. On or off your medicine."

"I'm sorry you feel that way," he whispered. "But I'm still me no matter what."

"I know you are," I said quietly. I leaned over and bumped my shoulder. "I just wish I had someone to talk to about stuff. Someone to goof around with. All you do is sit here. It's not good."

My head turned toward the door when it opened, and a few nurses rolled out with a cart. I frowned and pressed further back into the metal chair.

"What's happening?" I asked.

A wide smile crossed Kai's face, and he stood up. He looked down at me and took my hand.

"You're finally going to be fixed."

"I'm not broken," I told him, jerking my hand away from him.

A few patients close to the nurses started backing away, and as soon as I saw the needles, I knew why. I shook my head quickly and started to make my way to the door, but a nurse stopped me.

"You can't go anywhere right now. It's time for you to be fixed," the nurse told me. "Don't worry. It will only hurt a little bit."

The other patients started to panic. They tried to run around the nurses, but they were stopped and forced to sit. I saw all the people I knew thrashing around the place. Cady, the chess guy, the girl who played with leaves, even the bickering couple, were all being injected.

"Everyone will be getting the shot. There is no reason for you to resist. It will only help you," the nurse insisted before looking at me.

I shook my head quickly, my eyes squeezing shut.

"I don't want it. I don't need it. I promise. Please. I just want to go home," I cried. When I heard Kai gasp, I opened my eyes and looked at him. There was a small glimmer of something on his face, but it was gone within seconds. "Kai! Please. Don't let them do this to me. Don't let them do this!"

Another nurse came over and grabbed a hold of me. They pinned me to the ground, but I still thrashed against them.

"Please don't," I begged them.

I didn't want to forget again. I didn't want something bad to happen to me.

I just wanted to go home.

One of the nurses with a syringe came over to me and bent down my arm.

"Don't worry," she told me. "You'll be perfectly fine. Better even, so don't struggle too much, or it will hurt."

I squeezed my eyes shut as the needle slipped easily under my skin. I bit my lip hard to stop myself from crying out more. It was useless. No one was listening, anyway.

A cold feeling ran up my arm, followed by a sudden rush of heat all over my body. When I opened my eyes, I was looking up at the nurses, who were still holding me down.

Darkness started to close in around my vision, and I turned my head. The entire room blurred until I looked at Kai. I let out a small whimper before finally slipping into unconsciousness.

CHAPTER
TWELVE

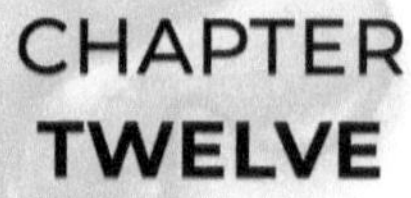

Dr. Faulkner walked into a conference room full of hospital leaders and prison wardens. All important people who were eager to buy his new serum. He grinned at them as he made his way to the head of the table and set down the briefcase.

"Good afternoon, ladies and gentlemen. Thank you all for coming," he said with a smile. He motioned for them all to take a seat before he walked over to the projector. "I know you're all here waiting to hear the good news about our new serum, Siero."

"Yeah, can you honestly cure the mentally ill with… with a single shot?" one of them asked.

"Please, hold your questions until the end. I'm sure I will answer most of them with this presentation," he assured them.

He grabbed a clicker and pressed a button on it. He looked up before turning to the others, with a slightly embarrassed expression, and pressed the button again.

When the screen lit up, he grinned and stepped back.

"There we are," he grinned, earning a few chuckles from the audience. "So, as some of you have already heard at Bellevue Psychiatric Hospital, we have perfected a serum that cures all mental illnesses. We have been working on it for years, and finally, had success just two months ago with a long-term patient of ours."

He clicked the button again, and the slide changed to show a picture of Kai.

"Here is Kai Hastings. We monitored his brain function for two whole weeks and watched as the parts of his brain that were affected by his PTSD were repaired by Siero. You can see the problem areas shrinking until they completely disappeared. It's a universal drug because it travels across the entire brain, finds which neurons aren't firing correctly, and rewires them. It doesn't matter what it is. We tried it on every single patient in our hospital, and we're cleared out. Not a single person on our beds. I've got people knocking on our doors, begging for this drug. Our goal for this is to make everyone a functional human being. Someone who can go out into the world and be… normal. They don't have to worry about how many times they've flipped the lights on and off before leaving the house, or about whether they're going to have to speak to anyone. They can simply be."

When he finished his presentation, his hands flew up. He grinned and looked at Joseph before giving him a small nod. He knew they were making history.

———

I sat in my parents' kitchen as the news played on in the background. I was staying with them because, when I was sent to the hospital, I lost my job, my education, and my apartment. They agreed to help me out as long as I needed, and even helped me get a job within my field of interest.

When I left the hospital after I woke up again, the entire world felt different. It was, all of a sudden, very underwhelming. I still wasn't sure if it was a good thing or not, but my mind never let me dwell on it for too long.

My parents were happy to have me back in the house, though. My mom baked cookies for me, and my dad sat with me, and we watched some crappy movies together. Dad spent a lot of time on that couch. I remembered him sitting there from when I was a kid. He'd never liked going out much and always said it was because he was shy. But I've heard Mom use the word "socially awkward" to refer to him.

Anyway, it was almost like I was a teenager again.

Or before I got depressed.

I couldn't really remember much of what my life had been before, but if it was anything close to what I was experiencing in that moment, then maybe, I was happy before everything went downhill. I never thought it would be possible to climb back up to the top.

I didn't do much. I was never one to go out and enjoy the nightlife. I would rather stay home and drink hot cocoa while snuggled deep in the blankets of my bed. This time, when I did it though, it didn't have the undertones of absolute dread. It was something I did just to do it.

Every now and then, I would think back to Kai and the hospital, but more often Kai, and my head would start to hurt. It was a dull ache that went away almost as soon as I started thinking, but I wondered if I should mention it to my doctor.

I wanted to remember Kai, at least. He was the good part that was weaved into all the bad memories at the hospital. It was hard not to think of one when thinking about the other. I tried to talk to my parents about it and tried to ignore the headache, but every time I started to dredge up some kind of emotion, I would stop and just smile.

I sighed as I saw Dr. Faulkner's face on TV and quickly shut it off. That was a face I never wanted to see again. If I still had dreams, I would probably have nightmares about him chasing after me. But there were no more nightmares. No more dreams. Thinking about Dr. Faulkner also gave me headaches, so I always turned the TV off as soon as he showed up.

That was another thing… I didn't have dreams anymore. It felt like I rebooted every night instead of falling asleep and waking up. It was so jarring, but every time I wanted to bring it up, my mind would put up a wall between me and the words I wanted to say.

I finished my drink and put the cup in the sink before heading back up to my room. It was exactly the same as it was when I was a kid. My parents hadn't even touched it. That was why I decided I needed to change it up.

I needed something new. I cleaned out almost everything that wasn't something I wanted, and I started to move around the furniture.

But when I moved my bed, I noticed a cardboard box. I frowned, not having remembered ever putting anything under my bed. I sat on the floor next to it and started to root through it.

There wasn't much in it. Just a few hair scrunchies, an old doll, and a diary. I smiled and pulled the diary into my lap before undoing the old latch. I started to read over the passages, laughing at how childish my handwriting was. Smiling at every single page I turned.

It was mostly just things about going through middle

school and the start of high school. There were entries about boys, about teachers I hated, about how I hated going to the Bahamas because my parents had forced me to go even though I was sick. It's not like I never wanted to go back. It's just that every time I thought about taking the trip, I felt sick. My father said that it was all just in my head, and I would eventually get over it.

There were also a number of dark passages. The handwriting was messy, and everything was so full of feelings. I never knew that I had gone so low in my life before. In the diary, I talked about ending my life and how nothing mattered anymore.

I squeezed my eyes shut after reading a few of the passages. It felt like something was pressing against my skull, and the pain nauseated me. I closed the diary and tossed it back into the box with the other things. I pushed the box over to the things I wanted to throw away. I glanced at it one more time before going back to rearranging my room.

———

One afternoon, I took my lunch break in the café down the street from my office building. I had been there a few times before I started working, but I preferred to sit at my desk and eat most days. But it was a nice summer day, and I wanted to have an iced coffee with lunch.

As I was sitting on the patio and sipping at my double mocha, I spotted Kai walking down the street. My eyes widened as I jumped up, nearly spilling my drink on the person sitting at the table across from me.

"Kai!" I called, waving my hand.

Kai spotted me and a smile split into his face.

"Constance," he said.

He walked over to me and motioned for me to take a seat as he took one with me.

"Aren't you going somewhere?" I asked as I sat down. "I don't want to keep you. I just wanted to say hi."

"Nonsense, I can delay my plans for you," he told me. He looked me up and down, nodding a little. "You've gained some much-needed weight. It looks good on you. You also look a lot less jaded."

I nodded my head slowly before taking a sip of my drink.

"Well, living at home, where my mother is cooking and not some random lunch attendant, helps," I admitted. I watched him with a smile, tilting my head to the side. "How have you been?"

"I've been okay," he told me. He tapped his fingers against the metal table before looking into the street. "I've been extremely happy all the time."

"Well, that's good, isn't it?" I asked.

It wasn't, and I knew it. There was an odd feeling to my happiness, like it was the only thing I was allowed to feel.

He chewed on his lip, and his knee started bouncing as he watched me.

"My mother died," he told me. "Last… last week. I think. I can't remember."

"Oh, no, that's horrible," I whispered and put a hand to my chest.

It wasn't that I was feeling sorry for him, but I knew I had to say something like that. My words held like lies.

Kai shrugged his shoulder and dropped his eyes to the table.

"I can't find myself to be sad about it," he admitted. "I can't feel anything about it, actually. Every time I do, I get this headache and, I don't know…"

"I get weird headaches, too," I told him. I rubbed my temple and closed my eyes. "In fact, I'm getting one right now. I don't know why I keep getting them, though."

Kai waved off the conversation.

"Let's catch up," he told me. "I want to know everything you've been up to."

We talked until I had to go back to work. I scribbled my number down on the receipt and pushed it into his hand. "Please, call me whenever. You're still my friend, after all, even if we don't get to see each other every day."

He nodded and tucked it away into his pocket.

"It was nice seeing you again, Ms. Fay," he said with a small tilt of his head. "Oh, and sorry. For a lot of things."

I shook my head.

"Don't worry about it. It's in the past. But it was nice to see you too, Kai," I laughed quietly. I got up and followed him out to the sidewalk. I pulled him into a hug, and I let out a sigh. "Soon. Don't be a stranger."

"I won't be," he promised as he pulled back.

He gave me a wink before he started to walk in the opposite direction.

I stood there and watched him as he walked down the street. I stuck my hands in my pockets and was about to turn when I saw his head turn slightly.

Kai looked back at me and gave me the first genuine smile since before he disappeared for two weeks. The same smile he had given me just before we tried to sneak out of the hospital. I was about to wave, but then all of a sudden, he turned and ran straight into the moving traffic.

A car struck him at the hip, and he was thrown onto the windshield, causing it to crack. He rolled over the top of the car and fell hard onto the asphalt behind it. The limbs of his body were spread out, and blood started to pool around his head from his cracked skull.

I ran forward, pushing people out of the way as they all ran toward him. As soon as I saw his limp and motionless body, I fell to my knees. I wanted to cry, cry for the loss of my closest confidant, but nothing came out. Instead, I reached for his hand and squeezed it as tightly as I could.

My head was pounding, so hard that I had to squeeze my eyes shut. I saw images of Kai on my first day in the yard. Saw him smiling down at me when I was on that horrible metal table. His smile had been the one thing to keep me sane, to help me pull through my worst of times. He'd gone against Dr. Faulkner, for me, and ended up hospitalized for trying to help me.

I remembered our chess games and the way he used to joke and laugh all the time. I saw him sitting next to me in the yard, even reaching over to grab my hand once when he walked me down the halls to our illusion of freedom.

My eyes twitched as all the memories clouded my mind, and I tried to be sad for him. I tried to shed tears for the friend I had just lost. But there was a huge wall between that past and my present. There was a wall blocking everything in, so I let go of his hand, blood coating my fingers, and I stood up.

Turning around and pressing my temples against the pounding headache, I walked back to the office to finish my shift.

CHAPTER
THIRTEEN

I sat toward the back of the small crowd that attended Kai's funeral. I didn't want to be seen, didn't want to be spoken to. I wanted to mourn my friend's death and then go home. But I was having a hard time even with that.

It didn't make sense. Why couldn't I cry? Why couldn't I feel remorse? Did I not care enough about him? Did he honestly mean nothing to me, and I just couldn't tell?

That didn't make any sense, either. I wanted to cry. My eyes hurt with the need to cry, but nothing came out. It made everything hurt, honestly. As they lowered the casket into the ground, I stepped back and started back toward my car.

I had enough. If I stayed another moment, it would be too painful. Not in an emotional kind of way, either. It was starting to feel like I couldn't feel those anymore.

When I arrived home from the funeral, my parents bombarded me with questions.

"How are you feeling?" Mom asked.

"Fine," I answered.

"Did you meet any of his family?" Dad followed up.

"No. I left before anyone left the cemetery."

"Do you really feel alright?"

I sighed and closed my eyes.

"I'm going to bed," I told them. "I've got work early tomorrow, and I don't want to be late."

They both frowned and shared a look.

"What?" I asked, tilting my head to the side. I smiled at them before letting out a laugh. "I'm honestly fine. You don't have to worry about me."

"Honey, your friend just died," Mom whispered quietly.

Her hands were twitching by her sides, and she was visibly nervous. I wondered if she was still taking her anxiety pills like she did when I was younger.

"In front of you," Dad added. He reached out and took my hand. "We're a little worried about how you're coping with this. It's okay to be sad. Someone close to you just died."

I shook my head and gave him a hug before giving my mother one.

"I promise you that I'm fine. I'm going to get some sleep. I don't feel that bad, anyway. I'm fine. I barely knew him."

They watched me walk away before looking at each other again. They knew that something was off.

"We'll keep an eye on her," Mom whispered before pulling her husband into a hug. "We won't lose her again."

————

A few weeks later, I was sitting with my mother and father in the living room watching the news. I found no interest in what was airing but wasn't going to change it; my parents were the ones watching, anyway.

"Dr. Faulkner's new treatment for all mental illnesses is once again blowing up the news in all hospitals and pharmaceutical companies," the anchor said.

My head shot up.

"Turn it up," I told them. "I want to hear what they have to say."

I usually just ignored these kinds of stories, but maybe losing Kai had changed that.

Mom turned up the volume and gave me a worrisome look.

"Isn't that what you were given?" she asked. "Oh, what's the name of it?"

"If you stop talking, I'll be able to hear it," Dad said, snatching the remote from her hand.

He turned it up more so we could all hear what had to be said.

"The death of Cadence Croix, aged 45, adds another suicide to the count from Bellevue Psychiatric Hospital, bringing the count up to a total of four hundred and thirteen. Many believe that Siero, the serum that was injected into all the patients at the hospital, is the main cause of it. There are other suicides that have been reported, and the police say they're inspecting each and every one of them for traces of the serum.

"Notes were discovered from many of the suicide victims who carried the serum, saying something along the lines of, 'I feel nothing. Everything is too perfect.' Ms. Croix ended her life by taking a lethal dose of sleeping pills, and professionals believe she didn't suffer. The notes left behind are leaving the police baffled, but they say they are looking into all possible leads—"

I tuned the reporter out after that, and I fell back onto the couch. I felt both of my parents looking at me, and I quickly glanced at them.

"What?" I asked. "I'm fine. I'm not going… I'm not going to kill myself like them. I've tried before, and I didn't like the experience, remember?"

"Maybe you should go see a doctor, though. Just in case," Mom suggested quietly. She motioned to the television. "Over four hundred people who took the same drug that you took have committed suicide."

"I know what you're saying, but I promise that nothing will happen to me," I told her. I gave them a smile before standing up. "Everything is perfect."

I didn't hear the words I used, but my parents paled slightly. I didn't tell them that I knew the patient. I had never known Cady's last name, but I was sure it was her. It would be like her to end her life with pills, the one thing she had despised and tried to avoid at all costs. It was ironic; it was something Cady would have done.

I quickly headed up to my room. I fell onto my bed and pulled a pillow to my chest. I wasn't going to lie; I was a little afraid of what was happening. It had to be a side effect of the drug. Had to be. Everybody I had known back at the hospital was probably dead. Not that I had been close to most of them, but we've been in the same place for so long, shared so many of the same traumas.

The idea left a bitter taste on my tongue.

I turned and saw the box that I had found my diary in. Slowly, I slipped from the bed and walked over to it. The notebook was still on top of everything. I picked it up delicately and brought it back to my bed.

I curled up with it and started to read every passage again inside it. I didn't know what compelled me to do so. Maybe it was the notes that were left behind by the suicide victims saying that they didn't feel anything.

Kai didn't feel anything.

I didn't feel anything.

Why couldn't I feel anything?

I religiously read the passages over and over again like they were Scripture, and I was praying for the chance to feel like I did before.

———

Over the next few weeks, I struggle with trying to find the right place for myself. Nothing feels right for me. I don't feel like I'm home, even with my parents around. I don't like my job, even though it's a stepping stone to my dream job. I don't like my life.

I know it's dangerous just thinking those thoughts, but it isn't like my mind allows me to think about it all that often. I have brief snippets of different emotions that slip through the cracks of the wall inside my mind. However, they are gone before I even really have a moment to feel them.

My parents are becoming more and more unbearable with each announcement of another suicide by someone who had Siero in their system. They don't want to leave me alone for even a second. They are afraid I'm going to end my life.

I want to tell them not to worry, but I can't stop myself from thinking about it. I feel nothing. All I can do is smile, even when I want so desperately to cry or hit something or do anything besides smile. I'm getting so tired of smiling.

There is nothing I can do to help. There is nothing anyone can do at this point. I am lost. Broken. I feel like a carbon copy of what "happy" is supposed to look like.

One night, I decide I've had enough. I know I can't fight anymore, and I need to find a way to feel something again. Anything.

I tell my parents to go out and have a good night. I don't want to bother them and ruin their lives by having them babysit me all the time. I promise them that I'll be fine. Just fine.

"No, better than fine. When you come back, I'll be a whole new person. I promise," I tell them as I push them out the door on a Friday night.

Guilt hits me for a second as I watch them drive away, but it's quickly replaced by happiness. I hate feeling happy. It isn't the right kind of happiness. It's too constant.

I make my way further into the house, and then into my parents' bedroom. I find the safe in the closet, where my father keeps his gun, and punch in the code. It isn't hard. It's my mother's birthday.

"How cute," I whisper when I type it in, and the door slides open.

I grasp the handgun and pull it out of the safe. I stare down at it, turning it over in my hands until I grab one of the clips, also in the safe.

As I sit on my bed with my father's gun in one hand and my diary open before me, I start to rock back and forth. There is no other way out, no other way to live. I'm not myself anymore.

I swallow hard as I press the barrel of the gun against my forehead. Tears finally break free and start to roll down my cheeks, leaving behind shining trails.

"Please, forgive me, Mom and Dad," I whisper, keeping my eyes shut. "I want to be able to feel again…"

I allow myself to remember every painful memory, hoping the pain would course through my body and give me that sensation. I think about my nightmares, about the black ink spilling down the walls, the creepy man with the bright yellow eyes, and take it all in. I think about the night I had tried to end my life, how I had carved words into my stomach in a desperate attempt to find help. I remember the leather straps that bounded my wrists to the cold metal table, and the feeling of piercing needles breaking into my skin.

I press the cold barrel of the gun harder against my head.

Piercing pain, shooting into my arm as they injected me once. Twice. Three times. They turned me into a lab rat, they tortured me, they stole everything from me. My choices. My life.

I press my finger against the trigger.

EPILOGUE

As the news spread about the suicides due to Siero, Dr. Faulkner starts to use his financial success to his advantage. He pays off the families of the patients, who are kicking up enough of a fuss, and stops news companies from reporting negatively on it. People stop talking about the suicides, and they almost seem to forget about it as the news reporters transition to talking about the wonderful benefits of Siero.

Dr. Faulkner then changes the serum to, hopefully, lessen suicide rates, and releases it to the public. Doctors start to prescribe it to more and more people until, within a few years, it becomes a standard for babies when they are born. It becomes the new measles shot.

Dr. Faulkner's name becomes known to society; he's a savior. The man who found the cure to every mental illness known to humankind. Suicide rates drop as there are no more symptoms of depression anywhere. Crime rates descend, and Faulkner considers running for Congress.

There is a new world. And the new world is gray.

People walk the streets just smiling at each other with no real feeling behind it. They politely hold conversations about the weather before going on their separate ways. There is no more art, no more movies, no more sports, nothing that sparks anything more than a mere mild smile. People get up, have their breakfast, and go to work. They return home to perfectly fabricated families, where no games are played, where kids play alone or sometimes in groups, but are not overly aware of what's going on around them.

Time goes by, and society forgets all about the tragedy of the almost five hundred suicides committed by patients of Bellevue Psychiatric Hospital after the first doses of the vaccine were handed out to all their patients. But even if they do remember, they probably wouldn't care.

People no longer live. They only exist for the sake of existing.

EMOTIONAL DEVIANTS

EMOTIONS BOOK TWO

EMOTIONAL DEVIANTS

EMOTIONS BOOK TWO

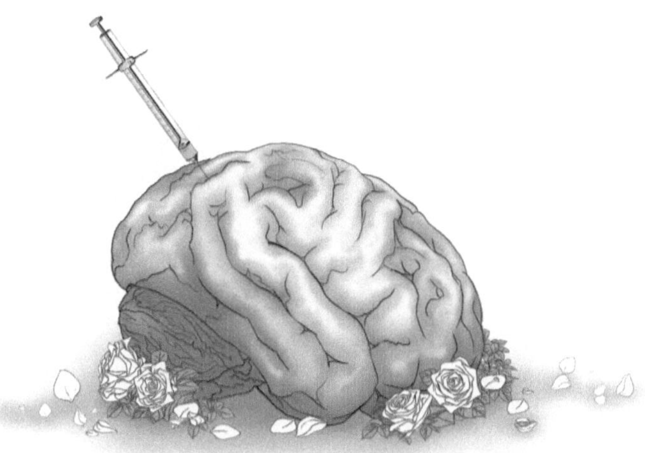

VIOLA TEMPEST

PROLOGUE

FAULKNER

The town of Bellevue was a desolate place. Not because there wasn't anyone around nor because the town was empty. No, the town was full of people: people who walked back and forth with their eyes glazed over, their expressions unreadable. It was desolated because it was empty of emotions.

Almost forty years had passed since Dr. Theodore Faulkner became the supreme leader of the town. His name had been plastered all over the city, his discoveries and the invention of Siero changed the lives of everyone around him.

The scandal after the first trials, where a whole psychiatric hospital had been emptied of its patients that later committed suicide, had almost been forgotten by the population. No one cared about it, because there was no sense in feeling bad about it, about something that had happened so long ago. Actually, there was no sense in feeling: because there were no feelings.

Not at all.

When Siero had proved its worth, Faulkner himself had run for mayor of the town. His face had been over every single post and window, and people had praised him for his discoveries. Mental illnesses were a thing of the past, and his discovery had changed the lives of many.

When the time for the elections came, Faulkner won without a struggle. He rose to power, and slowly, from the inside, he started to change everything. Siero became mandatory in his first five years in power, and within a few years, there was not a single person left in Bellevue who hadn't had the shot.

The vaccine kept changing through the years, and as Faulkner got drunk on his power, the vaccine mutated. People went from having no mental illnesses to having no feelings whatsoever. Babies were given the shot at birth and were raised to become what society needed of them.

In the present, no one could feel a thing in this desolate bubble town.

———

Faulkner watched people walking past from his window on the tenth floor, his mind far away as he thought about anything else that might be needed for that night's event.

The throngs of people looked almost organized as workers

headed home, and they formed lines to get onto the subway and buses. There were no arguments, no fighting over places in line, nothing. He still remembered how people used to get violent during this time of day, as if too eager to go home to keep being civil. He hated it.

Faulkner turned back to the desk and looked at the picture sitting there, slowly lowering to sit on his chair. The image was burned by the sun, but the happiness in his son's eyes was still unmistakable. He groaned as he sat, his joints making it hard to move, but he refused to use the cane unless he really needed to. So many years working on this, trying to make the best of this society, and now, the damned red reports filled his desk. He opened one, his shoulders sagging as he saw the statistics. More and more cases.

"I can't believe this is happening," he huffed.

More aberrations kept showing up, and his classified scientific team still hadn't figured out why, or how to stop it. Not many people knew about what was going on, and keeping the secret was getting harder and harder. Faulkner needed to get it over with, to cut the problem from the root, but he couldn't seem to find that root.

Some believed it was genetics. Others, faulty vaccines. He didn't care what the answer was, he just wanted results.

Almost ten years ago, he had managed to sell his vaccine outside of Bellevue. The version of the vaccine being shipped overseas wasn't the same one that he was using for his own town, no. He still needed an advantage, a reason for them to buy from him, and a way of making more money. The serum he had sent overseas was a milder version of the original vaccine, one that got rid of the mental health illnesses but allowed people to still feel. He needed wars so he could send his own heartless soldiers to fight those battles.

After all, the black market paid good money for his Black-hats, and he couldn't afford other places having an army as good as his own. The town's safety came first... but that didn't work if aberrations kept showing, and small riots kept taking place within the walls of Bellevue.

Annoyed and tired, he closed the files and headed toward the elevator. It was late, and he had to get ready for the party. The receptionist barely lifted her head to look at him as he passed, and didn't attempt to wish him a good night. She simply turned her head back down and kept working, as she was assigned to.

The Bluecoats' Annual Celebration was important for him and his reputation. After all, the Bluecoats were the ones who had his back, and someone from that tier would soon become the next leader, as Faulkner knew his days were numbered. He was getting old, and without any progeny of his own, he needed to pick a leader to replace him when the time came. He needed to find someone he could trust, someone who would make sure things kept getting better.

CHAPTER
ONE

ANNA

The party looked the same as every other year, and Anna Chaplin lingered around the banquet table, munching on the tasteless food as she looked around the room. The venue was huge, decorated with big chandeliers and flower bouquets all over the place. It was the definition of wealth, and even if she wasn't from the lowest tier in society and had attended the ball for years, she still felt out of place.

"So lucky," a girl by her side said.

Anna raised a single eyebrow while looking at the teen by her side, who was grabbing a heap of chocolates and shoving them in her mouth, one by one.

"Who's lucky?" she asked, unable to contain her curiosity when the girl kept looking around the room, her eyes expressionless and bored.

"The Bluecoats and their vials. I sometimes wish I could see what it's like, you know…"

With a shrug and a noncommittal grunt, the girl walked away, her expression back to being blank.

For a moment, Anna wondered if the girl could feel anything at all, but she shook her head, disregarding that thought. Of course, she couldn't. She watched the group of Bluecoats close by instead, and caught one of the men, just as he was grabbing a small blue vial from his pocket and tipping it into his drink. It was the group the teen had been watching, and the men there looked just about her age, maybe a few years older.

Joy, Anna thought with a sad feeling in her gut.

She felt the emotion creeping onto her face, and she made sure to shift her expression back to its usual blankness before anyone could see her. It was a trick she had learned real young, but still, once in a while, she felt things surging toward the surface.

She knew everything about the Blue Joy vial. After all, she was an intern at the same lab where it was being produced — the Emotions Wing at the Fox Lab. Blue Joy was a mixture of serotonin, dopamine, oxytocin, and even a touch of adrenaline. It was great for parties as it didn't have any adverse symptoms when consumed along with alcohol; it even heightened the effects of it.

The young girl from before was now lingering at the edges of the room, wandering with curious-looking eyes every time someone pulled a vial out from their pocket. Anna wondered if she was a Gray, but it couldn't be. Grays were never invited to Faulkner's parties, and that curiosity was surely something she was imagining. She wanted so hard to find feelings in anyone who wasn't a Bluecoat, that sometimes, her mind tricked her.

The party was mostly for Bluecoats — the businessmen and landowners of Bellevue — the ones who had been by Faulkner's side since the start and made sure to keep him in power. It was a celebration of everything they had managed so far, and a way for them to network and stay close together. They were a tight-knit group. This was why they were the only ones able to acquire the emotion vials — at least legally, as it was a way to reward them for all their hard work. They were also the ones with all the perks and almost none of the negative—

"Anna, darling. You shouldn't stare," her mother said as she showed up by her side, cutting her train of thought.

Glenn's shoulders were square, her chin held high. Her eyes blinked at regular intervals, her smile only showing when politically correct as she had been taught as a kid. The same teachings had come down to Anna when she was little, and she struggled to understand them at first. She had always been a smart kid, and it had only taken her a little while to notice that she was different. And only a little more to understand that *different* meant *dangerous* — that she had to blend in, to be invisible if she wanted to survive.

"I'm not. I was analyzing the composition of the Blue Joy vial in my mind, so I wasn't blinking because of the focus in my work," she lied with ease.

"Well, I admire your focus on your internship, but this is no place for formulas and work. You should go talk to some people. You know, ranking can get better if you connect with the right influences."

Anna nodded, "Of course, Mother."

Her mother barely looked at her as she walked away, her expression seeming almost bored. Whiteshirts weren't allowed to have emotion vials, so her mother had never experienced any kind of feeling. She knew almost everything about them from her work in the lab but had never experienced it for herself.

Same with her father. Frederik Chaplin, same as Glenn, was part of the administrative staff in one of the government bio labs that made drugs and serums, including the vials. This was the reason why Anna knew so much about the working of emotions, and why she had been granted the internship at the Fox Lab.

Having both of her parents working there had granted her easy access, and her future was almost set in stone. She'd work there her whole life, eventually be married off to some other Whiteshirt, and get some time off to have kids and keep the society working.

She hated it; she hated all of it. She knew she was lucky to have been born in the second most important tier of society, but still, she hated how her whole future had already been decided for her.

Tired of just watching and unable to disobey her mother's command, she decided to search for a group of people who looked high enough on emotions to be interesting. There was a group of girls about her age giggling, but that looked like too much — she might laugh at a joke and then have them figure out that she was only a Whiteshirt, which could get her in trouble.

Anna wasn't technically allowed to take emotion vials either, not even at a party like this. Looking around the room some more, she found a group of older gentlemen, about her parents' age, and made her way there.

"I can't believe the outrage of the situation between the Grays," a man was saying as she approached.

She tried to blend into the group, bobbing her head a little as the rest of the people did, and copying their postures as much as possible. She had been doing it for so long, that she wasn't even aware when she's copying the way other people moved or talked.

"I heard someone is smuggling out vials," another man whispered as if it were a secret.

Anna guessed it was, at least, among the commons. She couldn't believe her luck in overhearing such a conversation, so she perked up a little and listened in while saving each word the men said into her memory.

"I think Faulkner should put harder measurements in place to make sure this doesn't get out of control. Imagine all those Grays revolting because they're feeling too much. We could have the next Civil War coming our way."

"I think you're being dramatic, Mr. Tussels," the first man said.

"Not dramatic. There's no vial for that. I only took some enjoyment this evening."

A few people fake-laughed at the joke, and Anna bobbed her head a little.

"What about the fights? Did you hear about them? I heard they arrested a Gray last week who broke another man's nose. When they tested him, it looked like he had three vials of anger on him. I didn't even know those were still being stocked. I thought only positive emotions were being fabricated in the labs."

Anna bit her tongue so as not to get into the conversation. There was so much the Bluecoats were oblivious to. They might be the most powerful class, the ones with all the money, but they were also being manipulated by Faulkner without even realizing it. There was so much that was hidden from them, and Anna had only found out herself after lots of investigations.

Anger, betrayal, even fear… they were all used to enhance the reactions of the troops and make them more reactive. The Fox Lab had been running tests for months, while sending new troops outside of their borders, and Anna knew how they had gotten out.

"I think Faulkner is getting too old to know what he's up to," someone said in a low whisper that was almost inaudible.

"Careful what you say," another retorted.

That comment alone could mean prison time if the wrong person had heard it, and the man knew it. He was too high on confidence and joy to be able to worry about the consequences of his words.

"Well, that's why he's looking for a replacement. I hear he's having some interviews at the moment, looking for the next in line to take leadership."

Not being able to handle it anymore, Anna slipped out of the party and made her way to the terrace of the building, where she found herself alone. Listening to all those conversations was just too much, and hiding her emotions got exhausting after long periods of exposure. It was one of the reasons why she enjoyed being an intern at the lab so much, as most of the time, she was on her own, hiding inside the lab.

The lights in the town were on, looking like tiny spots from high above. She could see the city center, with many of the tiny spots, and how the lights dimmed a little as she looked outwards.

The outer city was where most of the Grays lived, between the Capitol and the huge walls that surrounded the town. Her home was a little to the west, nestled in between the Capitol and the outskirts, just where most of the labs and government facilities were.

"What is it like out there?" she asked out loud, enjoying the loneliness of the terrace and the sound of her own voice.

She had wondered that many times, but could rarely say any of it out loud. When she was younger, she had been naive enough to ask a few of those questions, and her mother had been terrified, explaining that she wasn't meant to ask any of those things.

Anna hadn't understood then, but soon, she did. She was different, and the things she felt deep in her gut were not normal. It was dangerous for her to voice any of it, and she didn't think she had done so since she turned six years old. It'd been hard to learn how to hide it all, every tear, every emotion, but her mother stopped worrying once she stopped showing signs of "illness," as Glenn had called it.

Working in the labs was the perfect way for her to find out more, to figure out why she was the only one in town who could... feel. It was scary most of the time, like she was walking among monsters that could tear her apart at any moment, but she had to keep going. She had to be invisible for as long as it might take until she had her answers.

Anna refused to play her part and simply survive. That was all she had done for years: being a survivor. Hiding in the shadows, pretending like pain and doubt didn't lace every step she took. Hiding the happiness she felt the first time she found an old record and listened to music, her eyes welling with tears that she quickly wiped away. She had hidden every emotion, every tiny thing she had ever felt, all to be one more in the crowd.

To be just another one of Faulkner's lifeless zombies.

But it was over. She wouldn't just survive anymore; she wanted to live. She'd find out the truth. She'd keep working in the lab and running her tests, figuring out how this all had come to be, and why there were still people who had feelings...

Even if she was the only one.

She refused to be a zombie.

CHAPTER
TWO

WINSTON

The town was oddly quiet in the late afternoon of that third Friday of the month. Winston had been stationed out there for a while now, and he had gotten used to the frequent brawls that he had to split up. There were more detentions in the past two months than there had been in years, and he wondered if something was stirring.

He was used to that particular Gray settlement by now, knew every street, every corner, and even some of the people were starting to look familiar after running into them over and over again. There was even a tavern in the south that he had gone to a few times with his pals on his days off, as it served some of the best beer that the town had to offer.

It wasn't that he wanted to feel familiar there. After all, it was a gray and sad place to be, but he sometimes felt more at home there than he did at his base. Maybe it was the memories of his mother and what she had told him, about what it was like to live there. Not that there had been any emotion to her tales, just simple facts, but ones that he had committed to memory.

"Mad Dog to Alfa One, do you copy?" His intercom beeped after the message, and he took it off of his belt, letting the memories slide to the back of his mind.

"Alfa One, copy," he said while pressing the button on the top.

He was walking down an empty street, the dim lights casting long shadows as he moved, and he looked around, making sure everything was in order. It had only been a few months since the Blackhats were deployed to the Grays' settlements, and it was unusual for them to send cadets to the field.

But since Winston was in his last year and close to graduating, they had made a few exceptions with his squad. They were treating it as some kind of advanced training, in which they could experience the work first hand — like an internship of sorts.

"There's a possible suspect of emotional abuse in the corner of fifth and fourth. I'm about to engage. Over."

"Copy that. Proceed with caution, Mad Dog."

He checked the map in his portable device and jogged toward the place of the disturbance. He wasn't too far away, and Mad Dog was sometimes stronger than he realized, so he'd just make sure everything was okay. Their shift would be over in half an hour anyway, so they could head back to the

Military Academy together. He set his hand on top of his gun, just in case, and quickened his pace.

A little surge of adrenaline kicked in as he got closer to the corner and saw a man lying on the ground, but he shifted his expression to nothingness.

"Mad Dog, report," he said once he was at earshot.

John was handcuffing the suspect, a knee on his back, and sweat pearled his features.

"Suspect fought back and rejected his sentence. He's being taken to the lab to test his blood for anger levels. I injected him with a sedative."

"I'll go with you. Let me send a command to base."

He quickly got his screen out and typed a message. The night had been pretty chill, so he was sure leaving a few minutes before time wouldn't be a problem. After all, the security was only there to find cases like the one they had in their literal hands. They pushed the man into the back of the van, and then as John, a.k.a Mad Dog, jumped on the wheel, Winston stepped into the passenger seat.

"Don't be an idiot, and don't speed."

There was a reason why they called him "Mad Dog." The adrenaline and anger shots seemed to have an incredibly strong effect on him, and whenever they went for their weekly shots, John went ballistic. Winston was one of the few who knew how to deal with his moods, and it was just because he knew anger pretty well himself. He had dealt with it his whole life. The fury of everything he had endured seemed to coil in his stomach, and he swallowed it all down, making it small, making it disappear.

"Who do you think I am?" Mad Dog replied as he turned a corner.

If he didn't know any better, he'd think Mad Dog had just made a joke, but no Blackhat was ever going to make one of those. After all, they weren't allowed any emotion vials apart from those that turned them into better soldiers. Blackhats were all either part of the civil police or the Military person-nel, chosen from a young age to serve Bellevue and the towns on the outside whenever required.

And that was exactly what everyone at the Academy was talking about at the moment. They were so close to gradua-tion that they were all wondering who was going to be deployed overseas and who wasn't. Bets were being placed on who was going to be deployed, but Winston had stayed away from all that.

"Thinking about deployment?" Mad Dog asked as if reading his mind.

"I was, actually."

"I still don't get why you always think so much about it; you don't have a say in it. And it doesn't make a difference, anyway," John said apathetically. "You bet on it, and then that's it. If you get some money from your bet, great. If not, nothing changes. You fight here, you fight out there, it's all the same... Patrol, get the bad guys, go home, sleep. Repeat." John lifted his shoulders in a shrug at the end, sounding bored as he drove toward the research facility.

Winston only nodded, trying not to give himself away.

He knew he shouldn't care, and he tried to pretend like he didn't. But as graduation got closer and closer, it was harder not to think about it. He was faithful to the regime, and he knew that the only way he could find out more about himself was to be deployed overseas when his training ended. That was why he had made an effort to be the best at everything.

He wanted to graduate, decorated with the most medals possible, so he could become overseas material. Out there, he'd be able to figure it all out: to see if there were more people like him. Handing himself in wasn't an option. After all, he wasn't suicidal.

"Your parents' health okay?" John asked in his usual chit-chat.

It wasn't that he cared, but John liked the sound of his

own voice, and liked to have the silence filled up whenever possible.

"Mom's fine. Dad… I have no idea."

"Same, dude, same. Haven't heard a word from my father in… eight years, I think."

Winston's mother was a Gray, which meant Winston had three younger brothers. Most Gray women were to have at least three children, who would be assigned to different tiers and jobs, depending on what was needed at the time of their coming of age.

Winston himself had been taken to the Military Academy when he was only twelve, due to his father being a Blackhat and part of the Military, too. John's case was similar, as his father was a Blackhat, too. He wasn't sure about his mother; he had never asked. Winston's father had been deployed overseas when Winston was only six, and he hadn't heard anything about him ever since. Most people who were deployed never returned, as they went off to fight whatever war was going on at the moment.

And that was what he wanted.

He wanted to go out and see for himself why no one returned. Why no one ever came from the outside of that huge wall and talked about how things were out there.

Was it all the same? Was the whole world an emotionless pit?

He couldn't help but wonder about it; he had done so since he was very young. After all, he had never met anyone else who had feelings — not like he did.

―――

The lab was quiet as they walked down the halls with the prisoner in tow. That wasn't unusual, but Winston often forgot how eerie and creepy the place was. He felt cold tendrils sneaking up his spine, and he shuddered.

"You all good?"

"Just cold," Winston said with a shrug. "Didn't put my thermal on today."

"Sucks," replied John.

He knew the halls well, and they took a turn to enter the Emotions Wing. It was right next to the Militia Lab, the one where they went to get their shots every week. Winston swiped his card at the entrance, and at the beep, they opened the doubled doors and signed in at reception. For the past few years, Winston had been to the Fox Lab regularly, just like everyone else on his squad. He usually went during the first hour of the morning to get his shot, so being there before dinner felt odd.

"Prisoner 1287B, found fighting on fifth and fourth," John said to the receptionist as she typed the details into the computer. "Suspected of being high on anger."

The man thrashed a little, fighting the restraints of the handcuffs, and John simply smacked him on the head with a bored expression as the receptionist kept asking him questions.

"How does he declare?"

"I'm innocent, innocent!" The man struggled some more, and John pinched his shoulder hard, numbing him until he was docile.

"Doubt that." The receptionist kept typing, not even flinching. "Okay, all done here. Take him to room four. Lock the door when you leave; we'll take it from there."

"Roger that."

They took the prisoner to room four, opened the door with the magnetic government cards, and shoved him in. John locked the door back and, as soon as it closed, a dense white gas came out of the corner of the room. The man looked at it with wide eyes, but he didn't struggle. He sat on the ground, his eyelids growing heavy, and a moment later, they knew he'd passed out. There was no point in waiting for it, so Winston and John made their way toward the exit.

"New subject to test?" a young girl asked the receptionist as they walked out.

Her hair was the color of fire, and Winston couldn't help but glance.

"Yes. Could you take care of it, Anna? He's already been sedated, should be passed out in a minute. Take the blood sample, and send it to testing."

"Yes, I've done it before. I'll take care of him."

Something in her tone caught Winston's attention, but he tried to keep his eyes on the door. He wasn't sure what it was, but the way she had said the last word, dragging it a bit longer than needed…

"Come on, man," John nudged him on the shoulder, and Winston realized that he was already standing by the double doors. With a shake of his head, he walked out. "What's up with you today? Did you take all your pills this morning? You seem a bit out of it. Are you sure you're not coming down with some sort of sickness?"

"I took all my vitamins, don't worry. Just didn't sleep well last night," Winston lied. "Let's get back to the barracks. I can use a nap."

They got out of the building and jumped back into the van.

"See you in a week, Foxy," John said, waving to the building as if it were a person.

"You know there's no need to be polite to buildings, right? Didn't they teach you that it's only for humans?"

It sounded too much like a joke, and Winston bit his tongue as he realized the mistake in it.

Luckily, John only shook his head. "Just practicing my skills for the day I run into a Bluecoat."

He shrugged nonchalantly, and Winston changed the subject to something boring, like the weather, as they made their way to their base. That way, there were no chances of him messing up.

It was getting harder and harder every week. The closer he grew to his squad, the harder it was for him to act like them and remain a cold and calculating soldier. Winston did care about them and their wellbeing. But no. He shook his head again and opened the window so the cool air would clear his head.

He couldn't care. He couldn't feel anything at all.

CHAPTER
THREE

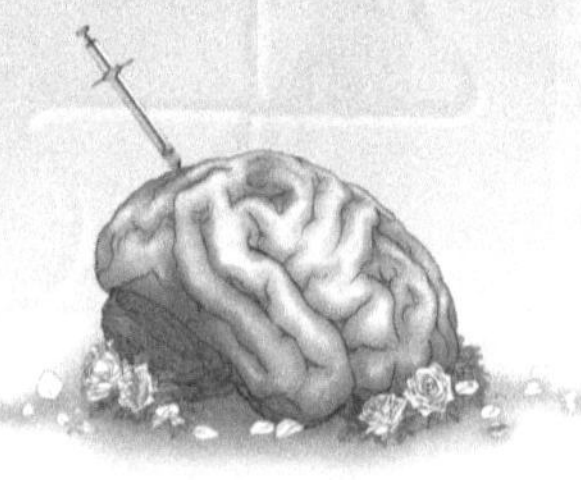

ANNA

As Anna walked toward the holding cell, she couldn't help but look over her shoulder to the retreating soldiers. She didn't usually pay them much attention, but she noticed the way one of them had stared at her — which was highly unusual.

A little curiosity settled in the pit of her stomach, and she bit her lip to avoid smiling.

What if…?

No, she couldn't be thinking like that. Getting her hopes up for a simple look was stupid, and she knew better than to project her feelings onto others.

She pressed the magnetic card to the reader on the door and opened it up. The subject was lying on the floor, unconscious, and she looked at his chart. Prisoner 1287B. No name, no nothing, just a number.

That was pretty much all the lab needed to know; the rest would go to court if the test results came up positive. She took the blood sample in a matter of seconds and went over to the testing lab to do the job herself. Results would be revealed in just hours, and she wanted to be the one to check it out and fill out the report.

———

"Anna, there's something for you."

It had been a few days since her encounter with the tall soldier, and Anna was still thinking about him as her mother knocked on her bedroom door and took her out of her daydream. She knew it was wrong, and that hoping was fruitless, but she couldn't help it. Anna had always been a dreamer.

"What is it, Mother?"

"A letter. It's got the government's seal."

She handed her the piece of paper, and Anna took it with trembling hands, dreading what could be inside.

She knew the odds, though. At her age, she would be either getting the lab's decision on whether her internship was turning into a hired position, or...

No, it couldn't be.

She was still young; she had at least another year or two before the other letter. Surely, this was just the confirmation of her hard work, and an acceptance into the lab as a hired and permanent staff member. It *had* to be.

"Come on, take it."

Her mother still had the letter in an outstretched hand, and Anna took it with trembling fingers.

Glenn crossed her arms over her chest in a comfortable position as she leaned against the wall and waited for Anna to open it. The girl took a deep breath and turned her face into nonchalance as she tore open the envelope. There was a single piece of white paper inside, and as she unfolded it, her stomach fell to her feet. Anna was glad that she was already seated, because her hands were trembling, and she thought she would have fallen, otherwise.

"And?" Glenn asked, ignoring her daughter's emotional response.

She was either blind to it or had deliberately decided to pretend it wasn't happening.

"It's… a mandate."

"Marriage?"

The word sounded so normal on her mother's lips. She couldn't understand how it didn't taste sour to her mother as it did to her.

"Yes."

It was barely a whisper that escaped between the huge knot in her throat, and Glenn only nodded before turning to leave.

"I guess it's time," she said as she walked out.

Anna stayed there, staring at the words and reading them over and over to try and make sense of them.

Anna Chaplin,

We hereby inform you that you have been selected for the Whiteshirt Marital Program. You are required to attend the marriage lab within twenty-four hours of receiving this letter to provide blood and urine samples.

The union will be arranged in the next sixty days as per protocol, and as declared by law, you'll be expected to be with child before the end of the year, after finishing the fertilization procedure.

A pamphlet will be provided to you at the lab with all the information on fertility you will need to read, the diet to follow, and prescriptions for vitamins. A full guide can also be found on our online portal in case any doubts arise.

Regards,

The Whiteshirt Marital Committee

She felt her eyes filling up with tears and looked up so they wouldn't spill.

"It can't be; it can't be…"

Anna needed more time. She needed time to figure it all out, to understand what was happening to her, to the world. To find a way out.

Trembling hands and all, Anna stood up, crumpled the piece of paper in her hands, and shoved it into her desk's top drawer before heading toward the dresser. She changed into her usual attire: a long white coat with matching white boots.

With her chin held high, she marched into the bathroom and did her makeup as she did every morning: just a little powder, a little eyeliner, and some lip balm. She willed the tears to stay away, the nausea churning in her stomach to settle, and the fast thumping of her heart to slow down. She stared into the mirror for a full minute, making sure the tears weren't about to spill.

Once she was sure they wouldn't, she grabbed her bag and went to the Fox Lab.

———

"Anna, there's something for you."

Not again, she thought. *Not again.*

"What is it, Alexa?"

"An envelope." Alexa, the receptionist, handed it to her, and Anna willed her hands not to shake.

It'd been just over twenty-four hours since the letter that'd turned her life upside down and put a death sentence on her life as she knew it, so Anna was almost unwilling to open the new envelope at the lab. But this time, she was certain of what she'd find inside. Her internship was about to be over, and the envelope held her future: whether she'd be given a permanent position at the Emotions Wing of the Fox Lab, or whether she needed to pack up her things and be sent else-where — to try her luck at another discipline.

Anna tore the envelope open and looked at the piece of paper inside.

"So?" Alexa was looking up at her, wanting to know if they'll keep working together or not.

"I'm in," Anna struggled to keep the smile from extending on her face, and instead, shrugged a little. "We'll keep working together."

"Great, you know what you're doing, not like the other interns. My job is easier with you here, so it makes sense."

"Yeah… Thanks."

"Have you checked on Prisoner A154 already?"

Anna's excitement deflated, and she nodded. "On my way."

She grabbed the folder from the counter and put the enve-lope away before heading toward the rooms in the back.

It was a morning like any other, following the charts and getting blood samples from the prisoners brought in the night before. After that, she headed to the main lab to run the tests. Most of them came back negative (thankfully), and the rest looked like they deserved their penalty.

One man had been brought in for killing a co-worker after a riot, and another for punching his wife in the face after she served him a cold meal. Anna's stomach churned with disgust, and she filled in the forms, stating that the analysis came back positive, and both prisoners had indeed used emotion vials.

I need to regulate what's going on with the Grays, she thought.

Things were getting out of control, and Anna couldn't

help but feel a little guilty. Grays were becoming addicted to the adrenaline rush they got from anger, as it was harder to come across joy for that fix.

In some ways, the compositions were similar. Both Blue Joy and Crimson Fury had adrenaline and serotonin. But while Blue Joy had dopamine and oxytocin, Fury was laced with endurance and strength drugs. The mix of creatine, caffeine, and beta-alanine created an almost "high" feeling as it kept the muscles going for longer and helped avoid fatigue.

The last case of the day was a young woman, and Anna felt bad the second she looked at the picture in her file. She looked so empty of emotion, like everyone else, dark circles under her eyes, and her skin was full of scratches and bruises.

Anna remembered the feel of her rough skin as she took the sample. The woman was probably a worker in one of the factories, where days blended into one another with the long hours of work. Her file stated that she'd refused arrest, violently, but didn't say anything about bad behavior before that.

Checking the charts, Anna noticed high adrenaline and norepinephrine, as well as high caffeine in her blood, but the rest of her parameters seemed normal... just like how an emotional person would react to a stressful situation.

She noted the woman's number, committed it to memory, and then changed the results, deeming the woman as not guilty.

She compiled the files back into the usual folder and walked out of the lab. It had been a long day, and it was already getting late, so she walked fast, wanting to clock out and head home to work on her investigation in private for a little while.

The memories from the day before, and her quick visit to the marital department, were still too fresh. She knew she should look at all the information they had given her, but she hadn't even taken it home, still holding it with her paperwork. Distracted as she was, she didn't look up when she turned the corner heading into reception — and slammed face-first into a solid human wall.

"Ow!"

"Sorry, are you okay?"

Anna shook the confusion out of her head and looked up to find a pair of deep brown eyes looking down at her. A few of the papers had fallen out of her folder, and she quickly crouched to pick them all up as she mumbled an apology to the familiar-looking guy.

"Sorry, I wasn't looking. I'm okay."

"Let me help you."

The soldier crouched in front of her and picked up a few of the papers, handing them back to her one by one as he did, his eyes never leaving hers.

"Winston! Are you coming?" another soldier yelled from the end of the hall, and the guy barely glanced up to reply.

"Coming! Wait for me outside!"

Anna glanced back at the retreating soldier as he nodded and turned his back to leave. He was the opposite of the man she had in front of her. While the other man was pure muscle, and as wide as he was tall, Winston was thin for a soldier, his tall frame making him look skinnier than he was. His skin was almost pale, and his short chestnut hair had a golden tinge to it.

"Are you okay?" Winston asked once more, helping Anna to her feet with a gentle hand under her elbow.

Anna then remembered why he looked so familiar. It was the same soldier she'd caught staring at her the week prior, and the way he was looking at her now…

"I'm fine; thank you for your help."

A little flush came up to her cheeks when she noticed the last piece of paper the soldier had handed her. It was the information on fertility that she had been handed the day before, a big stamp from the fertility clinic on the first page.

She quickly shoved it into the folder and tried to take a calming breath so her cheeks would stop burning.

"It's okay. I'm sorry for running into you. I should have been paying more attention. I'm Winston, by the way."

He stretched his hand forward, and Anna took it in hers, his warmth spreading up her arm, and her doubts from before multiplying ten-fold.

"It was all my fault for not looking where I was going. Once again, thank you for helping me pick it all up. And… I'm Anna, it's a pleasure to meet you."

"I guess I'll see you around, Anna."

With a nod of his head, Winston walked around her to follow his companion, who was long gone.

"You sure will. I'm here almost every day."

Winston turned around to glance at her over his shoulder, and something akin to a smile flashed on his face for a second before he turned again, and she was left looking at his retreating back.

What was that?

There was no way she had imagined it again: that bright sparkle shining deep within Winston's eyes. It took her a while to turn around and walk back to reception. Once she did and handed all her folders for Alexa to file, she bit her tongue. She wouldn't do it. She couldn't ask.

"Is that everything for today?" Alexa asked.

"Yes… Actually, no," she said too quickly.

"Yes, or no?"

Alexa didn't even look up, her fingers still typing quickly as she started filing the information from the charts on her desk.

She had already hinted at it, and she wasn't going to be able to forget about it, so she thought she might as well just go along with it.

"There's a squad that comes in every week for their shots. I just ran into them heading out, and it gave me an idea for my graduation project, now that I've officially been given the position. Do you think you can print their information for me? I want to look at their charts and see if any subjects might work for what I have in mind."

The lie was easy, and Anna felt guilty for it, but there was only one way for her to figure out if Winston was really who she thought, *what* she thought. By spending more time with him. And not even knowing his last name; that was the best way for her to find out more about him and get to know him better.

"Sure, I'll send it over to your email."

"Actually, can you print it out for me? I'll take it home and start looking at it tonight if that's not a problem."

"Sure." Alexa barely nodded and kept typing. Within thirty seconds, the printer started working. "Just grab it once it's done."

"Thank you."

As soon as the last paper was out, Anna snatched it all and put it inside a folder together with the fertility papers. Shoving it all in her bag, she headed out of the lab and toward her car, which was parked in the same spot as every other day. She jumped in, started the engine, turned on the heat, and took the folder out from her bag.

Her fingers drummed nervously as she scanned the names… until she found him. Heart jumping wildly in her chest, she read his information.

Name: Winston Hitcher
Tier: Blackhat
Mother: Gray
Father: Blackhat (deployed)
Age: 18 years old
Height: 6' 4"
Weight: 182 pounds
Assignment: Military Academy Cadet
Blood type: O-negative

Weekly shots: Crimson Fury, PED, modafinil

Anna read his whole file, her heartbeat an echoing thrum in her chest as she did. Maybe this was her way out. Maybe this was a sign that there was still hope, that her days were not counted, that she could get out of there, that she could do more than just survive.

When she finally drove home, determination was the only emotion coursing through her veins.

CHAPTER
FOUR

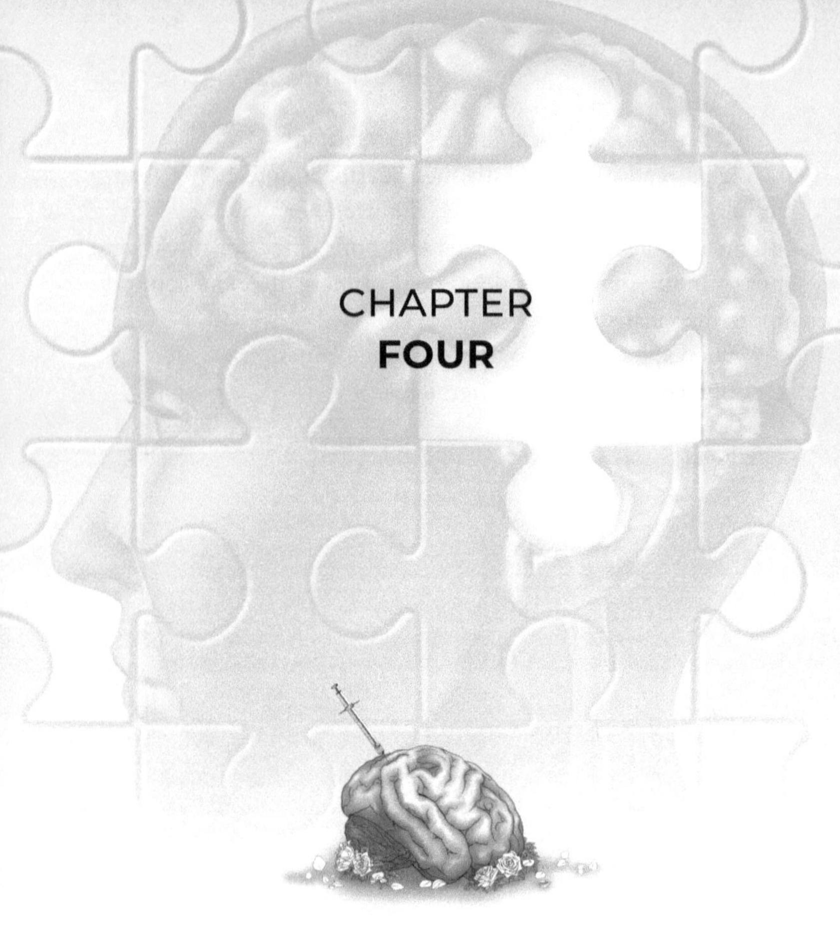

WINSTON

The next morning, Winston got up in the barracks, hoping his week would fly through. The look in Anna's eyes as their fingers had briefly touched while handing her the paper burned his memories, and he willed his mind to let go of it. It was stupid. There was no point in thinking about it. Anna had simply been polite, as it was her job to treat each soldier with respect. That had been all.

"Morning," John showed up at his side in an instant, jumping down from the top bunk.

"Mad Dog, slept well?"

"Like a drugged-up soldier."

It was his reply every morning, and Winston struggled not to snort. Unlike him, who was given modafinil to stay awake, Mad Dog was usually given melatonin to help him sleep. But it was a mild natural drug and didn't usually do much. With all the other pills he took, something stronger would mess up his system, so John simply ran on little to no sleep. He still did all the training as the rest of them, so as long as he wasn't causing trouble, the generals were okay with it.

"Strength training today?" he wondered, already knowing the answer.

"Yup, ready to go?"

"Always."

They marched out of the barracks together, only to run into a general standing outside the door and about to go in. They both saluted, clapping their boots together and taking a fist to their chest.

"General."

"Cadet Winston Hitcher, you're to report to the main office, now."

"Yes, sir!"

Winston saluted again and turned to head to the office, but not before glancing at John, wondering what was going on. John simply shrugged one shoulder, showing him a thumbs up as if wishing him luck. Winston found another official sitting at a desk in the office, his expression as bored as it could be. He glanced up as Winston entered, waving for him to sit.

"Cadet Hitcher, you have been requested to attend the Fox Lab. There's a new investigation starting, and they need subjects. Your name has been picked due to your response to the drugs being used. I believe there's a new drug they need to test, and your charts matched what they needed. You're to report there this afternoon." Winston knew better than to ask questions, so he bit his tongue. "Report at reception for procedure F25b at the Emotions Wing. You're dismissed."

With a bow of his head, Winston stood up and headed back to the training grounds.

His morning went by in a blur of motions, following the indications of the general as he did uncountable push-ups, climbed ropes, ran miles without end and with a twenty-kilogram bag over his shoulder, and then repeated the whole circuit again. And again.

By the time training was over, and he hit the showers, his every muscle was in knots. He let the cold water run over him aimlessly, untangling the dirt knots out of his hair and brushing the soil from beneath his nails. The whole time, his mind went back to that moment in the office.

Another drug trial couldn't be good. Every time the needle went into his arm, he felt a little less like himself. But it was what it was. It was his duty as a citizen and a soldier to do these trials, so he told that little voice in his head to shut up.

He scrubbed the rest of his body until no trace of dirt was left. All he had to do was fulfill his duties in society. After all, wasn't that what his mother had always told him?

Do as you're told, and they will leave you alone.

He didn't know how things had been before, as not many changes had occurred since he had been born, but his grandmother left a journal he often looked at when he was a child. She had been born before the vaccines were mandatory and had often written about her life.

After the vaccine had been given to her, the change was obvious, and Winston couldn't help but wonder if it had been one of the things that drove her to commit suicide. It was hard to picture, as the suicide rates in town had dropped to zero after the serum was improved, and the whole town immunized, but still, reading her entries... Winston had always wondered.

She had written a bit about Faulkner before getting the vaccine, and how he had gotten a liking for power as soon as he'd been named "supreme leader."

The serum was meant to make things easier, to guarantee a society where there would be no crime, no hate, and no violence. It had clearly worked for years, as during his whole childhood, Winston hadn't experienced or seen any violence around him. It had been something new to him when he joined the Militia, and the shot had been provided.

He felt it as a kid, but it had been easy to mask it, to hide it. But it was different in the Academy, where they were meant to get angry, to get the Crimson Fury shot and let it all out, punch bags without end, and shoot moving targets. Crimson gave a glint to men's eyes, one that Winston had started seeing in the men around the Grays' settlements during the past few weeks, which was concerning, to say the least.

At camp, they were meant to train to protect themselves from the outside world, not to monitor their own town, as they were doing at the moment. According to the history lessons, as soon as the whole town had been vaccinated, the outside world deemed them vulnerable, and attacks started. Faulkner then decided to isolate Bellevue, to turn it into a small self-sufficient town that didn't need the outside world.

That was exactly why Winston was so curious about being deployed outside of their bubble. It was said that politicians paid well to get Bellevue soldiers, and Winston wanted to know why. He wanted to know if the rumors of the vaccine going global were true or not.

He needed to see the outside world for himself.

———

"Winston Hitcher, reporting for procedure F25b," he told the receptionist amidst entering the lab that afternoon.

The woman typed a few things on the computer, and then looked at him.

"Room 36F, on the left-hand side of the hall, to your right. Trainee, Anna Chaplin, is waiting for you there."

Winston wasn't oblivious to the name given to him, and he remembered the redhead from the other day, wondering if this was a coincidence, and if, by any chance, he was about to run into the same woman again. He thanked the receptionist and followed her indications, knocking on the door to Room 36F only a minute later. His heart was already drumming in his chest, not knowing what he was getting himself into.

"Cadet Hitcher, welcome. Please, come in."

He wasn't sure if he was supposed to mention that they had met before, so he simply nodded and entered the small room, sitting on the bench to the side as he always did when in the lab. It was such a natural response that he wondered after doing it, if he'd done the right thing.

Anna closed the door and turned to him, half of her lips turning up into a small smile before she cleared her throat and pressed her lips into a thin line.

"Cadet, have you been informed of the reason for you being here?"

"Briefly," he said with a curt nod.

"Okay… My name is Anna Chaplin, and I'm a new trainee in this lab. I have recently finished my internship, and as a requirement to being formally introduced into the team, I need to conduct a study on a subject of my choice."

Winston listened, not knowing what to say, so he nodded once more. He was wearing his thick cargo pants and Military jacket on top of a standard singlet, and he felt the sweat gathering in his back and neck as he sat there.

Anna was standing close to him now, a stethoscope around her neck, her hand reaching up to place two fingers on his neck. He wondered if she noticed his fast heartbeat, and he forced it to slow down. Learning to meditate at a young age had saved him from many confrontations, and at that moment, he used every tool he knew to slow his metabolism down as much as he could.

"Your pulse is strong, seems a little fast, so let me check on that."

"Sure."

He squared his shoulders and took a few more calming breaths while Anna turned around to grab a tensiometer. By the time she tested him with the proper equipment, all the measurements came back normal.

"Maybe I counted wrong, seems like everything is perfectly fine. Do you get your weekly shot here?"

"I do, every Thursday."

"Any daily medication?"

"Just the standard vitamins."

Anna marked a few boxes on her sheets, and then approached him again.

"I'm going to get a blood sample. Is that okay?"

"Not a problem."

She turned again while she prepared the needle and sterilized all the equipment, and Winston couldn't help but stare at the curves of her gentle face, the shape of her lips, and the way her eyelids fluttered every other second.

There was something about her. It wasn't that she was beautiful, even though he thought she was. But he had seen many beautiful women before, and none of them had ever gotten his attention. No, it was the subtle ways in which Anna moved. The way her lips were constantly being tugged up, and how she moved her face back to nothingness when she noticed herself doing it. It looked like she was hiding something… in the same way he was.

Winston knew it was dangerous, but before he could stop himself, he started talking.

"So, are you satisfied with being picked to work at the lab?"

Anna glanced at him, and then grabbed an elastic band out of a drawer.

"I am," she said as she tied it around his arm. "Both my parents work here, and this is why I wanted to do it, too."

She smiled then, and it didn't look like those fake smiles that kids were taught to do when they were young. It seemed so real, so genuine.

"What about you? Is the Academy life good?"

No questions ever entailed feelings. It wasn't about if it was what he had wanted, desired, or dreamt of; it was always about the facts. About the schedule, and everyday life.

"Can't complain."

"I will just need a few vials of your blood," she explained as she plunged the needle into his arm, and the first vial of blood filled up quickly.

"Not a problem."

Anna pressed a cotton ball to the spot of the extraction and got a new needle. It was unusual to be punctured more than once, but Winston didn't argue or ask what it was about. He was sure that there was a motive for it. Finding another vein and tapping it with a finger, Anna got ready for the next extraction.

"What about your parents? What do they do?"

Winston felt the usual knot in his throat at the question, but he swallowed it and replied regardless.

"My mother's a Gray. She works at one of the factories in town. She's a seamstress. My father is a Blackhat. He was deployed when I was eight. I never heard from him after that."

"So sorry to hear that."

Anna followed her words with a needle, and Winston tried to breathe through it, to dissolve the knot in his throat, and to think about something else.

Anna pressed another bit of cotton to his skin, and then her fingers softly trailed his veins. He breathed deeply once more, trying to ignore the current of electricity that drove him crazy as her soft fingers kept moving across his arm. His shirt was rolled up, exposing every muscled bit of his arm, and Anna seemed to be exploring his skin as if she's never seen another human before.

He cleared his throat with little effort and tried not to jerk his arm.

"Anything unusual?" he asked.

"Oh, nothing. Excuse me, I was wondering which vein would be better for this last extraction."

Her fingers trailed down to his wrist, and she drew a circle there, then flipped his hand over and tapped some of the veins on the back of his hand. The way she held his hand was so foreign, her soft skin the complete opposite to his roughness.

"I think this one will do."

She looked up at him, a big and wonderful smile on her face, and he felt the heat in his cheeks, the drumming in his heart. He looked to the door as she inserted the needle, and when she was done, and he heard the syringe being placed on a metal platter, she still held his hand.

"All done."

She patted his hand once more, and he dared to look at her. That bright smile was gone, but the feeling in his gut was still there. He needed to get out of there before he did something stupid, but all words seemed to have left him.

Anna was back at the small desk, filling in some papers and taking some final notes, when the door opened, and a petite girl, with long dark braids down to her waist, entered the office. The girl closed the door behind her quickly and leaned against it. Her eyes opened wide as she saw Winston there, as if she were expecting Anna to be alone.

Winston looked between them, and both girls seemed

enamored and out of words for a second, after which Anna jumped into motion and rushed to the girl.

"Sammy, I'm sorry. I didn't know you were coming in today."

Anna glanced back at Winston, and her expression didn't give anything away this time.

"Sorry, Anna, I thought… thought you were alone."

"It's okay, I… I've already run those tests you asked for. We can discuss them after I'm done here."

Anna patted the small woman on the shoulder and opened the door for her. The movement was fast, but Winston's eyes were trained for details, so he noticed the moment Anna grabbed something out of her coat's pocket and quickly dropped it into the other girl's pocket. He saw a glint of blue, but the movement was too fast for him to know for sure.

Anna closed the door once Sammy left and nodded politely.

"We're all done here, Cadet Hitcher. Will see you again next week. Thank you for your cooperation."

She went back to the emotionless human she had been at the start, and Winston wondered if he'd imagined everything that had happened between them during the last few minutes. Not knowing what else to do, he rolled his sleeve down, got up, and nodded briefly.

"See you next week."

"Will see you then."

Winston left the lab, a knot of doubt and a huge cluster of questions swimming in his head.

CHAPTER
FIVE

ANNA

With the excuse of the test that she was running, Anna stayed until late in the lab again. She'd been doing the same thing, night after night, since testing Winston, too many wild ideas running through her head.

It was Wednesday already, which meant that Winston would be in for his weekly shot the next day, and in for another test with her on Friday. As she looked at his chart, her heart rate spiked.

"It's not wishful thinking; it can't be," she told herself.

It was the same thing she had been repeating over and over; saying it out loud gave it more weight. No one would have ever seen what she had seen in Winston's chart, because no one was looking for it. She had taken a few different samples, making sure to look for varying emotions in each of them.

When she asked him about his parents, she saw a pattern that showed distress. Thinking about his parents made him sad, which made sense, considering his father had been deployed years ago, according to his file. Anna felt a little creepy looking into all the information available about the cadet, but what else was she supposed to do? After dreaming about it for so long, she was sure she had finally found another human who was like her.

Someone with feelings.

She felt the tears prickling in her eyes and blinked away the dampness. Being alone in the lab was no certainty; anyone could still show up unannounced. Trusting the safety and privacy of her own lab wasn't a mistake she was going to fall into again. After all, Sammy had almost ruined everything for her when she stepped into the lab the prior Friday.

She had gotten her the vial in time, but it had been a close call. If Sammy got caught, then Anna surely would've fallen with her, and she couldn't risk it, not yet. Anna thought about Winston's last sample, the one she had taken after her fingers had trailed the soft skin on the inside of his wrist, and then traveled through his calloused palms. Her cheeks felt hot, and she covered her face with her palms as she giggled.

His dopamine levels had been off the charts on the last sample, and his adrenaline and testosterone levels had also been higher than they should've been.

"Don't be silly, Anna," she chided herself.

Opening the top drawer of her desk, she put the files away and closed the drawer, making sure to lock it with the small key hanging from her neck. She knew the lab wasn't the safest place, but she didn't want to take the papers home, either. She wasn't meant to take files home without a reason to and permission from her superiors.

When she finally left the lab that night, Anna drove home with a silly smile still plastered on her face. She made sure to get rid of it before entering the apartment, and greeted her parents with a simple nod.

"Make any advances on your project?" her mother asked.

"I think I'm getting there."

"What are you working on, again?" her father intervened.

That was the hard part about having parents who worked in the same laboratory as her: lying wasn't as easy. She couldn't just make something up and not have them doubting what she was talking about. So, remembering her plan, she started explaining how she was looking to make Crimson Fury better by altering the proportions of each chemical used in the vial and adding a new component.

"Hasn't that been done before?" her father asked after a moment.

"Not in the same way I'm doing it. All the previous attempts were only about the proportions, while I'm thinking about adding a retro-virus to the mix to also make the effects last longer. I think, if done properly, I could make it so the RNA in the virus attaches itself to the host, making the changes permanent. It would be a single-use vial that would be put into effect by taking a small weekly pill to keep the hormone levels steady, instead of having to get a shot every time."

It wasn't the most solid idea she'd ever had, and she knew it wouldn't work... it was just the lie she was telling her parents to make sure they wouldn't interfere in what she was really doing.

"I hope it works," her mother said nonchalantly.

Anna nodded and went down the hall to her room, where

she slumped onto the bed and closed her eyes. She let the image of ripped arm muscles and a twisted sweet smile cloud her thoughts, while a smile of her own tugged at the edges of her lips, making her cheeks sore from how much she'd been smiling lately.

Tomorrow, she thought. *Tomorrow, I'll probably see him, even if for just a minute.*

She wondered once again if he knew, if Winston understood how different he was, and in how much danger he was because of it. Anna didn't know what she'd do if Winston didn't know about his condition, but she had to talk to him about it. One way or another, she had to let him know that she was just like him, that they were different… but together, they could do great things.

When Anna closed her eyes for the last time that night, the image of Winston's attentive eyes was still lingering in her mind.

———

Thursday was a letdown.

Anna waited all day to run into Winston, but when she finally heard that the cadets were in the building, she was called to her boss' office to discuss her project. They wanted to know what she was working on, how she was contributing, and the plans she had for the serum.

She was also reminded of her duties that day when she received the results from the tests she'd gotten done the week prior at the fertility clinic. As it turned out, she was fertile, which meant she had been approved for the marital program.

Her time was running out, and anxiety clawed at her chest for the rest of the day, making it impossible to concentrate on what she was meant to do.

When Sammy entered her lab that night, just before her shift was over, she almost jumped through the roof.

"Sorry for startling you."

"It's okay, not your fault… It's been a rough day."

She walked to the door, her hand already fidgeting with the vial in her pocket.

"Same as last week," she said as she casually slid her hand into Sammy's pocket and dropped a vial into it. "Any news?"

"They're getting restless. There's not enough *blue* to go around, so they're going *red*. Not sure where they're getting that from."

Anna sighed and rubbed her temple as a light headache made her close her eyes for a moment. *Blue* was the code they used to talk about Blue Joy, the vial they had been smuggling into the Grays' settlements for months. Anna believed everyone should know what happiness felt like at least once, but people had become addicted to the adrenaline rush, and had somehow gotten their hands on Crimson Fury, instead. And she wasn't sure how to fix it.

"Thank you. You should get going."

As Sammy left, Anna turned around and looked at the closed drawer, where Winston's files were hidden. She wasn't sure what she was doing, but it had to be a sign. Why else would she have run into the only emotional soldier?

———

Anna waited at her lab, pacing back and forth as the clock ticked quietly in the corner. When she heard the knock on the door, she laced her hands behind her back and squared her shoulders.

"Come in," she called out.

At the last second, she sat on the chair in front of her desk and laced her hands over her lap, instead.

"Excuse me," Winston said as he opened the door and walked inside.

He made his way to the examination table and sat down.

"Thank you for coming," she said, even though it wasn't part of the protocol. "Having a good day?"

"Busy," Winston replied, one side of his lips curving up almost imperceptibly. A heartbeat passed, and then he casually took his Military jacket off, folded it, placed it on the table, and started to roll up his sleeve. "What about you?"

Anna walked over to him slowly, grabbing a piece of cotton and damping it in alcohol.

"Interesting."

She tried to control her tone, not wanting him to know she'd had a terrible week. People didn't have bad weeks.

She was so conflicted. On one hand, she wanted to scream from a rooftop, tell him everything… and on the other hand, she was doubting herself.

What if he's not what I thought?

But the tests didn't lie. They couldn't. This man felt something…

Winston extended his arm forward, and she gripped his wrist, cleaning his arm for the extraction. She grabbed the elastic band, wrapped it around his upper arm, and then tapped his vein with two fingers.

"Easy, isn't it?"

She looked up at Winston's question, confused as to what he was talking about.

"Excuse me?"

"My veins really pop out. I've been told before that extractions are easy on me because of it. My bunkmate, John, always takes the longest because his veins are really deep, and the nurses struggle to find them sometimes."

He was smiling as he spoke, and the conversation was so natural, so easy…

"Oh, yes, of course. Everyone is different, and you do make extractions… easy."

He didn't. It was so hard to get the needle in. Not because of the veins, not because of his anatomy, but because she was so scared of exposing him. *What if anyone else found the tests she was running and discovered something?* She had to get rid of his samples after she was done with them, and make sure to take his files home, make them disappear. She had been so selfish in her pursuit of truth that she'd missed the fact that she could be endangering Winston.

"Are you okay?"

She had finished the extraction, and she was just standing there, stunned. Her forehead was pearled with sweat, and she could feel herself going faint.

"I'm... yes."

Anna placed the sample on the tray, and then held onto the back of her chair. Her heart seemed to be beating too slow, and dark spots were showing at the edges of her vision. She knew it was stupid to panic like this, but she suddenly felt so scared that she was sure she was about to pass out.

"You look pale... Anna."

A warm palm settled over her shoulder, and she looked back. Winston was standing behind her, his eyes fixed on her, his eyebrows lowered.

"I'm just a little dizzy; it's nothing."

"Doesn't look like nothing... Here, why don't you take a seat for a moment?"

Winston helped her sit down and then ran to the corner of the room, where a water dispenser sat. He filled a glass with cold water and brought it to her, his hands wrapping around hers as he helped her hold the cup.

"Drink, it'll make you feel better."

His touch was warm and settling, and she felt even worse for what she'd done to him. He wasn't only feeling; he was kind and caring, too.

How had he gone off the radar for so long?

She had heard of a few cases in which people had been immune to the serum. Knowing if these stories were real or not wasn't an easy task, but she'd been getting classified information through her sources for a long time now, and one thing was for sure: none of those people were still around.

"Thank you."

She drank half of the water and placed the glass back on her desk. She closed her eyes for a moment, and when she opened them, she found Winston crouched in front of her, looking genuinely concerned.

"Should I get someone to help? Are you coming down with some kind of sickness?"

"No, no. No need for help. It was just… just a little dizziness, nothing unusual."

The last thing she needed was for someone from the lab to run tests on her. Winston bit his lower lip, gazed down, and then looked back up at her.

"Is this a side effect of the… tests?"

Anna raised a single eyebrow, unsure of what he was talking about. Winston's cheeks seemed to have turned a light shade of pink as he cleared his throat.

"I'm so sorry. I… saw the papers you dropped the other day when we met… about the fertility clinic. I know some of their tests can have side effects."

Her cheeks heated up so fast that she had to look away for it not to be that obvious.

"Oh, that… it could… it could be. I, you know, I'm not married. I have just been selected for the program, but I'm not paired, yet."

Why am I telling him so much? And why am I stammering?

She had the urge to tell him everything, to reach out to him, to open up.

"Well, congratulations."

Is that bitterness in his tone?

When she looked back at him, Winston was slowly rising to his feet, so Anna placed a hand on his knee, gently pushing him back down so he wouldn't.

"Apologies, I… I don't know what…"

Her eyes found his lips. The bottom lip was slightly darker than the top from how much Winston had been biting it, and Anna wondered, if only for a moment, what it would feel like to run a finger through his soft skin.

"It's okay." Winston's voice was raspy and, to her surprise, he placed a hand on top of hers.

No one had ever held her hand, not even touched her in any way that wasn't strictly necessary. And that's how she knew for certain. That's how all doubt disappeared from her heart, and she did the brave thing: she opened up to him.

"There's something I need to tell you… these tests I've been running with you. They were just an excuse to get you here."

Winston looked confused, but he didn't pull back. His hand was still holding her, so Anna hoped. She hoped with all she had that she wasn't making a mistake.

"I don't understand."

"When I met you in the hall, I knew… I just knew there was something different about you." Winston pulled back an inch, looking into her eyes with caution. "I want you to know that you are safe with me, that I understand… I know you're not like the rest."

She waited for him to say something, to deny it, to pull back. Instead, Winston held her gaze, unmoving. He opened and closed his mouth, then slowly moved his hand back. He was retreating.

She'd ruined it.

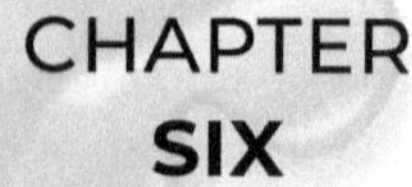

CHAPTER
SIX

WINSTON

I t couldn't be. There was no way Anna could know that he was different, that he wasn't like the rest of them. Winston's heart was beating wildly, the sound so loud he was scared that Anna would be able to hear it. Slowly, way too slowly, he moved back an inch. And then another. He was about to stand up, to try and make a run for it — anything — when Anna held his hand in hers, her eyes pleading.

"Please, don't. Don't run, don't go. I... I'm not a threat, I promise."

Winston shook his head. "I don't know what you're talking about. All my tests always come back normal. I have no clue what you're talking about."

Lying had always been easy but, for some reason, lying to Anna was ten times harder. She looked at him with a hurt expression, and another thought popped up in the back of his mind. But no, it couldn't be. That couldn't be guilt he was seeing; it was just wishful thinking.

As if reading his mind, Anna smiled.

"Here," she said softly, lifting his hand and placing it high over her chest.

She felt warm through the thin shirt she was wearing, and he stared at her for a moment, until he finally understood.

"Your heart is beating wildly," he said almost in a trance, unable to control what his tongue was doing.

"It's because I'm nervous."

The words were the faintest of whispers. The truth. A secret, a death sentence. Anna was risking everything by admitting out loud that she was feeling *something*.

Seconds stretched into what felt like minutes as they stared at each other, and then he snapped out of it. Winston stood up so fast that he hit the table behind him, the loud metallic bang reverberating in his head. He turned around, grabbed his Military jacket, and put it on in one swift motion. Before he could think about it further, he was walking out the door.

He walked as fast as he could without looking suspicious, and was out of the building within a minute. The fresh air filled his lungs, but it wasn't enough. He felt out of breath, his chest tight, his mind racing so fast that he felt dizzy.

Was this what Anna felt? Like there wasn't enough air in the world to make her feel satisfied? He breathed in deeply using the exercises he had learned as a kid to keep his heartbeat under control. Winston knew he had to keep moving, so he walked toward the Military truck he had borrowed and jumped behind the wheel.

Buildings turned into trees as he got closer to the Academy and the barracks, but his mind wasn't on them. He was numb.

Anna knew he had feelings. Anna could feel, too. And he had run away, like a coward. But it was the right thing to do. It was dangerous to be caught, and Anna wouldn't say anything. After all, he could tell if she told on him. He was safe as long as he stayed away. It was going to be okay. He'd tell her next week that she needed to leave him alone and find another subject for her tests. He'd get on with his life, graduate from the Academy, and get deployed. Everything was fine. Just fine.

"Are you okay? You seem a bit off since yesterday's tests."

John was running by his side, and Winston barely looked at him before nodding.

"Fine, just a bit tired after it."

"What's the test about, anyway?"

"New drug trial," he said nonchalantly.

"Any good? Do you… feel anything?"

Winston's pace slowed for a second before he caught up again. They were doing laps around the camp and still had another eight laps to go before they'd be let free for lunch.

"No, not really. Just tingling."

John seemed a little disappointed as he shrugged and kept on running. Tingling at the tips of the fingers or toes was a common side effect of most of the drugs they took, so it was a safe bet whenever someone asked about "feeling" anything. He didn't like lying to Mad Dog. After all, he was the closest thing he had to a friend. But it was the safe thing to do, and he knew it. His whole life had been a lie.

Ever since he could remember, he had lied about his feelings. Lied about not feeling anything, when inside, he was a mess. He'd been angry more times than he could count, had cried while hiding in his closet when he was just a boy, and had learned early on how to hide everything.

Make a ball with your emotions, and let it drop to the bottom of your stomach. Imagine the emotions dissolving into nothingness, being eaten by the enzymes in your stomach. Let go of them.

He did that again as he ran, the adrenaline from the fast pace helping, even if just a little.

When they finally stopped for lunch, he ate the tasteless food without paying any attention to what he was consuming. Anna's hopeful face was dancing in front of him, his mind unable to come up with anything else. She had been so scared. She'd almost fainted in front of him, probably from the fright of everything she was about to tell him, and what had he done? Run away. He'd run away from her and left her alone.

I'm an asshole.

———

The weekend went by in a blur between training sessions and, come Monday, Winston and John were sent to the Grays' settlement to patrol.

It was a cloudy afternoon, and Winston had his jacket tightly wrapped around his body and his thermal on. It was colder than usual without the sun, and he walked aimlessly along the roads, searching without really looking. His boots echoed on the almost empty street as he took a turn and found himself in front of a well-known tavern.

Mingo's was a cozy and small tavern where Grays and Blackhats alike were welcomed. It was an unusual place, known for its delicious beer and chill service. No brawls ever took place there, and the owner prided himself in having the best drinks and food in all of Bellevue. He'd visited the place with some of his bunkmates before, so he decided to poke his head in, just to see if he could get any information.

"Mingo, is everything okay here?" he asked as soon as he reached the counter.

"Business as usual," the owner replied.

"Seen anything out of the ordinary?"

"Nothing at all." Mingo was polishing glasses as he spoke, his expression bored as usual. "We have venison stew tonight if you want to come in for dinner. It's good. I got it fresh from the forest this morning."

"I'll think about it."

Without knowing what else to say, Winston went back outside and kept patrolling. He wasn't sure why that tavern always called to him. Maybe it was because it was one of the few places where he felt safe. Drunk people didn't pay attention to what others were doing around them. It was one of the few places where he didn't need to constantly mask who he was… just as he'd felt with Anna.

No. He couldn't go there. Not again.

Anna was dangerous. Being around her was a bad idea, and nothing good could come out of it. After all, what was she going to do? There was nothing to be done that could make a difference.

"Forget about her," he commanded himself.

———

When Thursday came around, Winston walked into the lab with his mind resolved: he'd ignore Anna if he ran into her and pretend as if nothing had happened. But that was easier said than done. As soon as he was close to the Emotions Wing, he started looking around for her.

Every turn he took, he expected to see her. His heart beat wildly, his palms were sweaty, and every time he turned a corner and didn't find her, his heart sank a little deeper.

He got to the lab without running into her, got his shot as usual, and then walked out, a little deflated. He knew he shouldn't want to see her, but he couldn't help it. Anna was everything he'd been able to think about lately, and he told himself he just needed a glimpse of her smile. Just a second to see that she was okay, that nothing had happened, nothing had changed.

Then he turned another corner — he was almost to the exit — and that's when he saw it: a glimpse of hair as bright as fire.

"Anna," he whispered.

"Excuse me?" asked John by his side.

"Oh, it's, ehm… Anna Chaplin, the investigator who's doing my testing. I need to catch up with her because of my appointment tomorrow. I'll see you at the car in five."

Without waiting for an answer, he ran after the redhead, who was now turning another corner. When he got to her, he called her name again, a little lump forming in his throat as he did.

"Anna."

He felt so guilty for how he had run away, for how he had ignored the opening of her heart. Anna had been vulnerable with him and, in exchange, he had left her alone.

"Cadet Hitcher," Anna said sternly as she turned around.

Oh, he had fucked up. She wasn't even using his first name anymore. Gathering all his courage, he straightened his shoulders.

"I wanted to apologize for the way I acted the last time we saw each other," Winston said almost politely, looking discretely around to make sure no one was close by to hear him.

Anna arched an eyebrow. "Are you really?"

"I shouldn't have left the way I did, and I apologize for it," he reiterated, hoping, with all his might, that she'd understand just how sorry he was.

Only a few minutes ago, he had told himself over and over that he wasn't going to approach her. That he'd go in the next day and tell her she needed to find a replacement but, upon seeing her, all that had disappeared. He needed her. He needed to know more about her, about himself. If she was the only other emotional human around, he needed her help understanding. Understanding what was wrong with him, why he was different, and if there were any more people like them.

"I accept your apology," Anna said, letting a small smile form on her lips for a second.

That simple gesture warmed Winston's heart, and he let the feeling spread through him. She was like the warm sun on a winter afternoon, and he basked in it.

"I'll see you tomorrow, then?"

"As usual," replied Anna, "There's still a few more tests I need to run for my project."

Her lips tugged up, and after looking quickly over her shoulder, Anna looked back at him and winked.

Winked. His heart fluttered, and Winston found himself smiling broadly.

Anna brought a finger to her lips as if silencing him, and he made a huge effort to hide his feelings from his face.

With a nod, he took a step back.

"Until tomorrow."

"Until then."

Anna turned around, leaving him alone in the hall, still stunned.

———

Friday couldn't have come any slower. Every second seemed to drag as Winston waited for his appointment with Anna. He was so nervous, he kept wiping his palms on his pants, his hands perpetually damp with sweat. The early morning training went on as usual, and when it was finally time to get to the lab, Winston was beaming.

He felt like how he did when he was a kid, and his mother would make his favorite food. She never understood why he got so excited over it but, for him, those were the best days.

Walking into the lab with a spring in his step, Winston made his way to the room and knocked before entering.

"Come in."

He opened the door with almost trembling fingers and quickly closed it behind him. Instead of going to his usual spot at the examination table, he stood there. His back against the door, his heart hammering against his ribcage.

Anna stood at the opposite end of the small room, half-sitting on her desk, her hands laced in front of her.

She parted her lips, and her voice came out as soft as a caress.

"Winston?" A question.

"Anna." An answer.

CHAPTER
SEVEN

ANNA

She walked to the middle of the room, deliberately slow, while her eyes stayed on Winston's. He was waiting for her, but she didn't know what she was doing, what she was about to do.

"Any tests you need to run today?" Winston asked playfully, a cadence to his voice she hadn't heard before.

After he'd run away the week prior, Anna feared she'd doomed herself. She had spent all week as a ball of nerves, unsure of what was going to happen. Having Winston tell on her wasn't an option; she knew he wouldn't do it for the fear of her doing the same, but she had feared losing him before even having a chance to get to know him.

Learning what it was like to interact with someone like herself was an experience she'd been looking forward to her whole life.

"Maybe a few… practical tests?" she replied sheepishly.

Winston pushed himself away from the door, his lips curling up into a smile, and his eyes full of fire. Anna felt the room charging with energy, and an electrifying feeling that ran from the tip of her toes all the way to the top of her head. She was breaking every single rule she had made for herself over the years. They were going against every natural instinct for survival. But she wanted it. She wanted all of it.

She slowly broke the distance between them, standing right in front of him. They approached each other the way a wild animal approaches a friendly-looking creature: with curiosity, but also with fear of being bitten for making a sudden movement.

So, they gravitated toward each other instead, one of Anna's hands stretched forward, Winston's breaths coming in quick succession. When they were only an inch apart, Winston lifted his arm, grabbing Anna's hand softly between his own and running his thumb through her palm.

"Have you ever…" He broke the silence first, his words a soft whisper between them, "ever met someone like… me?"

Anna shook her head softly. "I haven't. And you? Have you met anyone like… me?"

Feeling. Someone with so much inside of them that they struggled to keep it all contained. Anna wanted to dance, a euphoric feeling taking root in her heart. Neither of them had said it, but they both knew what the other knew — they both recognized each other as equals.

"No, no one."

She observed the way his fingers moved through her hand, and she grabbed his, doing the same. Drawing the lines in his palm with her fingertips, she met his eyes again.

"What does this feel like?" she wondered.

"You tell me," he replied, mimicking her movements.

"It tickles," she said with a giggle. "But also, it's like… I don't know. Nothing I've experienced before."

"Do you… like it?"

Anna giggled once more, a sound so foreign that she barely recognized it.

"I do. You should… take a seat. I should take some samples for my files."

Winston grabbed a seat as usual, and Anna got the equipment ready while glancing at him every other second. There were so many questions she wanted to ask, but she knew the lab wasn't the safest place to do so. She needed to find a way to see him outside of the lab, but was too scared to even suggest it.

So, she didn't.

Instead, she got the samples, filed them, and basked in the simple presence of another emotional human for as long as she could before having to let him go.

"I'll see you next week," she said begrudgingly when he was leaving.

"See you then."

———

Anna's life was always busy. Being at the lab and doing her job, trying to gather information illegally, constantly pretending to be something she was not. But lately, her weeks seemed to only occur for the sake of waiting for Fridays.

For Winston.

That was why on Thursday, when she finally got home

late after briefly running into him in the hallway, she didn't notice the letter addressed to her sitting on the table.

"What time will dinner be ready?" she asked her mother.

"In twenty minutes. Have you looked at your mail?"

Her heart dropped. She turned around, seeing the formal envelope on the table. She knew what it was.

"I've already opened it," her mother said unceremoniously.

"Is it the date?"

"Yes, your husband will be here for a formal meeting in a matter of weeks. They have narrowed the search down to three suitors, and they're waiting for the DNA test results to figure out the best match. In two weeks, you'll meet your husband. In three, you'll be getting married and moving in with him."

She couldn't breathe. It was all too much.

"Okay. That's… okay."

Anna grabbed the letter from the table and almost ran up to her room, moving as fast as she could without seeming improper. Upon closing the door, she leaned against it, her legs giving out as she slid to the floor.

The tears rolled down her cheeks, uninvited, but she couldn't stop them. For a moment, she felt powerless. All the research she was doing in the lab, trying to figure out the workings of society to get out of it, and it was all for nothing.

In three weeks, she'd be married, and they would make her have kids, if she wanted to or not.

But no. She was done with that, done with surviving. She had an ally now; she had hope. And that was all she needed.

Standing up, she brushed the tears away and threw the letter into the trash bin without even looking at it. The next day, she'd talk to Winston. She'd find a way out. It wasn't too late.

CHAPTER
EIGHT

WINSTON

Getting up in the morning, Winston had to repress the smile tugging at the edges of his mouth.

"I hate Fridays," John grunted beside him as he jumped down from the bunk.

Raising a brow, he wondered why out loud. John didn't have any feelings, so hating something was unusual for him.

"You've got the test, which means you're not running with

me. My time is worse without you because I lose my pace. My charts look worse, which means they send me to bathroom duty almost every weekend."

"And what's so bad about that?"

"The smell."

Winston suppressed a laugh. Even in a world without feelings, some things could still be physically upsetting, he guessed. He clapped his bunkmate on the shoulder.

"Try to find a way *not* to lose your pace. I'm sure I'm not the only thing setting it when I'm there. Use your watch; you have it for a reason."

The watch that counted their steps and time was a useful tool to keep the pace of their training, but John wasn't great with technology, and that was why he avoided using it a lot of the time. He simply didn't understand it.

"I'll try."

With that, both cadets went their separate ways. Winston jumped on one of the Military trucks they used for everyday transportation and drove straight to the Fox Lab. Once there, he used his magnetic key to go inside. The morning was still early, but plenty of people were walking back and forth down the halls.

He presented himself at the front desk, filled the usual form, and then marched toward Anna's lab. The last time he'd been there, it had been… exhilarating. The softness of Anna's skin still lingered in his mind as he knocked.

"Come in."

He opened the door and found her in her usual spot by the desk. Her hair was up in a pony, her cheeks slightly pink as usual, and the freckles on her cheeks seemed to call him over, to get closer… close enough to count them.

"Good morning," he said in his usual polite tone as he closed the door.

Unsure of the protocol for this new relationship, he went

to the table and sat down when Anna didn't approach him straight away.

"Morning."

"Blood?"

"Uhm, yes. Roll your sleeve, please."

He did as she asked, taking his jacket off and rolling his thermal up. Her fingers were careful as she got everything ready for the extraction, and she seemed almost detached from the situation as she took the sample and then pressed the cotton ball to the inside of his elbow.

"Are you okay?"

"Yes, I'm…" Anna looked to the door, and back to him. "It's been a rough day, that's all. Keep pressure on this."

Instead of taking over, Winston covered Anna's hand with his. Their eyes met once more, and he leaned in a little closer.

He had never done anything like it, but there was an ingrained being inside of him that was taking over his body. It was as if he didn't know what he was after, what he pretended, but his body knew well what he needed. They shared their breath for a moment, their faces so close together that their noses were almost touching before Anna pulled back. She turned around, put away the sample, and then sat on her desk chair, rolling until she was in front of him.

Placing a soft hand on his knee, she sighed. "This is so complicated…"

"I know this is all new and unconventional, and…"

"I know."

Anna glanced at the door again, and suddenly got up. Getting to the door in two steps, she latched the lock and returned to the chair in the exact position she had been in.

"I… I'm sorry, but I think we need to talk."

"Yes, of course, you're right."

He leaned in closer so they could whisper and still hear each other.

"I know…" She sighed. "I know we both know about each

other, and that it's probably not safe to say certain things out loud. But I want you to know for certain that my intention isn't to tell anyone about this."

Winston knew exactly what she was talking about, and he was glad she was the first to say it. Anna was better with words than he was.

"Of course, I'd never say anything, either."

"You know this is dangerous, right? Us, out in the open, is already dangerous. But us together? We need to be extra careful of what we say and do."

For a second, Winston felt a little annoyed. He wasn't stupid enough to risk his life, not for this, not for anything.

"I know," he said almost rudely, in the monotone he had learned from listening to other people talk.

Anna might have taken it as a bit of a joke because her smile lit up the room.

"I'm sorry if I'm being a little too intense," she said then, placing a hand on his knee again.

He'd never thought another person's touch could do so much for him. That Anna's hand could brighten the world in the way it did. It was almost as if his senses were more invested in his surroundings when she was there, and he was appreciating the way light came in through the small window high up on the wall and danced around, lighting her hair on fire. He could smell the soft perfume she was wearing, and the touch of her hand on his knee was warm and inviting.

"It's okay, I understand. This is… unprecedented." That was to say it lightly.

It was more than that; it was dangerous and on the verge of stupid. It was wrong. *They* were wrong, but together… at least, he knew he wasn't alone. He now had faith that when he's finally deployed, he could go out and find more people like him. Know a little more. He'd fight his battles, but he wouldn't fight them alone, hopefully.

"I was thinking..." Anna leaned in even closer. "Is there any chance I can see you outside of here?"

Winston recoiled.

It was as if a bucket of cold water had been dropped onto his head, and the water was dripping down his back, making his muscles taut, his heartbeat a little faster. The hurt in Anna's eyes was immediate.

"I... I don't know. I'm not sure if I can risk it."

Even though her eyes said otherwise, Anna nodded. "I understand."

He left the lab a minute later with a heavy feeling in his heart. He felt a little guilty for what he'd done, but at the same time... There was no way he could risk it all and see her outside of the lab. It was stupid, and anyway, what was the point?

———

On Sunday, Winston couldn't sleep. He lied in bed, staring at the roof, and thinking about Anna. The curve of her lips, the cross between her brows when he'd said no. The hurt expression in her eyes, the way she'd looked the other way as if embarrassed.

Monday's training was a hit or miss. He had good sprints when he managed to clear his mind, and then a terrible round as Anna's face showed up uninvited in his head. Guilt was a new feeling in his dictionary, but he was sure that's what it was. It was as if her expression of disappointment was drilling into his mind.

During lunch on Tuesday, he concluded that he'd done the right thing. There was no point in risking more than he already was. He was close to graduating, and within a month or so, he'd be deployed if everything went according to plan. That was everything he'd ever wanted.

That night, he was on patrol, and he convinced himself that Anna was not on his mind. He didn't see her when another ginger woman walked past him, even if she looked nothing like Anna. He didn't see her when a little girl seemed to almost smile at him as she walked past. And he was certainly not thinking about her again that night when he lied in bed, a burgeoning pain within him.

All his resolutions were almost broken by Wednesday, when he woke up thinking that there were high chances that he'd see her the day after during his shot.

Why is this woman driving me crazy?

It was almost as if she was the only thing he could think about.

Disappointment was his only company on Thursday when he looked for her in every corner of the lab and still didn't see her. Maybe if he saw her outside of the lab, then he'd get to spend a little more time with her… just a little. Just as a way to explore his own feelings, to learn about the way she'd survived without being noticed. It was purely experimental. Logical, even.

———

"I apologize if I was rude last time, but you have to understand that with the Military… it's hard for me to get out without being noticed."

Anna had been a little colder than usual while taking his blood sample, almost as if she were disappointed in him. But at his words, she turned around, a bit softened.

"I understand this is not… easy."

"I was thinking…"

He gestured for Anna to come closer, and she patched up the extraction mark while standing close to his side. Winston looked up, and he thought for a brief moment that having her this close… he could almost kiss her. Just needed to lean in a bit…

"I'm on patrol on Tuesday. I can sneak out after it. We sometimes go for drinks, so no one will question my disappearance for a little while."

Anna's lips were merely a breath away as she replied. "Where?"

"Meet me on fourth and third, Grays' settlement. There's an alley to the side…"

"I know the place."

Winston's eyebrows shot up, but he didn't ask why she knew her way around the Grays' area. No Whiteshirt ever went that way; they were too good to go there, and they had no reasons to.

With his heart thrumming, and his nerves a little on edge, Winston left the lab that day puzzled.

Tuesday at eight — it couldn't come fast enough.

———

"Mad Dog to Alpha One, do you copy? Over."

"Copy. Over."

It was almost eight on Tuesday, and Winston's nerves were on edge. He was scared, but mostly, excited. He could see Anna out of the lab, really see her. Touch her. Feel her. Know her.

"Drinks at Mingo's. Tonight. Over."

"Not today, Mad Dog. Over and Out."

He checked his watch. Five minutes to eight. Winston walked toward fourth and got there with two minutes to spare. He could see the dark alley close by and waited until eight to send the command.

"Alpha One, the watch is over. Returning to base late."

It was usually code for when cadets needed to go home to

get something from their parents: a change of clothes or to take something to them. Military cadets were free to roam when they weren't on duty, and it was known among the ranks that with the number of drugs they took, with all that adrenaline and testosterone… cadets were usually out all night, trying to ease their calling.

"Roger that. Alpha One, dismissed," came a metallic voice on the other side.

He walked to the alley, and when his feet found the cobblestone path and the lamps from the street dimmed behind him, a hand poked him on the side.

"Hey."

He almost jumped, and he was glad that his reflexes and training were spot-on because his hand had gone to his gun so fast, he wasn't sure how he wasn't pointing it to Anna's head.

"You scared the living hell out of me," he said in an exhale.

"Sorry, Cadet Hitcher." Anna's tone was a playful thing, but she eyed Winston's hand hovering over the gun as she said it — as if aware that she'd stepped too close to the edge.

They almost ran down the dark alley together, and then took a corner down a small street, and another, and another. At first, Winston was leading the way. He wasn't too sure where he was going, but he knew a few areas where there weren't many people, and they could, hopefully, talk uninterrupted. But soon, he realized that Anna was the one guiding him.

"Where are you taking me?" he asked as they rounded another corner.

Buildings were scarce over there, lots of them abandoned as they were getting close to the outer wall.

Anna turned quickly and pressed a finger to his lips, silencing him. She was on her tiptoes, her red hair hiding under a hood, but her eyes bright as the moonlight above them.

"Quiet, or they'll hear you."

"Who?"

"You'll see."

She smiled wickedly, and Winston had no clue anymore what his heart was attempting to do inside his chest. This woman was going to kill him.

In a matter of minutes, they found themselves by the edge of the forest. Anna guided him with such ease, as if she'd been down that track a thousand times. She probably had. The moon was almost full above them and guided their steps, but just in case, Anna had taken a small torch out from her pocket as soon as they stepped between the trees.

When they got to a clearing, the woman finally stopped and removed her bag from her back, leaving it on the grass.

All around them, the trees rose high into the sky, giving off the sensation that they were so far from everything. The stars shone in a way Winston had never seen, and he wondered why he never paid them any attention. No one did.

"What is this place?" he asked while Anna got something out of the bag.

"Just a little clearing in the woods that I found when I was younger."

She pulled out a blanket, and she stretched it onto the grass for them to sit on.

She sat down and patted the spot beside her, so Winston sat, too. He removed the heavier parts of his armor, leaving all his guns and bits and pieces by his side. What was left, was the same uniform that Anna was used to seeing him in.

"Thank you for agreeing to this, it's... weird, but also so refreshing to be out here with someone else."

"Thank you for bringing me to your hiding spot," Winston replied with a twisted smile.

Anna took a little container out of her bag and placed it

between them. It was full of small pieces of fruit, and Winston eyed them warily. All the food at the camp always tasted the same, and the texture of fruits wasn't his favorite. He wasn't really hungry either, but he thought it would be rude to turn them down.

"Don't look at them like that; they're not like the crap they give us. They're wild. I picked them myself from this forest."

Winston still eyed them with disbelief, and Anna might have seen his expression because she grabbed a small berry between two fingers and lifted it to him.

"Open."

Winston rolled his eyes but indulged her.

Anna's fingers brushed his lips softly as she placed the berry on his tongue, and he closed his mouth in slow motion as she watched him expectantly. He bit into it, the juices coating the inside of his mouth, and the sweetness of it taking over his every sense. It was like nothing he'd ever tried before. It was delicious. He closed his eyes for a second, reveling in the feeling, and then snapped them open.

"Can I have another one?"

Anna laughed brightly and passed him the container. He ate another one, and when he was about to eat a third, he changed his mind. Slowly, as if approaching a wild animal, he took it to Anna's lips instead. She opened her mouth without taking her eyes off him, and he placed the fruit delicately between her teeth. When her mouth closed, his thumb brushed her bottom lip, and his eyes were glued to the spot as she swallowed — his hand still lingering in the air between them.

In the tense silence that preceded, Winston counted his heartbeats.

Can I approach her? Touch her lip once more? See what she feels like?

He wondered what it'd be like to hold her in his arms, and then, out of nowhere, a loud shriek pierced the air. They both jumped back, and then Anna started laughing, tears running down her cheeks as she held her stomach.

Winston was looking around frantically, his gun already in his hand.

"It's just… an owl," Anna said between the laughter.

"An owl?"

"I'm sorry; that's why I told you to stay quiet before. This area is full of wild owls."

As Anna laughed again, the beating of wings was heard above them, and a white and gray blur flew quickly over their heads — an owl.

"I'm starting to think that you're trying to give me a heart attack."

He couldn't help but laugh then, joining in together with Anna's giggles.

"Sorry."

Anna wiped the tears that were running down her cheek, and Winston found his hand gravitating toward her face again.

He ran the back of his finger down her cheek as carefully as he could. Anna closed her eyes, leaning against the touch. When she opened them again, she leaned against him, placing her head on his neck as she looked up at the stars.

"I hear people used to watch them all the time… Did you know that the stars are so far away, that when you look at them, you look at the past? The light takes so long to get to us, that what we are looking at might not even be there anymore. These stars saw people with feelings. They saw them argue, fight, but also laugh, and fall in love…"

Winston's arm was around Anna's shoulders, and he squeezed her a little — as if saying, "I know."

"Things have changed…"

"But why? Why did they change? To whose benefit?"

Winston tensed, unsure of what to say. Anna's body against him was the warmest thing he'd ever experienced, but her cold words were laced with treason at every corner. And he didn't know what to do about that.

He was a soldier.

He couldn't betray the army for what his heart desired — for Anna.

Could he?

CHAPTER
NINE

ANNA

Getting used to the new routine had been easy for Anna, maybe too easy. She spent her days in the lab, as usual, but did more work behind the scenes than ever. She was gathering information about the government, Faulkner, and the vaccine as fast as she could. There was a sense of urgency that was making her push herself to the limit.

The time to meet her husband was only around the corner and, any day now, she'd get another letter with the name of her future spouse. Anna knew she'd have to get out before that — or else she'd be stuck there forever.

She found a bunch of papers in the old files that hinted at individuals with feelings, but had found nothing conclusive. Yet. With the help of Sammy, she'd managed to get more Blue Joy vials out to the outskirts and Grays' settlements, and was slowly teaching her how to acquire the samples on her own so as not to raise suspicions.

Sammy was the daughter of Bluecoats, and she was the only one Anna trusted with the truth inside the lab — the government was up to something, and this emotionless world didn't make sense. Even if it's just one vial at a time, she was giving the people back what was rightfully theirs.

And finally, that week, she'd gotten a new lead. She had something to hold onto.

Almost every night, for the past week, she had snuck out to see Winston, even if just for a few minutes. Anna didn't know how to stay away from the sense of high she got every time she was around him. She finally had someone she could be herself around and was learning how to open up, how to let laughter bubble up in her throat, and how to openly feel. It was a whole new experience, one she never thought she was going to have, but one she didn't think she could ever let go of.

Anna felt freer than she'd ever had, like the world was suddenly lighter, easier — the weight on her shoulder a little less burdening. But she also knew it was only the start. Their lives were in danger, and if she wanted to survive this mad town, she'd have to find a way out.

Figuring out how to destroy Faulkner's regime was paramount if she wanted to be free. If she wanted the whole world to be free, for the serum's effect to be reversed. So, she needed Winston, needed him to help her follow the new lead, so together, they could save the town, maybe even the world.

She needed him because he had access to areas that she didn't. Like the waterways.

———

That Tuesday night, she found Winston in the same alley once more and took him over to the forest on silent feet.

"You seem a little quieter than usual today. Are you okay?"

Winston stood by her side as she laid the blanket on the grass.

"I'm okay, it's just… I can't keep going like this. I need to do something else, something bigger."

"What do you mean?"

He sat by her side as he usually did and threaded his fingers through hers.

"What Faulkner did to Bellevue is not right, and you know it. I know it… But the world doesn't know it, and it needs to. We need to do something. Things need to change, Winston."

His face went pale under the light of the moon, and his fingers fell slack in hers.

"You're talking treason, Anna… That's not… That's not why I'm here, you know that."

He was shaking his head, and she wanted to slap some sense into him.

"You and I both know what it's like… what it's like to feel, and everyone should be able to know, too! I don't understand why Faulkner thought he needed an army of emotionless beings, but you and I know it's better… better like this."

She traced her fingers down Winston's arm slowly, and he closed his eyes, his expression unreadable.

He had to understand.

"We're the only ones who can make a difference, Winston. We have to. How are you going to live with yourself if you don't do anything? I don't know why we're different. I'm trying to figure it out, but I know it's what allows us to make a difference. We need to act!"

"I'll be deployed in less than two months, Anna. I can't do anything to ruin that."

She stood on trembling legs, shaking her head furiously. "You can't be serious. This is bigger than you and me!"

"All you're going to do is get yourself killed, Anna. Please, promise me you won't do anything stupid!"

She shook her head again, still not able to believe that she had read him so wrong.

"I can't promise you that."

Anna gathered her few things and shoved them into her bag without waiting for an answer. With the night as her only companion as she rushed back to town, she let the tears silently rush down her cheeks in a way she hadn't allowed herself to in a long time.

———

The young woman was certain things couldn't get worse, but when she got home late that night, she found the dreaded letter sitting on the table. She took the envelope to her room and opened it with trembling fingers.

Inside, the name of her future husband stared at her mockingly. She didn't know who he was, but she had an appointment to meet him the following Wednesday. Nausea crept up her throat, and Anna made it just in time to the bathroom to empty her stomach into the toilet bowl.

She was running out of time.

The night, Anna thought. Thought about how far she had come, how much information she had gathered, and how much she still didn't know. In the morning, she'd get what she needed. No matter what it took, she'd find a way to get out of there. She'd find a way to implement her plan and rid them all of this insufferable tyrant.

She sent coded messages to all her contacts: the Grays, people who had helped her get vials to the minorities, and those who claimed to feel something but really didn't. Most of them were junkies, but at least, they wanted things to change. Unlike Winston, at least a few people were willing to do something.

———

Anna wasn't ready for the knock on her door Friday morning, and had almost hoped Winston wouldn't show up. She was still deeply hurt by his inaction the day before, but there wasn't much she could do. After all, it seemed like it was still her against the world.

"Come in." She tried to keep her voice steady, but it wavered.

The door opened slowly, and Winston stepped in, staying far away as he leaned back against it.

"Anna Chaplin," he greeted her.

"Not for long," she huffed.

She hadn't meant to say it, but the words slipped her lips unprompted.

"Excuse me?"

Anna shook her head and waved for him to sit.

"This will be your last visit. I will let your unit know that our testing has finished. I won't be in your way much longer."

Winston seemed tense as Anna placed the rubber band around his upper arm and got the needle ready.

"I'm sorry for the way I reacted, but you have to understand—"

"Understand what?" Anna snapped, plunging the needle fast into his arm and making him hiss as her cold fingers wrapped too tightly around his wrist. "At least, you have a way out. You're being deployed. I shouldn't have trusted you to help me. Why would you? You'll be out of here in no time." She let out a labored breath as she threw the sample onto the tin tray. "Meanwhile, I'll become Mrs. Thomlinson," she added under her breath.

She turned to her desk and placed her hands on the cool glass while trying to calm her breathing. Losing control wasn't appropriate, and it was dangerous, even inside her own little lab. A soft hand on her shoulder startled her, and she turned around fast, finding Winston only inches away.

"Mrs. Thomlinson? Have they assigned you a husband already?"

"Why do you care?" she asked softly while looking down.

She didn't want pity; she wanted out.

Winston's calloused finger pushed her chin up softly. "I don't want to care, but I can't help it... I care too much. I care about you, Anna."

She shook her head again, unable to believe his words in full. He wasn't ready to leave everything behind for her. He was a soldier, a man loyal to Faulkner, and she'd been an idiot for believing that she could trust him. She could feel the entire world crumbling upon her, her shoulders being pushed down, her chest tightening with the fear of being stuck in Bellevue forever, and not being able to help society in the way she'd always envisioned.

Getting into the lab had only been the first step, and she thought she'd have more time. The serum she'd been working on over the past weeks wasn't ready. She needed time, and a husband was almost like a death sentence. They'd take her away from the lab as soon as they met. She'd have to concentrate on going to the fertility clinic, and wouldn't be able to return to work until she provided the town with at least three children. It was Hell, Hell incarnate. And she couldn't breathe.

"Hey, Anna, I need you to breathe with me, okay? I'm sure you used to do this plenty of times when you were a kid and got upset, right?"

Anna nodded, remembering how, at a very young age, she had to learn how to control her emotions.

"In through the nose, out through your lips. Slowly. Good, you got this."

His hands were on her shoulders, rubbing small soothing circles, his breath mingling with her own as he kept talking to her softly. When she felt better, she managed to look up, finding his deep eyes piercing hers.

"Are you okay?"

Still unsure if she could speak without crying, she nodded.

"I'm sorry that I was so harsh last night. I should've known to put you first, but I just... I've been convinced my whole life that I was the one who was broken. Wrong. And the Military gave me everything. But I... I can't let them simply ship you off to a husband. I can't..."

His hands shook against her shoulders, and she placed one of her hands on top of one of his.

"Does this mean you will help me?"

"Do you have a plan?"

Winston smiled, and something in Anna's chest loosened enough for her to release a small laugh.

"I do. Meet me at the usual spot tomorrow night. There's someone I need to go meet, and then I'll see you there. Now, go. You've been in here for too long, and we can't allow suspicions."

Winston held her eyes a little longer before begrudgingly letting go of her shoulders and slowly walking to the door.

"Tomorrow," he whispered as he walked out.

Tomorrow.

It had only been a couple of days since the new insight had reached her, and she had been unsure of trusting it, but it was time. With a husband less than a week away waiting for her, it was time to take a risk.

————

Anna woke up earlier than usual the next morning, got changed almost in the dark, and headed out to meet with the new lead. Sammy had been the one to point her in the right direction. Somehow, a woman named Valerie had heard about her and the vial trades, and had asked Anna to contact her.

It wasn't unusual for people to enquire about "the trader" — as she was known among the Grays — but this seemed different. The woman wasn't after vials, but after Anna herself. The enquiry had come from mouth to mouth, alley to alley, and she had been asked to go to the local hospital first thing in the morning if she was interested.

So, there she was, first thing Saturday morning, walking to the back entrance of the hospital and slipping into the staff room as she had been told. Unsure of what she was going to find there, she was a little surprised to see a petite, but imposing, woman with medical scrubs on.

"I assume you're the famous trader."

The woman was sitting on a small couch, her posture relaxed. Anna lingered by the door, her hands in her pockets, trying to look uncensored.

"I'm Anna, simply Anna. And you?"

It was a rule to never give more than her name. She didn't often give the real one, but seeing how this woman already knew it, she found no point in lying.

"Valerie. Please, take a seat."

She gestured to the empty seat in front of her, and Anna sat right on the edge, ready to flee if anything weird happened.

Silence settled between them while both women evaluated

each other, and then Valerie clicked her tongue loudly and leaned forward.

"I have met many people like you throughout the years," she said.

Anna tried not to express any emotion on her face, which was hard to do at such a statement, "People who are not like the rest."

"I don't know what you're talking about."

It was a swift lie, one that had come out of Anna's lips way too many times. She kept her shoulders relaxed, even though her legs were ready to flee, the door to her side her main point of focus in her peripheral vision.

"I think you do. Look, Anna, I don't have any way of proving to you that I'm telling the truth." Valerie leaned in closer, her voice barely a whisper. "But I know what it's like. I know how it… feels to be so different."

Anna flinched back.

"Yes, that word is… powerful, right?"

It wasn't one that was thrown around lightly. Anna nodded and waited. She wasn't going to say anything incriminating yet, but if Valerie had information, she needed it.

"Would you like me to explain why I contacted you?"

Anna nodded, her eyes quickly darting to the door, just in case.

"I have been meeting with people like you for some time now. There aren't many left, and we're not easy to spot, but between us… there are certain things we see that others don't. Small things that show us we're one and the same. A little flinch, a small tear in the corner of an eye. You know what I'm talking about, do you?"

Breathing deeply, Anna finally spoke up.

"Are you saying that you're… that you have…?"

She let the words hang in the air, unable to say them out loud. It was too dangerous.

"Yes." Valerie smiled, a small but almost adorable smile

that crinkled the edges of her eyes and made Anna's heart flutter. After a second, she shifted her face back to nothingness, and Anna almost had to wonder if she had imagined it. "There are more of us, and if you're willing, I can help you get there."

Could it be true? Could this woman be talking about what she thought? Was there really a community of people with emotions, living far from the government and gathering their forces?

"Where?"

It was the only thing she could ask. She didn't want to get her hopes up, but her heart was already racing.

"It's a community up north, far from the government's control. People live there, like they did in the old days, if you know what I mean. I can take you there, Anna."

Valerie smiled again, but this time, the smile stayed on her face. Anna felt her own smile slowly spreading on her lips. Everything she'd been working on, everything she'd dreamt of, might become real.

If there were more people like her and Winston, then she had a better chance. She could gather some forces, mass-produce the secret serum she'd been working on for months. Together, they could make a difference. They'd start with Bellevue, but what could stop them from helping the world? With a community behind her, she could do much better. She could help more people, make a difference in the world.

When Anna opened her mouth to reply, a single word came out.

"When?"

CHAPTER
TEN

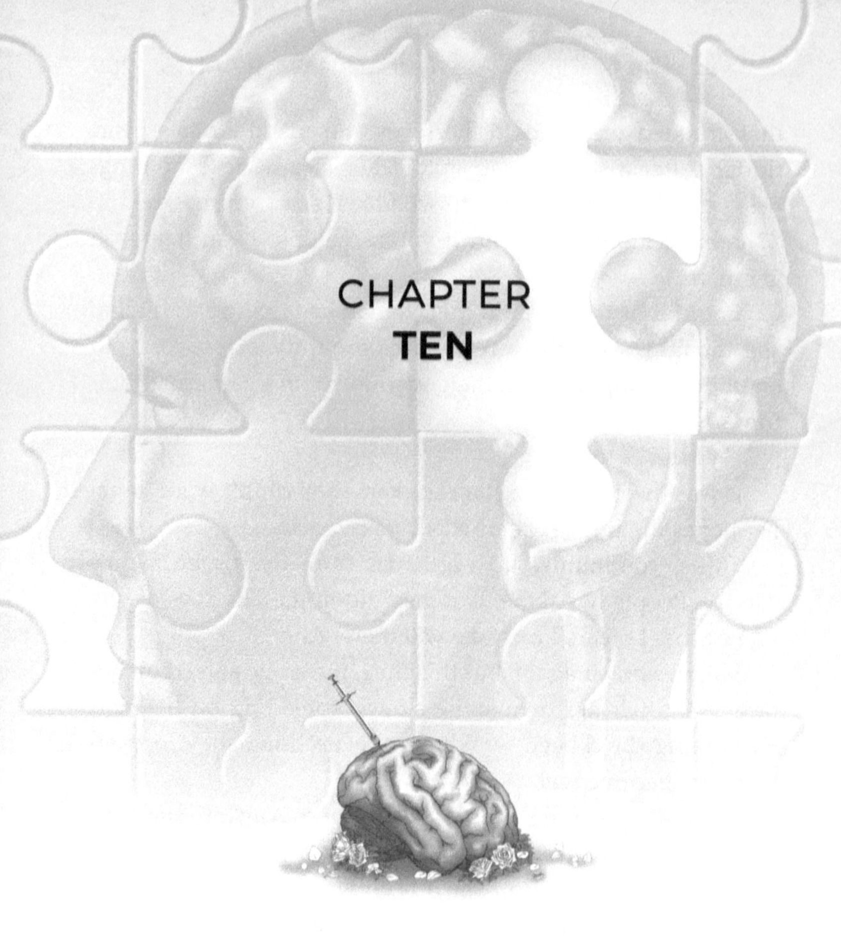

WINSTON

Winston waited for Anna in front of the usual alley, his heart thumping in his chest. John had started asking questions, wondering why he was spending so much time out of the barracks, and he was scared of being caught. He was doing his best to make up excuses every time, but there were only so many things they could do outside of duty.

He was running out of plausible excuses. But Anna was

about to be handed to another man in less than four days, and he could not let that happen.

She found him a minute later, appearing out of thin air. Grabbing his hand, she ran toward the woods. They followed the same path they always went down, both of them so familiar by now that they could probably do it blindfolded. Once they got to their spot, they were both a little out of breath. Anna was worse than he was, bracing her hands on her knees, taking in pockets of air and wiping the sweat off her forehead.

"You okay?"

Anna nodded and slowly straightened her back, taking one last deep breath before she suddenly broke into a smirk.

He'd never seen her smile like that. It was such a bright and beautiful thing, and his heart ached at it. Ached to get closer, to hold her against his chest, to see that smile every single day of his life from then on.

She only looked at him, so he broke the silence.

"What's that smile for?"

"I have great news! I… I can't believe it, oh, my, oh! You won't believe this." Anna spoke fast, her words stumbling, one into the other, as she didn't even stop to breathe. "I met this woman. She's… her name is Valerie. And she's part of some community. There are more people like us, Winston. We're not alone! We're not the only ones who can feel. She told me that there's a small settlement to the north, and she can take us there…" She finally took a deep breath, her eyes a little weary as she repeated the last bit, almost like a question. "She can take us there."

Anna's face was as bright as the moon, her smile brightening up everything around her. But still, a little cloud of doubt poked Winston on the chest.

He didn't want to let her down, didn't want to say anything that would ruin the moment, that would wipe that smile off her face. So, he thought. He thought about a way in which he could possibly express his fear without breaking her. Thought about the pros and cons of the situation, and of what would happen if they left with this mysterious woman.

Trust had never been his forte, but he trusted Anna. Trusted her enough to nod slowly, biting his lip not to grin like an idiot when Anna's smile widened — if that's even possible. He couldn't let fear out, not when she was there, looking at him the way she was.

He couldn't let Anna get married, wouldn't accept it, and taking her away seemed like the only way to stop it from happening. So, he nodded once more.

"Is that a yes?" Anna jumped on the spot, taking a step closer so she was right in front of him.

"I guess… Yes, it's a yes."

Anna jumped into his arms, and he caught her just in time, his strong arms holding her as Anna's legs wrapped around his middle.

"Thank you! Thank you! Thank you!"

She followed each word with a kiss to his cheek, his temple, his forehead. Anna was giggling again, and it was so contagious that Winston found himself laughing, too.

"I can't believe we can actually do something, get out of here, show this kind of emotion out in public for once!"

"I can't believe it, either."

He couldn't. It sounded too good to be true, but he had to trust her. It was the only thing he could do. Anna's smile dimmed as she stared at him, her hands still wrapped around his neck, her legs around his torso.

"Sorry." She breathed. "Was this too much? I feel like my emotions overflowed just then…"

She started to pull away, to loosen her hold, to lower her legs, but he held her closer. He squeezed his arms around her, begging her to stay where she was. She was so small, almost weightless in his arms, and he thought he could hold her forever. He wanted to hold her forever.

"No, it's okay… You're okay… And you can stay here for a moment longer if that's okay with you, just a little bit… Let me hold you, feel you…"

Anna's pupils dilated as she looked at him with an adoring smile. One of her hands let go of his neck, and she cradled his cheek. He leaned into that touch, the softness of her palm like nothing he had felt before. His eyes closed, his heart beating so loudly that he knew she could probably hear it.

He felt the soft pressure of a finger trailing his bottom lip, and he let his eyes flutter open once more.

"May I?"

Anna's question was a small whisper, one full of longing and adoration.

"You may," he said simply, his voice a little hoarse, a little rough.

She closed the distance between them, her lips the most delightful thing he'd ever tasted.

He watched Anna as she stared up at the stars, admiring how they reflected on her eyes.

They were lying on their usual blanket, their legs half tangled together, their hands held with their fingers intertwined and sitting across Anna's stomach. They had been like that for a little while now, and he didn't want to break the moment, but he had to.

"What's the plan, then?"

They had gotten too distracted in each other's arms, but it was time to go. They couldn't stay in the forest forever, and before they left, they needed to have a solid plan. Anna turned her face to look at him, her smile not as confident as it had been earlier.

"I spoke with Valerie for as long as I could, but time was

short as we couldn't risk getting caught. She told me to pack light and meet her by the hospital parking lot at sunset in two days. She'll smuggle us on one of the ambulances when she's going out on her rounds, and from there, we'll transfer onto an untraceable car that she'll have waiting for us just outside of the city. She said she'll be with us every step of the way, that someone will take the ambulance back so there's no suspicion. Said she's been doing this for a while, that it was safe."

"But you still sound worried. Is there something else you're not telling me?"

Anna bit her lip, and her shoulders slumped.

"After speaking with her this morning, I went to the lab for my usual shift. I wanted to find something, anything that could help me get more relevant information that we could take to these people, something that would make a difference. If there are more people like us — hiding — then I want to be able to help them, too. I broke into the company's server, and—"

"You, what?!"

He let go of her fingers, staring at her in disbelief. How could she do something so blatantly dangerous?

"It's not the first time I did it. Don't worry." She patted his hand and held it again, rubbing her thumb on his palm. "There's no way I'm getting caught for it."

"That was dangerous and stupid, Anna." He tried to control his rage and speak calmly, but it was hard when he knew she was going around risking her life. "Why would you do something like that when you're finally so close to getting out? Isn't that what you've always wanted, to get out of here?"

"I do, but I also want to help other people. There's no point in getting out if I'm the only one doing it. And I don't want to live my life hiding. I already do that here." She reached out and grabbed his hand again. "And don't worry about me, okay? I've been doing this for a long time. I've been tapping into their network, stealing vials from the lab…"

She let the words linger, as if waiting for him to move away from her again.

"You did what?" He couldn't believe it. Well, actually, he could. What he couldn't believe, was that he hadn't realized it before. The vial he saw her dropping into Sammy's pocket that first time in her lab, the rumors, the way she always looked so sneaky, how she knew the alleys like the back of her hand, it was all making sense now. "You're the one getting the vials to the Grays?"

She didn't even flinch. "Yes."

"Why?"

It was the only thing he could ask. He understood the rest, wanting to help. But why make them violent? Why get them in trouble?

"Because they deserve it. They deserve to feel something, to know what they're missing out on. I wanted them to feel, to give them a reason to want more than what they have…"

Some of that made sense, but… "But why give them Crimson Fury?"

"I never did. I mostly got them Blue Joy, but I think a small shipment of Crimson Fury was smuggled out right under my nose. That wasn't me. I think it was all a plan by the government to arrest people and get some troubled workers out of the way. I think they targeted people they suspected of having feelings. But it's just a theory. I can't be sure… There's something else I found when I got into the system today…"

"What is it?"

He didn't know if he could take any more; it was a lot, but they were running out of time. She moved closer, almost as if not wanting anyone to hear what they were talking about. But they were in the middle of the woods, the trees their only companions.

"I found some information regarding the vaccine, something that helped me with a project I'm working on, a serum I've been developing in hopes of counteracting the effects of the original, but it wasn't only that..."

He wanted to ask about how she was working on a cure on her own. He couldn't believe his ears, but after all, Anna was fierce. He knew she was a force to be reckoned with the first time he saw her crimson hair whipping around as she walked, the first time he admired the way in which her hips swayed when she moved, her chin held high. But Anna was still talking, so much information being dumped on him that he was struggling to keep up.

"I also found several mentions of a place called North Camp. I'm not sure if this has anything to do with the settlement that Valerie had spoken to me about; it could just be a coincidence. But I think it could also be that Faulkner is aware of the settlement and is trying to do something to get rid of those people. It almost seems too coincidental that Valerie found me now, now that I have you, and now that I'm finally so close to getting my sample of the serum finished. But... I don't know. I have this gut feeling telling me that if I don't try, I will never know. We still have two days; maybe that's enough. Maybe I can print out all the information I found, look at it, find something else that will help us. Maybe I can get the serum done by then."

He waited for a single heartbeat before replying, wanting to make sure that she knew his decision was final, and that he was sure of what he was doing.

"Whatever you decide to do, I will follow your lead. I don't know if I like how this all sounds, but there's no way I'm letting you go with Valerie alone. So, if you're in, I'm in."

Another truthful smile spread on Anna's face, and he couldn't help but mirror it. She leaned in, pressing her forehead against his. He breathed in her scent, the smell of lilacs mixing with the perpetual aroma of alcohol and sanitizer that was always around Anna. She smelled the same way her lab did, but he didn't mind it. He actually liked it.

"Do you think we can do this?" she asked after a minute of silence, their foreheads still touching.

"Together, we might be able to do just about anything."

He didn't know where that answer came from, but deep down, he believed it. He believed that there wasn't a single thing he couldn't do with this woman by his side. She was his muse, his reason to push forward, to do better, and the only reason he would go against the government.

Without her, he would've never been where he was now. He'd be thinking about graduation and stressing about getting deployed.

Now, he was stressed about running away, about risking their lives for something bigger than themselves. But for Anna, for Anna, he'd do it. He'd put his life on the line, do whatever it took.

They stayed under the trees for as long as they could, holding each other, basking in a kind of intimacy they had never experienced before. And when it was time to go, Anna kissed him goodbye, the promise to see him again in the parking lot of the hospital being the only reason he managed to walk away from her.

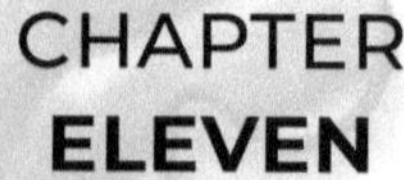

CHAPTER
ELEVEN

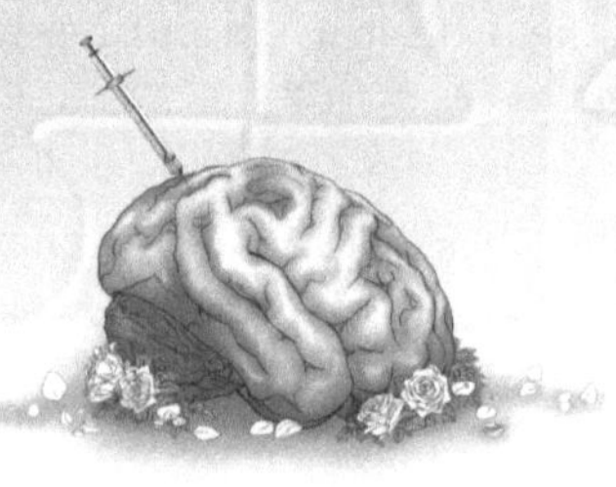

ANNA

Heart beating wildly in her chest, Anna arrived at the parking lot precisely as the sun was setting over the horizon, a bright orange ball of fire barely visible between the tall buildings. She lingered on the outskirts of the parking lot, a small, but heavy, bag slung over her shoulder.

Saying goodbye hadn't been an option. She told her mother that she needed to take some files back to the lab, and simply walked out the door. Her escape bag had already been packed in the car since the morning, as she didn't want to risk anyone seeing it.

Anna looked around, waiting for a Military van to pull up at any minute. She knew Winston was probably going to be in one. After all, his camp wasn't close to the hospital. She felt as if she wasn't breathing as she waited, her head light and dizzy.

What if he doesn't show up?

She brushed the thought away from her mind the minute it popped up.

Winston will be here. She was sure of it.

When Valerie walked out through the back door and jumped onto one of the vans, her heart went wild. Her pulse was audible in her eardrums, cold sweat clinging to her whole body. The bag over her shoulder felt as if it weighed a ton.

Valerie started the engine, and the lights flickered twice.

It's the signal.

She looked around, her throat closing. And then, there, at the edge of the lot on the opposite side, another flash of lights. A Military van started up, drove a few meters, and parked next to the medical vehicle.

He made it.

Anna almost ran to the van, opened the back door, and jumped in. Winston stepped out of his vehicle and jumped in right behind her. Breathless, she held his hand, and he squeezed it back as he closed the door.

"Ready to go?" Valerie asked from the front seat, looking at them through the rear-view mirror.

"Good to go," Anna whispered back.

The engine roared, and the van slowly pulled out of the parking lot, as if it were just another night of usual rounds. The streets were busy enough, people going back home from work, a few full buses around them.

Anna and Winston lowered their heads and sat on the

floor, their hands never breaking contact. She needed that steady pulse against her fingers to know that Winston was there with her.

"Stay low; we'll be out of the city in an hour."

They hummed an agreement, and Valerie kept driving, her eyes always on the road. She looked unconcerned, as if she wasn't smuggling them out. As if nothing out of the ordinary was going on.

"Are you okay?" Winston whispered in her ear a few minutes later.

"Good," she replied, finally setting her bag onto the floor.

It made a loud thump, and Winston raised a brow at her.

"I thought we were supposed to pack light."

"It'll be light once I read through all of these papers, commit them to memory, and burn them," she replied with a smug smile.

"Papers?"

"Yeah, I took a bunch of files from the lab before leaving."

She undid the zipper and pulled the first yellow folder out of the bag. She flicked through the pages, unsure of what she was going to find inside. These were highly classified files, something she couldn't have taken out earlier without risking being exposed.

But now that they were out, it didn't matter anymore. Authorities would surely find out that she was gone in the morning, and she knew she was never going back. It'd mean certain death.

Anna moved closer to Winston, talking in a whisper so Valerie couldn't hear them.

"Should I tell her that I read about North Camp in the files?"

"I don't know. Maybe we can keep that one out. She's only one woman, and I'm sure I can take her down if it comes to it, but I don't think we should risk it, at least, until we get there. Let's see where she's taking us, and then we can decide."

"Okay."

She traced circles in his palm as she opened the file on her lap and started to slowly go through each page in front of her.

Soon enough, a repeated word started to pique her interest. There were a lot of personal files in between what she had pulled out: people who lived before their time, some of them their age, some of them older, some younger. Way younger. Some were marked as deceased, some without enough information to know for sure. But there were too many deceased children, and Anna's stomach was starting to feel uneasy — and it wasn't the motion sickness.

"Look at this," Anna said, pointing at the red stamp on the file. "I've been seeing this in a lot of files, but haven't found the meaning yet."

"Aberration?" Winston read the bold red word out loud as a question. "What do you think it means?"

"I'm not sure, but if my gut feeling is right... I don't like this."

"Let me help you." Winston grabbed another file, and together, they started to classify the pile into personal files and informational ones. The red stamp with the word "aberration" kept appearing, and all those people were marked as deceased. Anna's gut was twisting with concern, and she didn't like the look of any of it. Between the stacks, a blue folder caught her attention. She opened it, looking through reports and essays.

With further investigation, we have determined that not everyone is susceptible to serum PX320 as originally expected. A few individuals have been immune to it, the immunity not traced to any genetic marker or phenotypic characteristic. The cause of this immunity is unknown, but subjects have been tested and proven to be immune at different levels. Some of them only show certain patterns of behavior, while others seem to have a full range of emotions. These individuals have been classified as "aberrations."

Anna felt the sweat gathering on her lower back, and she nudged Winston.

"Read this."

She passed him the file, and he read it with his brows tucked together, his expression looking more and more worried each second.

"They know about us; they're aware that we exist."

"Are you talking about the government?" Valerie asked from her seat, quickly glancing at the mirror.

"Yes, they know that there are people like us," Winston repeated.

"Of course, they do. They're not *that* useless."

"Did you know that they classify us as aberrations?" Anna asked, unable to hold her tongue any longer.

Valerie didn't even flinch at the word. "I've never heard of that term before. Where did you get it from?"

"Some files I got from the lab before leaving. They're classified reports from the highest functionaries in the Fox Lab. The word "aberration" has popped up many times now."

"That's interesting," Valerie muttered. "We're almost there," she added louder. "We're going to stop here for the night and move first thing in the morning. We're far enough from the city; this place is safe."

"Where are we?" Winston asked, peeking out of the window.

It was dark outside, but the moon illuminated enough for them to see a small facility a few meters ahead. It was a building with plain white walls, tattered and worn by the years.

"It's an old research facility; it's been abandoned for a long time."

When Valerie parked, and they departed the van, Anna could see that the place was deserted. There wasn't a single soul around, only a worn-out road leading to the building, and a thick forest stretching all around it. It was sheltered from peering eyes, so Anna thought it was smart for the resistance to use such a place as their own.

She slung her bag over her shoulder again and walked next to Winston for a bit before he helped her with the bag, a gentle smile on his face.

"I can take that for you," he offered.

It wasn't necessary, but it was a nice gesture, so she let him.

Valerie guided them to a door on one side, which she opened with a key she pulled out from her coat pocket. Inside, the facility was almost vacant. Most of the equipment had been taken away, the worn-out marks on the floors and walls still visible. It was freezing inside, the windows so small and high up that the sun probably never got in. She shivered, and Winston wrapped an arm around her shoulder.

"What's the plan?" he asked, addressing Valerie.

"We'll get some wood to get a small fire going, and then get some sleep. In the morning, we keep going. It's too dangerous to drive through these roads in the dead of night. No one does, and it would be suspicious. But once the sun is up, no patrols will be in this area, so it'll be safe."

They nodded, and Winston got a small sleeping bag out from his pack, unraveling and putting it onto the floor. It was a very compact sleeping bag, and Anna was so happy to see it that she sighed in relief. She hadn't thought to bring a blanket, as it would have been too bulky. But the army had always had the best equipment.

Winston smiled and nodded at her, as if giving her permission to grab a seat on it. She sat down, her legs crossed, and pulled some folders out of her bag straight away. There were still a few blue folders for her to go through, and she wanted to use the little moonlight they still had left.

"Is it okay if I start on this?" she asked, looking up at Valerie and Winston.

"Of course. I can go get the wood," Valerie offered.

She didn't have a pack, so there was nothing for her to get rid of before walking the few steps back to the door. Winston placed his bag onto the floor, and he was about to sit by her side when Valerie looked over her shoulder, her hand on the doorknob already.

"Big guy, would you give me a hand? There's only so much these tiny ones can carry," she said, showing her palms.

She smiled at him, and Anna almost felt a pang of jealousy at the way she looked at Winston. As if he was a prize or something.

Winston shared a look with her before agreeing, making sure she didn't mind being left alone for a moment. Before getting up, he pressed a sweet kiss to her temple, making her insides melt into a pile of goo, and then he took off his jacket and placed it over her shoulders.

"Be back in a minute," he murmured against her skin.

Anna returned to the files, pulling her arms into the sleeves of the jacket and losing herself in the information. Her nose was almost pressed against the paper, the letters barely visible in the near darkness.

It is impossible for the government to know who is a proper member of their caste, and who is an aberration in the early stages of life. Kids are unpredictable, and some of them do cry and show small signs of emotions in their early years before they're fully developed. If a kid still shows signs of emotions by the age of seven, tests are run, and the subjects are eliminated if the test results come back positive. Aberrations must be eliminated as soon as possible.

Anna felt bile crawling up her throat, but she made herself keep reading. She couldn't believe everything that was going on behind the shadows, and she had never known. For a moment, she wondered if her mother knew. If that's why she had paid such close attention to her as a child.

She shook her head, getting rid of the thought. It wasn't time to be thinking about family, a family that wouldn't even miss her now that she was gone. She flipped the page, and then pulled the sleeves of the jacket over her cold fingers as she kept on reading.

Only a very small percentage of aberrations grow to become full adults. In this case, an agent is sent to infiltrate them.

Anna's heart rate doubled.

Redwatchers will usually pose as a member of their caste, pretending to be aberrations too, in order to get these emotional beings to trust them in full. Redwatchers are the government's newest acquisition, running under serum PX550, a newer and deadlier combination that produces the most advanced and deadly soldiers.

Valerie's cold smile made an appearance in her mind, and Anna shuddered, reading the last sentence with difficulty as the paper shook in between her trembling fingers.

Redwatchers will earn the subjects' trust as fast as possible, drive them to a desolate area, and kill or capture them one by one.

The words blurred as Anna's world stopped. Desolate area. North Camp.

They were in danger. In mortal danger. Without time to come up with a plan, Anna stood on trembling legs. She ran toward the door. A pipe was leaning against the door, so she took it. She turned the doorknob with trembling fingers. Adrenaline rushed through her system. Even if she wasn't ready for what was to come, she knew she had no other option. Winston was in danger, so she'd do whatever it took to help him.

CHAPTER
TWELVE

WINSTON

As soon as they stepped out of the building, the air around Winston felt hotter. It had been so cold inside — as if no one had been in there for centuries. Which was probably the case.

He was glad he'd left his jacket with Anna; she'd looked so cold and worried. He really hoped that they were doing the right thing. For her, Winston would go to the end of this damn world if needed.

When did it happen? When had she gotten tangled so deep into my soul? Had it been when she'd held me in her arms a few days back? Had it been the first time I'd tasted her lips? The first time I had looked into her eyes?

He didn't know, but he didn't think it mattered anymore.

Picking up a log and looking back at Valerie, he thought about the road that had gotten them there. He wasn't sure if he could trust the woman yet, but at least, they were in a deserted enough spot for him to notice if anyone came up the road. After all, it was the only way in.

They lingered at the edge of the forest, Valerie picking up some of the smaller branches to start the fire while he tried to find bigger chunks that they could use.

"An axe would've been helpful," he joked.

"It would've," Valerie answered, her tone dull and bored.

He could hear her a few steps behind him, and he glanced over his shoulder, seeing her kick a small branch with the tip of her combat boot, and then crouching to pick it up. Her pants rode up as she lowered to the ground, and the way her boots shone made something in Winston's stomach churn. He knew that gleam all too well. After all, he saw it every single day when cleaning his uniform.

Something isn't right.

"I think this is enough to start a small fire; we should get back," he offered, trying to sound casual.

He eyed the building, thinking of Anna inside. He'd rather keep this woman away from her, but if he could get to his pack, then he could get his gun. He wasn't sure who this woman was, but his gut wasn't usually wrong. Those boots were Military provided, and if she had them, she'd either killed someone for them or was working for the government herself.

He'd have to act fast before she suspected something, just in case she was armed. He couldn't see any obvious weapons, but her coat was big, and she could be hiding pretty much anything in there.

"Sure, we'll come back for more in a minute," Valerie replied.

Winston smiled, a fake and small thing that made him feel sick. He didn't want to smile at this woman, but he didn't want her to doubt him, to realize that he was already planning a way out of there — that he needed to get rid of her.

He walked two steps closer to the building. The back wall wasn't far, but they'd still have to go around the corner to return through the door they'd come out of. Pulse quickening, he took another step. It almost felt as if the world was moving in slow motion. Valerie tripped, the twigs in her hands falling onto the ground with small rattling noises. Out of instinct, he reached out to catch her, his own logs falling.

That was his first mistake.

The second his hand closed around her upper arm, Valerie spun in the air, her free arm swinging in a wide circle and clipping him on the chin. It'd all been an act. The blow made him stagger backwards, white dots clouding his vision. Valerie seemed to be made out of air as she pushed forward, moving with the speed of a gazelle.

Another fist to the jaw, and Winston's guard was finally up. He dodged the third strike and threw a hook. But she was too fast.

The woman dodged again, and her leg swiped down, hitting his legs and throwing him onto the ground. Air rushed out of him in a loud hiss. Valerie didn't give him time to try and get up. She was on him in a second. Her legs pinning his torso and legs, her hands going to his throat. The incredible strength with which she squeezed made his vision blurry at the edges. His hands flew to her arms, trying to pull her away.

Who is this woman?

But he wasn't going to get an answer. No air was flowing

down his pipes, and he needed to act fast if he didn't want to pass out. One hand pushed Valerie away as the other tried to reach his boot. He had a knife there, and if he could get it, he could have the advantage. Maybe.

"You're done for, darling! And your woman is next."

She spat the words at him, and he pushed harder, his finger digging into her right eye socket. Valerie grunted, pulled her head back. And then, her head was busted to one side.

Anna stood behind her, a pipe in her hands. She'd just swung it like a bat, smacking Valerie on the side of her face. Winston used the distraction to punch her hard enough to get her off him. Anna swung again, her eyes wide in terror as she got Valerie on the shoulder. The woman rolled to the side, and Winston staggered back an inch, getting back to his feet with some effort and pulling the knife out of his boot.

"Winston…"

He didn't get to answer Anna's scared eyes.

That was his second mistake. He'd underestimated Valerie's strength and speed. Valerie jumped to her feet and lurched toward Anna, going for her throat as well.

"No!" It was almost a breathless scream as he ran toward both women.

He slashed at her back, but Valerie didn't even flinch. He stabbed her between the ribs, getting her kidney. She barely squirmed and kept on squeezing Anna's throat. The pipe had been dropped to the ground, slightly bent. He picked it up and swung. Valerie toppled to the side, blood pouring out of a gash on her forehead. Anna struggled to breathe, and he was by her side in a second, helping her to her feet while she coughed and panted.

"Come on, love, we gotta move."

He picked her up from under her armpits and half carried her weight as they rushed back into the building.

"She's… she's a Redwatcher… highly trained Military…"

"I sort of figured that out. Save your breath; we'll be safe in a minute."

He needed to get inside, get to his gun, just in case Valerie wasn't completely out of the game. It had been a strong blow, but if she was built stronger than a normal soldier, he didn't think that would've been enough. He was pretty sure John would've survived that hit if he were high enough on Crimson.

They got to the door and rushed in. Anna was running now, almost completely recovered. She grabbed her pack at the same time as he grabbed his. He went straight for the gun, keeping it in his hand.

"Are you okay?" asked Anna.

"I'm fine. Are *you* okay?"

"I think so…"

"Stay behind me, please."

Anna did as he told her and lingered behind his shoulder as he inched toward the door. Inside, they probably had the advantage. There were places to hide, more shelter, and only one way in. But outside, Anna could get a chance at running away if Winston got tangled in a fight.

So, outside it'd be.

"If I get trapped into a fight, I want you to run, okay?" He looked at her for a second, her eyes filled with concern, her eyebrows lowered. "Please."

Anna nodded begrudgingly. He risked a second of valuable time to plant a kiss on her temple, and when he turned back to the door, a shadow lingered on the threshold.

"So romantic; that's the word for it, right?"

"You picked the wrong humans, Valerie." Winston shifted to cover Anna completely.

"Oh, I think I picked you perfectly."

There was blood covering her face, the front of her clothes, her hands. But she looked unphased by it.

There was no emotion in her words, either, only a hint of

disdain, probably an effect of the adrenaline that she was running on. He had no time to think; he needed to act. Raising his gun and damning any small chance he had of ever returning to the Military, he shot twice. He got her right on the chest. Valerie staggered back, took a hand to her abdomen… and then straightened.

His heart dropped. It was worse than he'd expected. He had no clue what kind of drugs she could be on, but she wasn't even human anymore.

She ran straight toward him. He shot again. He wasn't sure if he got her that time, her body slamming against his like a bull. She tried to pin him to the ground, but he rolled.

"Run!" he yelled at Anna.

They rolled onto the floor, kicks and punches being thrown indistinctly as they wrestled. He thought he saw Anna's shape moving toward the back wall on hesitant feet. He'd lost the gun, so it was only them. Only strength.

They were a tangle of limbs fighting for their lives.

No. Valerie wasn't fighting for her life; she was fighting under orders. And that was the difference between them. She didn't have anything to lose. He did. He used every single tactic he had learned in the army, but also let his feelings help him. He let the adrenaline fuel him, the anger move his fists, the terror of losing Anna pumping through his muscles.

He managed to pin her down, and he let blow after blow fall to her face. He hated himself for hitting a woman, but he had to remember that this was not a woman. It was a soldier. A minion from the government. Valerie was almost unstoppable, her legs held onto his torso with incredible strength as she punched him right on the throat, choking him.

She twisted and got on top again. She had the advantage. His hands flew to her throat at the same time that hers flew to his. They both squeezed, and it was a battle of endurance he didn't know if he could win.

And then, there, in the corner of his eye, he saw Anna. She hadn't run.

Run, he thought.

She'd picked up his gun with trembling fingers and was aiming it at Valerie's head. She was right over Valerie's shoulder, her eyes on him. His vision was blurring, and he wanted to tell her so many things. That it was okay. That if she did it, she wasn't a bad person for it. He knew how hard the first kill was, knew by experience. His vision went dark, his hands slacking.

A gun was fired.

———

"Winston, Winston, please, wake up!"

The desperate plea woke something inside of Winston more than just his body and mind. It seemed to wake his soul.

"Anna…"

His eyes fluttered open, finding Anna lingering over him, her hands cradling his face on top of her lap. It was dark inside, but he could tell that her cheeks were tear stricken.

"Winston, are you okay? I thought, I thought…"

"Shh, shh, I'm okay. I'm okay."

His hands flew to her face, and she wiped the tears, now falling in earnest.

"Valerie?"

He tried to look around, but his head spun with the effort. He felt dizzy and tired.

"I think she's dead… I thought you were dead, too. You weren't waking up, and you lost so much blood. I'm so sorry. I'm sorry. I never… I never wanted to…"

Anna kept choking on her words as her tears dropped onto his chest, and Winston tried to understand what was going on through the fog in his mind. Blood? Why had he lost blood? He wasn't injured. It was just his head that hurt; it hurt so badly. That's when he noticed that only one of Anna's hands was cradling his face. The other was pressing hard against his shoulder.

"What happened? It's okay. I'm okay. I just need to know what happened."

Anna sucked in a deep breath and closed her eyes for a second before regaining her composure.

"I thought you were going to die. She was choking you, and I... I got the gun..."

"Yes, that was okay. You shot her, right?"

"I did, but the bullet... it..."

Anna looked down, and he followed her eyes, finding the spot that she was pressing on. His shoulder was bleeding heavily. The gun had small bullets — bullets strong enough to break through armored vehicles. So, of course, it had gotten through Valerie's skull and came out the other side. Anna had saved him by shooting Valerie, but she had gotten him in the process, too.

"Anna, it's okay. Look at me." He guided her face to his with his good arm. "I'm okay, and you're okay. We'll be okay. Did you check Valerie's pulse?"

"No, but it's been minutes, and she's not moving. There's..." Anna gagged and covered her mouth.

"Shh, shh, it's okay. It's over, Anna. Look at me; it's over."

Anna's eyes found him again, and he did his best to smile up at her. He was injured, but he was sure he'd survive. He had a small first aid kit in his bag, and if they could bandage his shoulder, they could get out of there, take Valerie's van, and live. That was all that mattered now; he wanted for both of them to live.

"I need you to do one more thing for me, okay? I'm going to guide you through the process. But first of all, I need to know if there's an exit wound."

Anna nodded and slowly pulled him up, checking his

back and nodding. He bit his tongue, not wanting her to know how much pain he was in.

"There's an exit wound," she said quietly.

"Then we're fine, Anna. We're fine. There's a first aid kit in my bag. I need you to get it and dress the wound for me. After that, we can get out of here, okay?"

"Yes, yes, I can do that... I can do that." Anna breathed deeply once more, and then gently lowered him to the floor. "I work in a lab, with blood all the time, you know? This is nothing new; I can do this."

"Of course, you can, love."

Anna chuckled and returned to his side with the kit, a soft smile on her face.

"That's the second time you called me that tonight. Did you know that?"

"Is it?" He felt a smile tugging at his lips, unable to hold it back. He hadn't even been aware of doing it, but he liked how it sounded. "I hope that's not an issue for you. I can stop doing it."

Anna chuckled again and threaded a needle with amble fingers. "I don't mind it, at all. But you might call me some other names once I'm done with this wound."

"Never."

Without much more to do, Winston bit the inside of his cheek as Anna started cleaning and sewing his wound. It had been a close call, but they were both alive. And they would make it. Even if it was the last thing he did with his life, he'd make sure Anna got out.

"Okay, here we go!"

Without waiting for an answer, Anna plunged the needle into his skin. But this time, it wasn't to get a fake blood sample; it was to save his life.

CHAPTER
THIRTEEN

ANNA

"Are you sure you can stand?"

"Anna, I'm okay. I already said it five times; my legs are perfectly fine. You shot me in the shoulder, not the calf."

Anna scowled but couldn't stop a small laugh from bursting out of her lips. What a situation they were in! She'd been terrified when she found out about Valerie, but seeing Winston struggle for his life had been worse.

She was going to run. She told herself that she was ready for it, that she was going to run, just the way he'd told her to. But she couldn't do it. Valerie was going to kill him, and the gun was there, just sitting there. And she'd done it. She had to.

"You did the right thing," Winston reminded her, running a hand down her cheek.

It was as if he could tell where her train of thought had taken her.

She had taken a life.

"It was her or us; you did the right thing," he repeated.

"I know, but that doesn't make it any easier."

She shook her head to stop the tears from falling. She didn't want to cry anymore; she wanted to move on, to get out of there. With an arm under his armpit, she helped Winston to his feet.

"I know it doesn't. But make sure to remind yourself that it was the right thing to do every time those thoughts come looking for you. Because they will. You will come back to this moment many times over the next few weeks, and maybe even months. Or years. Killing someone is not something you just forget about, but you learn to live with it. If it's them or you... I want it to always be you, okay?"

He held her face in a warm palm, and she pressed her cheek harder against it. Gently, Winston lifted his injured arm and placed it on her waist, moving his other hand to the back of her head and cradling her softly against his chest. The steady thrum of his heartbeat gave her hope.

He was okay. He was a strong soldier, made to endure battle, and a single bullet wasn't going to stop him. He was going to be okay; they were going to be okay.

"Thank you," she murmured against his warm chest. "Thank you for everything."

"For you, I'd do anything and more."

She glanced up, finding his kind eyes on her. She got lost in there for a moment, in the intensity of that simple gesture, in the warmth that a pair of eyes could radiate. In his embrace, she felt whole. For the first time in her life, she felt complete. Not because she had him, but because she had experienced love. Because she knew what it felt like to be terrified of losing someone, and that made her want to fight even more. She had one more reason to give this cause everything she had.

"Love… You know, how you used that word earlier?"

"Hmm?"

The hum traveled down his chest and vibrated against her cheek, against her whole body.

"I want you to know… I do, too."

"Do what?" It was almost a breathless question, his face already tilting down to be closer to her.

"Think of you as love."

She smiled, mirroring the expression that was taking over Winston's face.

"I love you, Anna."

"And I love you, too."

Softly, too scared to hurt him even more, she raised onto her toes and pressed a soft kiss to his lips. They had kissed before in the woods, but this, this was different. It was softer, gentler, full of love and care. It was a kiss that said how much they cared about each other, and how much they had already given for this. To be able to be together. To be able to return this kind of feeling to the rest of the world. Because if they could have this, then the world deserved to know about it and to have it, too.

"What's next?" asked Winston when they finally pulled apart.

"We head north. I don't have any better ideas than that. I don't know if anything that Valerie had said is true, but we can't go back. So, we will keep heading north and see if there's really a camp there. Maybe there are people the government hasn't managed to get to. And if not, we'll start over from there."

"I think you're right; that's the best we can do."

It was still late at night, but they had decided that they should be on the move. They couldn't stay there any longer and risk being caught. If Valerie didn't report soon, they were sure someone would go looking for them. So, they had to move, and they had to do it as fast as possible. They had already spent too much time healing Winston, probably a good half hour or more.

"Let's go."

With an arm around his waist, and Winston's arm over her shoulders, they walked out of the building together. The air outside was cold, but not as cold as the inside had been. And she still had Winston's jacket, so she was okay. They pressed on, step after step, slowly inching toward the van.

They were about halfway there when Winston tensed, his arm dropping from her shoulder.

"Is everything okay?" she asked.

"Shh… I think—"

Winston's words were cut short by a beam of light. Both their hands went to their faces on instinct. Clicking sounds came from all around them, and Anna's blood froze. Guns. It was the sound of guns.

"Raise your hands over your head, and do as you're told, or you'll be shot." The voice boomed through the forest, metallic and deprived of any emotion.

Her eyes adjusted enough to look around. There were Military vehicles surrounding them from all angles, bright lights pointed at them. And behind the lights: soldiers. Black-hats and, probably, Redwatchers too, all with guns aimed at them.

Anna looked at Winston's chest, at the red laser dot there.

And then she looked up. She found his pleading eyes on her, regret plastered all over his face. And fear. So much fear.

"I'm so sorry, Anna. You should run…"

When the words left his lips, Winston lunged toward the army in a sprint.

CHAPTER **FOURTEEN**

WINSTON

His mind was almost blank as he raced toward the army in front of them. There was only one thing that mattered: giving Anna a chance to run. He knew it was slim, he knew it was almost impossible, but he hoped that having all the attention on him would give her the small chance she needed.

It was all so fast. Barely seconds.

He ran, his feet kicking up dirt. Anna screamed his name.

The closest soldier shot a dart into his bad shoulder. The electric shock sent him to the ground.

"Winston!"

He wanted to turn, to look at her, to tell her that she should be running. But his entire body was convulsing on the ground, the mixture of a potent electric shock and a mild sedative already taking hold of his body. He knew those weapons too well, and knew that he was done for.

Knowing was probably the worst of it, because it took his hope away. They had nothing. Nothing else to do, nothing else to fight for.

Anna was by his side in a second, her hands cupping his face, tears splashing on his torso.

"I… told you… to run," he managed to gasp out.

"And you're an idiot if you thought I would leave you."

The loud thump of boots intensified, and Anna was yanked away from him. He tried to scream, his throat raw and unwilling. They had her handcuffed in a second, her legs kicking, her eyes fixed on him.

It was the most horrible thing he'd ever seen. Her scared eyes, her thrashing limbs, the too-rough hands holding onto her upper arms and probably leaving bruises there.

He felt the little hope he had leaving his body and shattering against the ground.

Tears streamed down his cheeks as a soldier flipped him onto his back and handcuffed him, too. His eyes never left Anna, never. They took her onto a van, shoved her in the back. They got him on his feet, and he took a step toward Anna, not caring about the handcuffs, the unbearable pain in his shoulder, anything.

"And where do you think you're going, Romeo?" the soldier asked nonchalantly into his ear.

He was shoved back, his body twisting in peculiar angles as he tried to keep his eyes on Anna. They were taking him to a separate van.

"No, no. Take me with her, take me with her!"

He tried to squirm out of the soldier's hold, only to have a finger shoved into his bullet wound. He doubled over and was pushed onto his knees again.

"Cooperate, or you'll get worse than that."

No, no, no. It couldn't be happening. It couldn't! He looked over his shoulder, just before the doors of the van closed, and Anna was shoved out of his life.

"Anna..."

"Move, soldier."

He was lifted back onto his feet and pushed toward an empty van. Winston didn't know what else to do.

What's the point in fighting anymore? We'd tried it all and failed.

As he was thrown into the back of the van and the door closed, he closed with it. He pushed it all in, deep down, as he had done when he was a kid.

There was no more hope, no reason to keep going.

CHAPTER
FIFTEEN

ANNA

As the door to the van closed, and Winston's eyes were taken away from her sight, Anna screamed. She had fought with tooth and nail trying to get away from the Redwatchers and the Blackhats, and her fingers were bloody and sore, her cheeks covered with tears. But none of it mattered. They had gotten so close. They knew they weren't the only ones, and that the government was indeed eliminating people with emotions.

She was aware that was probably her destiny. She'd be taken into a prison, probably be given a sort of deadly serum that would wipe her out for good. Her records would disappear from the public eye, and it'd be like she'd never existed. Anna's parents would be told to never speak her of name again or risk death. And they would agree, because they didn't care. They couldn't care. She'd become another file with a red aberration stamp on it.

The van started up, and the gravel under the wheels marked the movement of time for the next hour while she was taken back into the city. There was no other place they could take her to, so she knew that'd be it. She'd never heard of prisoners before, so she wondered where they were taking her. She wondered where they were taking Winston, too. Probably back to the Military, where they'd attempt to brainwash him or hang him on the spot.

It was painful to know so much about how Faulkner dealt with things and be able to anticipate his moves. It pained her. With her hands tightly bound behind her back, Anna used her shoulder to wipe away the tears.

Those would be the last of them.

She wouldn't cry anymore, wouldn't allow them to see her weaknesses. She was strong, and she could make it. She was going to make it. Finding a way out was her first priority, so she started looking around the van, hoping for any small thing she could use to her advantage.

But there was nothing.

Too fast, the van stopped. It was getting bright outside, and when the doors opened, she was almost blinded by the first morning rays.

"Get down."

The male soldier pointed to the ground, and Anna obeyed. She was going to get out, but she also needed to know which battles to pick. An armed soldier wasn't the one.

She jumped down and looked around. A tall building was

to the front, a big parking lot all around it. Weeds were growing between the paving stones, the place clearly abandoned. The yellowish walls of the building had pieces of paint falling off, and some windows were broken and boarded.

As they walked closer to the building, two soldiers flanking her, a sign came into view.

Bellevue Psychiatric Hospital.

Her blood chilled, and her bones ached, at the sight of it. Anna knew the place. Hell, everyone knew that place. It was where everything had started, where Faulkner's reign had grown from nothing, and where the first Siero serum had been created. Where hundreds of patients had been vaccinated and later committed suicide.

She was taken inside through a side door protected by a code and accessed with a magnetic card. Inside, the place seemed deserted. They walked down a hall and there: another human. A woman with a medical coat was standing in a small room, a syringe in her hand. Anna squirmed, trying to get away from her, but the woman approached in silence and — with the help of the soldiers — took her jacket off and plunged the needle into Anna's upper arm.

Her vision went blurry in an instant, and the only thing she could think of was the jacket the nurse now held in her hands. Winston's jacket.

Don't take it, she wanted to say, but the words failed her as the world turned pitch black.

———

When she woke up, the room she was in was almost dark. A small lightbulb flickered on the ceiling. A little confused, she looked around. The metal frame of the bed squeaked as she tried to sit down and found that she couldn't move. A little desperation clawed inside her throat, and she pushed up, but nothing happened. Both of Anna's wrists were restrained with thick leather straps, and she could barely lift her chest enough to look around the room — a room that was more like a prison cell.

There was nothing but a chair and a doorless closet to one side, which was empty. A small glass window was high up on the wall, barely a shred of light coming through it. The mattress she was on was thin, and she could feel the metal underneath, each plank digging into her back. She was wearing a thin medical robe, Winston's jacket nowhere to be seen.

Panic made her heart race, and Anna did her best to breathe deeply through her nose. In and out. In and out. When calmness finally took over her, she was left in silence, her breathing and the ticking of a clock behind her back the only thing breaking the stillness.

She couldn't turn enough to see the time, only heard its incessant ticking.

Tick. Tick. Tick. Each second felt like a lifetime.

Where is Winston? Is he even alive? Why haven't they killed me yet? How can I get out? I need to get out.

Tick. Tick. Tick.

Minutes passed, and no one came. So, Anna screamed at the top of her lungs. Screamed for someone to come and help her. For someone to tell her what was going on. For food. For someone to let her go to the bathroom. She screamed until her throat was raw.

Tick. Tick. Tick.

She screamed in anger, in frustration, in pain, and in fear. But she didn't let a single tear roll down. She wouldn't let them see her cry again.

When nothing happened, and her voice started to fail her, Anna closed her eyes. She saw Winston there, his short hair and fearful eyes. His lustful eyes. His hopeful eyes. She saw Winston, his face contorted in pain as he was taken away from her — their last memory together. Anna snapped her eyes open and stared at the small window, seeing how the light dimmed in slow motion.

She couldn't think like that. Couldn't let fear and pain rule her. She was smart; she would figure something out.

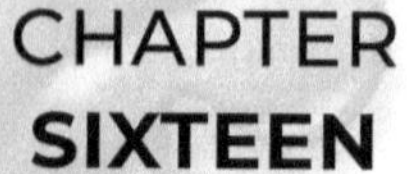

CHAPTER
SIXTEEN

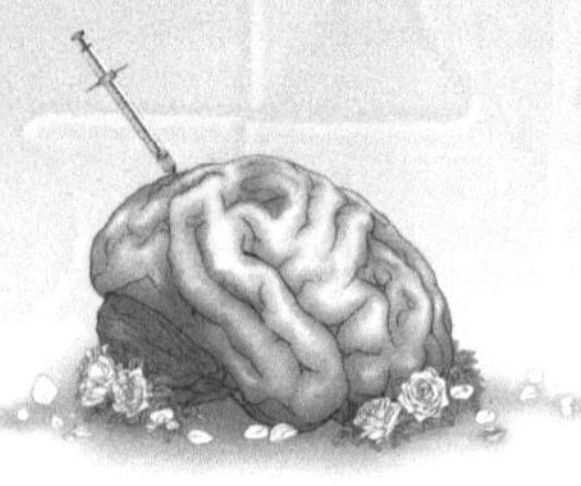

WINSTON

Expecting to be taken straight into the woods to be hung or shot, Winston was surprised when the van rolled to a stop, and he was let out to find a familiar camp. *His* Military camp.

Instead of heading to the barracks, he was taken to one of

the furthest buildings... the ones where only the highest-ranking soldiers were allowed. He was taken in shackles, his head hanging low, his soul hanging in tatters. Halls merged one into the other as he was taken further into the heart of the building, away from the outside world, away from the comfort he had learned to find in his barracks.

A few floors down, and too many halls to recall where he was, Winston stood in front of a thick metal door.

He was thrown inside the cell; the door closed behind him.

And then, darkness was his only company. Darkness and despair.

ANNA

Time was a curious thing. A curious and twisted thing. Had it been days? Hours? Weeks? Silence was everything she had. Silence, and the dreaded ticking of that damn clock. She wished she could rip it down. Hit it with a hammer. Slam it against a wall.

Food was delivered at irregular intervals, time such a slippery thing that she couldn't understand it anymore. Anna was so tired. Just so tired. She had fought against the restraints, her wrists raw, her head pounding with the echo of her own screams. But nothing had worked. They hadn't let her go. She was sure that days had passed, maybe even a week. Or a month. Time was so curious, just so curious.

The familiar loud click of the lock sounded, but she didn't even turn.

What's the point?

They'd give her some food, and then be gone. She hoped it was the chicken flavor thing, not the other disgusting mixture they usually gave her. Maybe they'd give her another shot, monitor her vitals as her body seized and convulsed. She wondered what kind of concoctions they were trying out on her, and if they were attempting to erase her emotions once more.

She had become a lab rat.

The large nurse's shadow loomed over her, but still, Anna didn't look. She told herself she was waiting for the right moment, for a flicker of hope so she could escape. But the truth was that she was losing whatever hope she'd had.

She had asked to speak with someone, to be let out, to be able to talk to her parents, Faulkner, a Blackhat, anyone. But none of her questions had been answered. All they did was give her different serums, some food when she was lucky, and then leave her alone once more.

Is this what the first subjects felt like? Like they were losing their minds?

She wasn't sure if her emotions were duller, or if there was nothing to be felt among those four walls. Her mind... her mind was the last thing she'd lose. She pictured Winston, his hopeful eyes, his scared ones. The scared ones were the ones that came to her more often than not those days.

She seemed unable to forget about the look on his face just before the van's doors closed between them. The last time she had seen him.

Would it be the last?

No. She couldn't think like that. She had to find a way out, a way to fight... but she didn't even know if Winston was still alive.

WINSTON

Trying to count the passing of days had been fruitless. Winston wasn't sure what was real and what was not anymore, his face too bruised to even open his eyes properly, his body an aching mess.

The physical torture wasn't even the worse, no. He knew physical pain, and it was easy enough to deal with. The hard part had been the live videos they made him watch: Anna's almost expressionless face, the fight leaving her body.

At first, he had seen her struggle against her restraints, scream, fight. But now… now she was simply there, her body almost limp. The image was a little grainy and in shades of gray, and he thought that was so fitting.

Their lives were a dull shade of gray now. They never let her out of that bed, and he watched how they pierced their skin with needles over and over.

He couldn't help her.

Every time he was kicked on the ribs, he was asked if he was ready to forget about her, to rejoin the force. Every time, he said her name.

"Anna."

It was a plea for them to stop; it was a last wish to see her once more, to touch her, to feel her.

"Anna."

It was a desperate attempt to get those ruthless soldiers to feel something. To snap out of their expressionless lives, to feel a tinge of what he was feeling.

"Anna."

It was the only thing that had mattered. It had been the hope that a different life was possible, that he could have more than he had ever wished for.

But as the days passed, it was harder and harder to even say her name.

What's the point? What am I even fighting for?

———

ANNA

"Rise and shine," a bored voice said as the door opened once more.

Unfamiliar to words lately, Anna jumped, a little startled.

The nurse went to her side and, to Anna's surprise, started unlatching her restraints.

Is this it? Is this my chance to get out?

She tried not to move, not to react. She had to wait for the perfect time, that had been the plan, right?

After loosening both restraints a little, the nurse gave her one more shot, and then completely undid the leather straps before quickly leaving the room and locking the door. She had left the used syringe on the small side table, and Anna couldn't believe her eyes as she grabbed it. Her eyes darted around the room once more. Nothing had changed… Nothing but the jacket that had shown up, hanging on the back of the metal chair while she slept.

"Winston…"

She stood up on trembling legs, her muscles so sore that it felt like pins and needles stabbed at the sole of her bare feet as she made her way toward the Military jacket — the syringe still tightly clutched in between her fingers.

Anna barely made it there, walking the short steps that separated her from the jacket being the hardest thing she'd ever done. Her legs gave out, and she slid against the wall, all the way to the floor as she tried to find any remnants of Winston's earthy scent on the jacket — but there was nothing. Nothing there.

A gentle click of metal against the floor made her look down at the syringe she had dropped — the only weapon she had. Her only way out. She could inject air into the nurse and make a run for it. It was the only way. She picked it up again and saw the name of the drug on a small label on the plastic tube.

Siero — prototype I.

5 ml.

Her blood chilled, and her bones seemed to ache.

"No, no, no..."

———

WINSTON

A hard fist collided with his cheek, and Winston tasted the blood coating the inside of his mouth. It was the flavor he was most used to by then.

"Are you ready to rejoin the force?"

Silence.

A kick to his stomach as he tried to curl up on the floor and protect his internal organs.

"Soldier Hitcher, are you ready to plead allegiance to Bellevue and Faulkner, and rejoin the force?"

Winston's lips parted.

"A..."

Can I even say it? Can I even say her name again?

He hadn't seen any videos in what felt like weeks, and he didn't even know if Anna was still alive. Any small shred of hope he had of seeing her again was leaving his body, along with the blood pouring out of the corner of his mouth.

He swallowed and curled his arms, holding onto his knees, his head resting on the cold floor.

"Make... it... stop."

The soldier's leg stopped halfway to his face. Winston waited for another blow but, a moment later, the door to his cell closed with the familiar click of a lock, and he was left in darkness again.

———

ANNA

"Why?" she asked the empty room. "Why now?"

Anna wondered what had changed. Had they broken Winston and gotten him to speak? Was he dead? Had they decided that she wasn't useful anymore? She knew what Prototype I was like. She knew it had been the one to wipe out emotions so badly that the side effects had led hundreds of people to kill themselves.

"I will never do it," she chanted to herself. "I will never give them that satisfaction."

But wouldn't it be better? A voice asked inside her head.

If she was going to die, she would rather do it by her own hands than wait for the scientists and government to kill her. *Right?*

Anna clutched Winston's jacket as hard as she could, trying to remember every little moment when she was by his side. The feel of his fingers on her face, of his hands wrapping around her waist, of his lips pressing on hers. It was hard to do, but she had to. She had to believe that she had the strength to remember it, to feel it.

How long had it been since they'd given her the shot? She'd been unable to stand from her spot against the wall, but she thought days might have passed again. Time seemed to pass so slow and so fast all at once. She could see the clock on the opposite wall now, but its hands were stuck on three and two — unmoving.

With her head pressed against the cold wall, Anna breathed slowly, trying to stay present. Her fingers found a few lines on the wall, as if someone had been counting days in there. She started counting them, but got lost somewhere around seventy-eight, or maybe ninety-eight. The marks were small and jagged, as if scratched with a nail or something that wasn't too sharp.

Anna's nails were long after being there for so long, so she slowly moved her index finger up and down until she added one more line to the count. The days didn't matter, but she wanted to leave a little something to show that she'd been there.

More marks appeared on the spot where she was leaning against the wall, so she pushed back and sat with her legs crossed, looking at the wall.

And there, under more and more lines… something different. Curved and small lines made with careful precision gave her a name: Constance.

Someone named Constance had spent days and nights in the same cell, just as she was doing. Anna picked up the syringe again, and with the sharp end, scribbled her name underneath it.

Constance.

Anna.

———

WINSTON

"Soldier Hitcher," an emotionless voice said as the door to his cell opened once more.

Winston braced for the torture, for a kick to his ribs, but nothing happened.

"Stand up. You're being taken to see the general."

Winston stood up, and the light outside was almost blinding when the soldier put a hand on his shoulder to usher him forward. A second soldier was waiting outside the door, and as he walked with his head hanging low, a flicker of something he knew caught his eye.

He looked up, "John?" The soldier didn't even flinch, so he asked again, "Mad Dog?"

His bunkmate barely glanced at him and kept walking, taking him over to see the general.

Winston didn't know what he was in for, but all fight had left him already.

How much worse can it get?

CHAPTER
SEVENTEEN

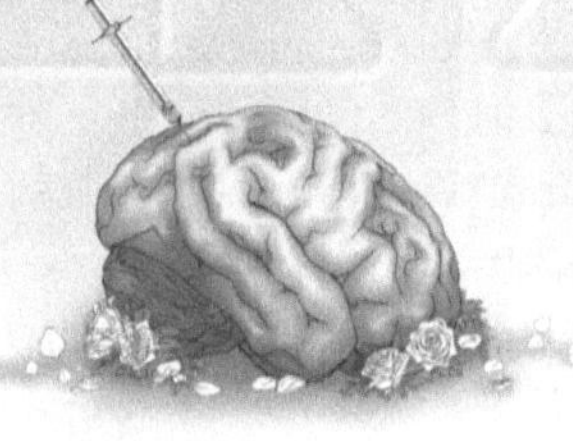

ANNA

The next time the clicking of keys sounded on the other side of the thick metal door, Anna was ready. She didn't have much left to fight for, didn't remember what it felt like to be held in between Winston's arms, but she knew that the small room wouldn't be the last place to hold her. She knew the jacket she was wearing belonged to someone she'd cared about, even if she couldn't make herself feel like she cared anymore. Thinking of Winston was like thinking about the broken clock on the wall — she felt nothing.

Instead of waiting for the nurse by her bed, she quietly dragged herself behind the door and stood with her back against the wall. She'd never seen anyone other than the same nurse who came in every day, so it should be easy enough. It should be.

Her breathing was steady, and her heart was beating consistently as Anna waited. Her head was clear — she knew exactly what she had to do. She might not have felt a thing, but that didn't mean that she was willing to die in that room alone.

If there was something she was sure of, it was that old Anna would have wanted her to do this. To get out. To see the world one last time in hopes of feeling a little something.

The door opened an inch, two. She heard one step. Anna pushed the entire weight of her body against the door as fast as she could and heard the nurse groan. She loosened the piece of metal that had been keeping her locked for so long as fast as her legs would take her.

The nurse was on the floor, clutching her bleeding forehead. There was no time to worry about her, so Anna ran. She ran like she would've run if her life depended on it. Did it? Maybe it did, but Anna couldn't care about it. She ran for old Anna, for the memories of what she'd been, for the feelings she couldn't remember.

———

WINSTON

"Soldier Hitcher, I hear you're ready to negotiate your return to the force," the general said as he sat in front of him.

Winston didn't say a word, too stunned to think straight.

Is that what they thought? That I'm ready to return? Am I?

"We're offering you your old place back. You'll be graduating in two months, and when you do, we'll recommend you for deployment. You'll be taken onto the front lines like you've always envisioned. All you need to do is commit to your old schedule. Forget about the woman."

The woman.

Anna.

"Anna...."

The general nodded, and the soldier standing behind him placed a screen on the desk that separated him from his superior. He turned on the screen, and images from a security camera showed up. It wasn't the room he was used to, but a hallway. And in the middle of it: Anna. She was running and about to turn a corner. But she couldn't see what he saw: a guard posed at the end of the hall that she was about to turn into.

Winston's heart hammered in his chest, cold sweat gathering in the back of his neck. He kept his face expressionless as he watched, nausea creeping up his throat, fingers clutching the edge of the desk as hard as he could.

Anna.

ANNA

Anna turned a corner and skidded to a stop. A few feet ahead, a soldier stood against the door that she thought would take her outside. He pointed the gun at her, his eyes invisible behind the shield of his helmet. Anna lifted her hands slowly as her eyes scanned her surroundings. Then she darted to the left and took the stairs, two at a time.

She didn't know the building, but if out wasn't an option, she'd at least go up. So, up she went. Up and up and up, heading toward the stars that had been her only company for so many lonely nights.

She could almost remember what loneliness had felt like. She could taste it on her tongue, but even though she knew that she should be feeling lonely in the middle of nowhere, left alone to rot, she couldn't. She didn't.

So, Anna kept running up as fast as her legs would take her. One floor, then two, then three. The sound of boots heavy against the steps followed, but she didn't slow down. They yelled for her to stop, yelled for her to surrender.

Surrender? What do they know about surrendering?

Anna had already surrendered everything she had and everything she was. There was nothing left. Nothing but the stars high up in the sky, waiting for her to join them.

———

WINSTON

His heart was wild in his chest as the image on the screen changed from a security camera to a Military one. He knew those too well. They were small cameras placed on soldiers' helmets so they could report directly to the base and have their generals know what was happening.

And now, he was watching Anna's back through that soldier's camera, her small figure disappearing behind the turn of the stairs over and over again, and reappearing once more.

What's she doing? Why's she going up? There's no way out up there!

"This ends today, soldier. You have to make a choice. Who do you stand with? That woman, or us?"

Anna was out of screen once more, and a second later, the soldier reached an exit door — a door to the rooftop. It was half-open, and the soldier pushed it, stepping into the moonlit night.

———

ANNA

She hadn't known that it was nighttime before stepping onto the roof, but she had almost felt it inside, like a knowledge she simply possessed. The stars were glistening all around her, and she tried to recall what it had felt like to be so small, to have the world in front of her. But she couldn't.

She walked over to the edge of the roof, stood on the ledge, and looked up. Then down. Trees stretched far beyond, and the ground seemed to be so far away.

How many levels had I climbed? How far up am I?

She didn't know, but she didn't think it mattered anymore. The night had seeped into her; it had taken over her heart and turned it into a black pit.

Or is that the serum?

"Anna Chaplin, step off the ledge, and turn around with your hands up."

She wanted to laugh but couldn't remember how to. So, she turned.

The soldier who faced her had his gun pointed at her, the red dot like a small firefly dancing over her chest.

"I will not shoot you unless you make me," the soldier said in a bored tone. "I have orders to return you to your room if you cooperate."

"And spend the rest of my days in a closed room? I have lived all there is to live, but I can't remember what any of it feels like."

Anna opened her arms wide and took a step back, her heels tasting emptiness as she almost toppled back into the abyss behind her.

"I'm sorry, Winston," she said out loud, hoping that he was already with the stars and listening to her. She looked up and drew a smile on her face, the muscles used to the movement even if her heart wasn't anymore. "I think I love you."

WINSTON

His fingers hurt where he clutched the edge of the desk as hard as he could. He thought he'd splinter the wood as he watched Anna standing on the ledge. She opened her arms wide, and her lips moved, a soft smile on her face — but there was no audio on the video.

"She'd been given the chance to surrender," the general said.

Winston barely heard him over the roaring of his own heart.

And then Anna fell back.

CHAPTER
EIGHTEEN

WINSTON

An official entered the barracks and woke them up. The soldiers jumped from their bunks, Mad Dog landing on the floor with a loud thump.

"It's a six-mile run today," John said as if reminding himself of the fact.

Winston barely nodded, got ready, and together, they got out of the barracks and onto the track. They ran side by side as they had done so many times before. They ran side by side, as if the last two months of their lives hadn't even happened. Like nothing had changed.

But everything was different.

Winston had found someone like him. He'd learned that love was possible. He had given his heart and soul. And then, both of those had been ripped from his chest. He'd been tortured and made to watch the woman he loved fall to her death. The grainy image of Anna's sprawled body in the distance, recorded from the soldier's camera, was ingrained in his mind.

"Nothing left to lose, soldier," the general had said. "Are you with us?"

He couldn't remember replying, but he must have.

The next day, he had woken back in his cot, his body drenched in cold sweat from the nightmares that now clouded his every night.

Failing Anna wasn't even the worst of it.

But what do I have left?

At least this way, he'd be deployed and leave this place. If he were lucky, he'd be sent to the front lines and be shot in the head, so he wouldn't have to think about her anymore. It was too painful to do so.

So, Winston ran because he had nothing left to do. He ran, and he showered. He fought, and he patrolled. He practiced his aim with a gun and spent his nights surrounded by those he blamed for Anna's death.

It was his third week back when he returned to the labs for the usual shot. He hadn't been getting any because the generals knew he didn't need them, but they wanted him to be more reactive — so he was back in the dreaded place where he had met her.

Winston fought hard to keep his expression neutral as he swiped his card and walked in. The white walls of the halls made the place look so big, but there was not enough air inside. The hallway stretched forever until he found the door he was looking for. He walked in, found the usual nurse, and was injected with the shot in barely seconds. It was all the same as usual, but Winston couldn't help but look for a tinge of copper hair in every corner.

But, of course, he didn't find her.

Instead, when he was almost out, he heard someone murmuring his name. "Winston?"

He turned around and found a familiar girl standing beside him. She had dark braids, down to her waist, and equally dark eyes that looked right into him.

"Sammy?" Winston remembered the girl that he'd seen in Anna's lab, and the connection to her almost broke him.

Sammy quickly ran to his side and almost bumped into him. Her fingers twitched at her sides, and her pupils were dilated, making her eyes look almost black.

"Sorry," she whispered as she placed a hand against his chest to steady herself. "I need to watch where I'm going. Just wanted to say hi." Her tone was loud enough for the few people around to hear them.

Sammy looked around to those lingering about, but no one was paying them much attention. She looked a little nervous as she leaned in closer and whispered against his shoulder.

"Anna wanted you to have this if anything happened to her."

With that, the girl turned around and disappeared between the workers coming and going. Winston felt the piece of paper the girl had smuggled into his pocket, and he dug his hands in them, pushing it to the bottom and walking out of the Fox Lab as if nothing had happened.

————

Winston had been too scared to look at the paper in front of anyone, so he had ignored it for almost two days before he finally got the weekend off and claimed that he had to go drop some supplies off at his family's home. It wasn't unusual for soldiers to take provisions to their families, so no one questioned him when he signed his leave for the day.

Taking one of the Military vehicles, he made his way to the suburbs. He walked the familiar streets to the unmarked door and knocked.

It was only a minute until a plump woman opened it. "Winston, come on in."

"How's everything going, Mother?"

"Same as usual. Everybody's working, so I'm home alone. I can get you some food if you're hungry."

Sara barely looked at him as she went into the kitchen and kept working on what she was doing.

"That'd actually be perfect, Mother. Thanks. I will be in my old room for a moment and would appreciate not being disturbed."

"Of course." Sara waved a hand his way and kept stirring a pot of something that smelled like rabbit stew.

Winston crossed the small hall to the room that had been his when he was younger. Before that, the house had belonged to their grandparents, and Winston knew it would've been his grandma's.

He was about twelve years old when he'd found the secret compartment under a loose floorboard, where his grandmother kept her journals, and he'd never told anyone about it. His grandma, Cady, had talked about emotions, about things Winston understood but knew he couldn't talk about, so he had felt a strong connection to them from the start and made sure to keep them a secret from the rest of the world — even his own family.

Back in his childhood room after so long, memories assaulted him, but he tried not to let them get to him. He closed the door and locked it before sitting on the single bed that now resided in the room in case anyone ever stayed the night. He fished the piece of paper from his pocket and stared at the folded note.

When had she written it? It had to be from before we fled if Sammy had it, but why? Had she known something could go wrong?

He rubbed his fingers on the edge of the paper a few times before gathering enough courage to open it up.

As soon as he unfolded it though, he had to blink away tears in order to see the words scribbled there. The image of Anna falling backwards played in his mind over and over again, so he shook his head. This was everything he had left of her; he had to be strong. Slowly, he read the words.

Winston, if this gets to you, it's because things haven't gone as we planned. I know I'm making a hot-headed decision by choosing to trust Valerie and follow her to who-knows-where, but I have to take the chance. My whole life, I've been waiting for chances like this. I never knew anyone like me, with enough feelings to know what it meant to be me.

But then you showed up. You showed up in that lab like you were a God-sent, and that comes from someone who doesn't even believe in a god. But seeing you there, I had to believe in something.

I've been working on something for a very long time since the first day I stepped into the Fox Lab. It had been my Plan A for a long time, but when you showed up, I had to give Plan B a go. I had to risk it all for you... How could I not? The way you look at me and hold me in your arms make me believe in the possibility of a better world. A world where people can be like you and me, where there can be love, hope, and beautiful memories being created every day.

We're living like empty carcasses, being led by other people's choices, but we can't keep going like this. There was a world before us that was better. A world where people could love as you and I can. And I want to give that back to the world, to Bellevue. I don't know if things outside the wall are the same as here, but I choose to believe that they are not. I have to believe that, by returning the emotions to Bellevue, I will be doing what's right.

But Winston, if this gets to you, it's because something went wrong. It means that I'm not around anymore, but for some reason, you are. Winston… I love you. I love you like I never knew I could love another human. I love you so much it hurts. It hurts to know that so many people are deprived of what we have. We have to give it back. We have to allow people to feel this.

So, if this flimsy piece of paper is between your hands, I have one favor to ask. You have to take over my Plan A.

Winston took a deep breath and wiped the tears streaming down his cheeks before he finished reading Anna's plan. And then he read the whole thing again. And again.

"I love you," he whispered, knowing that she'd never hear those words again.

Even though he had things to do and places to be, Winston allowed himself a moment with Anna's letter. He read it so many times that he had almost memorized it by the time he stooped onto the floor and got the loose floorboard out.

He took his grandma's journals out from the inside and looked through them one more time. As a kid, he'd looked at them with fear. He'd checked a few pages here and there, read his grandma's stories about love and death, and then put them away, fearing that someone would find him with the diaries in his hands.

Now, having almost nothing left to lose, he opened them up and marveled at them slowly.

He read the first few pages, where his grandmother talked about a love so great that it had driven her mad when she lost it. He read about the short years Cadence had spent in a mental health clinic while her sister looked after her child because she was unable to be a good enough mother to Sara.

"Bellevue is a tricky and treacherous place," Cady had written. "There are needles that pierce, but others that soothe. There are people who stare, but others who listen. Walls that listen. Lights that blind. Trees that whisper."

From what he'd gathered, his grandma, Cady, had been at Bellevue when the first Siero serum had been created. She had been released and was allowed to go back home, where she had written most of her diaries. But her time had been cut short. Her handwriting had gotten neat and almost perfect, but then it had gotten messy all over again. She had written loose phrases here and there that scared twelve-year-old Winston.

"No one is safe."

"They'd doomed us all."

"People are dying everywhere. Everywhere. My friends are dead. The ones I loved are dead. The ones I hated are dead. They're all dead."

The last pages were plagued with cuttings from local newspapers. A note about a woman who had jumped from a roof. Another who had taken enough sleeping pills to kill an army. A man who had jumped in front of a moving vehicle.

That one had a small note on the side that said, "I remember him."

Winston read the entire article, which described the death of Kai Hastings, a man who had been a scientist at the psychiatric hospital but had later been a patient after some unconfirmed diagnosis of mental illness. He had been a patient at the same time as his grandma had been, and Winston wondered if they'd been friends. The man had simply jumped in front of a moving vehicle, taking his own life.

The last note was one from a woman named Constance Fay. There was only a note by its side that said, "I'll join you soon, Connie." Winston had been too scared to ever ask how his grandmother had lost her life, but after reading so many articles, he knew suicide had been the cause of it. Almost four hundred lives had been lost that year to the first Siero, but it was something almost no one talked about. Winston put everything away and read Anna's letter one last time.

He knew what he had to do.

CHAPTER
NINETEEN

WINSTON

Before leaving the house, Winston planted a kiss on his mother's forehead. Sara looked at him as if he had just done the strangest thing in the world, but he simply walked off. He had no time for emergency goodbyes. If he was going to do it, he had to do it before he changed his mind. Before he chickened out, or someone found out about the note.

Just like Anna had done a few weeks back, he was making a hot-headed decision. He was throwing everything in. He jumped back onto the Military van and drove over to the alley, where he'd always met with Anna. She'd told him in her letter that he was going to find the rest of the plan and what he needed in the place where they had kissed for the first time. It was coded to make sure only Winston would find what Anna had been working on, and he felt a surge of emotion in his chest that he couldn't give a name to.

Maybe it was pride. Pride that she had chosen him for the task, that she had believed in him in a way he hadn't even believed in himself. If it wasn't for Anna, he would've never considered leaving the army in the first place. He would've never considered ditching the only place he had ever known as a home. His barracks, his bunkmates. But he couldn't even call them his friends. And Anna? He had called her his love. Winston had known with her something he hadn't known existed otherwise. And now, she was asking him to do one last thing for her, for all of Bellevue. And in her memory, he'd do everything in his power to make it a reality.

He'd give the town their emotions back.

The alley was deserted, and the sound of his steps resonated in the emptiness as he ran toward the forest. No one paid him much attention, but he looked both ways before entering the edge of the forest, in case anyone was following him. But no one was.

The clearing opened up in front of him within a few minutes, and Winston dashed over to the tree that they had leaned against. The one where Anna had laid a blanket for them to eat grapes and berries together. The one where he knew Anna had hidden what he was looking for. He walked around the trunk, looking for any marks, until he found a small hole in the bark.

Inside, was a small plastic bag with a note. He ripped the plastic and unfolded the piece of paper. The same hand-writing as before greeted him, and Winston read Anna's plan. Read how she'd trusted Sammy because she was the only emotionless human she had met who was smart enough to understand that life with emotions would've been better.

Anna had given her vials of emotions as often as she could, so Sammy could understand what Anna was talking about. The only other person besides Winston that she had trusted with her secret. And the one she had gone to before leaving with Valerie, in case anything went wrong.

Anna had told Sammy to give Winston the first note at the first chance she got if Anna didn't return. In that first note, he had been told to return to the forest and look for the next clue. And now, he sat under the well-known tree and read the words of his lover one more time.

Follow the map until you find what I've been working on.

So, not having any better plan than to listen to her, Winston followed the map of the forest toward a stream.

It was a half-hour hike that led Winston to a frigid stream. The water was almost freezing cold to the touch, and Winston knew immediately why Anna had left her investigation there. She needed the serum that she had created to stay cold for as long as possible in case she couldn't return to it for a long time. In case anything failed.

And it had.

According to her first letter, Anna had been working on a cure for years. Knowing that the chances of administering it to humans as a shot was slim, she had worked on a new formula that could be drank like cough medicine. Before leaving, she had tried the serum on Sammy, who Anna claimed had regained her emotions after a few short days.

The formula was now a concentrated version that Anna had planned on releasing to the waterways so that it would get to the entire city. It wasn't the best plan, but Anna had known that it was the best she could do without a bigger team of people supporting them. After all, they were alone.

Winston dug between the rocks that Anna had marked with a red cross, and started piling them by the side of the stream, his fingers going numb after a few minutes. When he was done, he found a small cooler that had been hiding in plain sight. He took it out and opened it. Inside, one last note waited for him, along with two glass vials.

Winston, I'm leaving you with my legacy. With everything I've ever worked on. With this note, is a map of the water purification plant and the entry points that you can use to sneak in. Once inside, find the purified tanks and drop the contents of one of the vials into it. If you find the chemical tanks, you can drop the contents there, instead.

Keep the second one so other investigators can replicate my work once the town has their emotions back. If this has spread to other cities as we've been led to believe, they'll need this to produce more and help others, too. Thank you for this. Thank you for everything. If you're reading this, and I'm gone, I want you to know that I don't regret any of it. I chose the life I chose, and I chose to allow myself to love you. And I would do it a thousand times over if I could.

Live for me, Winston. Live for us. Make this world better.

With love, Anna.

"I will. I promise, I will."

Pocketing both vials, Winston returned to his van. The water purification plant was on the edge of the city limits, just inside the wall, so he made his way there without delay.

He'd been a soldier. A lover. A fool. But above all, he knew he had his training to rely on. So, Winston steadied his own heart as he jumped over the fence and snuck inside the plant. The building didn't have much security, as there was no point in guarding a place like it, so immobilizing the guard at the back entrance had been simple enough.

Winston was a soldier, a human madly in love, and a fool. Because of his haste to do what Anna had asked of him, Winston forgot the basic running of the Military. He forgot what those people were capable of. So, when he found his way to the tank, and a group of ten armed soldiers pointed their guns at him, he knew he'd messed up.

"Soldier Hitcher, put your hands up, and step away from the water tank."

Winston's heart dropped to the ground at the sound of Mad Dog's voice.

Why him? Why'd they have to send him?

He'd only been inside the building for a few minutes before the armed forces barged in. He had been a fool, such a fool. And now, he was going to die because of it. One act of treason, the army could deal with, but him going rogue twice? He knew he wouldn't leave the building in one piece.

"You've been tracking me, haven't you?" he asked, trying to win a little bit of time.

The vial in his right hand felt sweaty, and he held onto it harder so as to not drop it.

"Yes, Hitcher, we have. Your van is rigged. As soon as you took the road out of the city, we started following you. What are you doing here?"

He'd never tell them. He wouldn't tell them a thing.

"This is not right. And I wish I could show you why. I wish I could show you what life feels like without that damn Siero messing up your brain."

John didn't even flinch. His arms were steady as he pointed the gun to Winston's chest. The men around him stood waiting, all guns pointing at him, too. The water tank was just behind him, a huge cement pool that he could access through a ladder on the side. Even if he ran as fast as he could, he would never make it to the top. He would never be able to drop the vial inside.

But it was okay. Everything would be okay.

Winston looked up to the ceiling, wishing that he could see the sky, instead.

"I'm sorry, Anna. I have to break my promise."

Before he could change his mind, Winston turned to the side and raced to the metallic ladder.

Gunshots resounded in the enclosed space, like explosions being detonated right inside his head. He fell against the ladder, his fingers barely brushing the first step, and the vial falling to the ground with a clinking sound that no one heard. His back burned as if a thousand whips had scorched his skin, and his breathing came out ragged as he struggled to hold onto his life — even if just for a second longer. Even if just to remember what Anna's smile looked like.

Before everything went dark, Winston managed to smile as his left hand felt the empty vial in his pocket. He had been a fool, but the Military had been too slow. The second vial had been the decoy, and the first had already been emptied into the tank that contained the chemicals used to purify the water.

He'd broken his promise to live for the both of them, but at least, they'd be reunited soon.

EPILOGUE

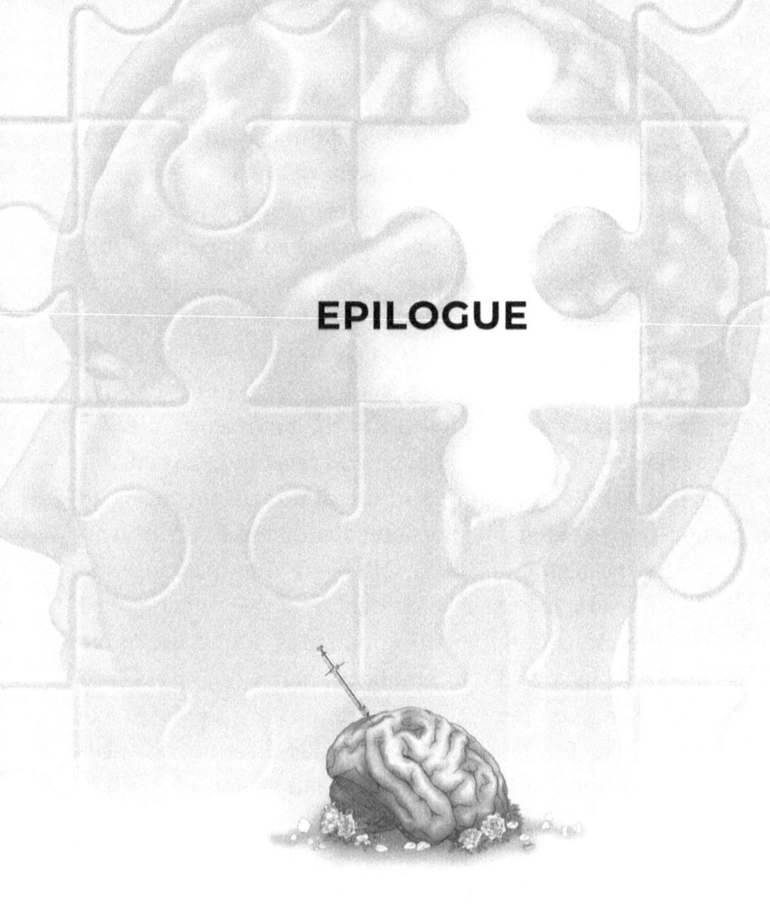

FAULKNER

The town of Bellevue was a messed-up place. The working class was outside Faulkner's building, and he knew it wouldn't be long until they found their way into his office. It was a raging war outside, and Faulkner hid for as long as he could, making desperate calls to try and save his city. A city that was messed up because everyone's emotions had returned in full, and many had lost their minds to it.

Anna Chaplin had come up with a serum right under his

nose, one to return emotions to the entire population. And with the help of soldier Hitcher, she had managed to leak her formula into the water supply of the entire town.

Within less than twenty-four hours, people had regained their emotions. Within two days, riots had started. Within three, his own Military had turned against him. Almost forty years had passed since Dr. Faulkner had become the supreme leader of the town of Bellevue, his name had been plastered all over the city, his superiors had praised him, and the government had allowed him to run the town as he pleased as an experiment. And now, no one was returning his calls.

He had the second sample of the antidote that they had retrieved from soldier Hitcher after his demise, and he was pretty sure the results of the revolts were due to a dose too high. The formula had been so concentrated that, when mixed with the chemicals in the purification tanks, it had backfired. The town had lived without emotions their whole lives, and with everything coming back in full so quickly, they had lost their minds, The few who had been used to the emotions vials still regained some of their sanity and had stayed by Faulkner's side longer, but they were all angry at him, regardless. They all wanted him to be taken down.

When the phone finally rang, he picked it up in a blink. He was desperate.

"Faulkner, here, what's taking so long? Why is help not on the way already?"

"Dr. Faulkner, we allowed you to run this town under the premise that the rest of the world wouldn't hear about it. You claimed to have everything under control, and your soldiers helped the nation with wars on multiple occasions. But now, with the Military turning against you and the town completely out of control, we have no choice but to let you loose."

"Let me loose?" Faulkner paled as he slumped in his chair. He could hear the people getting closer. The devoted army at the front of his building had probably fallen. They were coming for him. They were coming to eradicate him for what he had done. For trying to help them. "You're fools! Fools! I have done everything and more for this town. I have provided valuable assets to the Military. I have done everything, all for my country! For this nation! I demand that you send a helicopter to my roof and retrieve me right now!"

A loud bang sounded below him, and Faulkner hung up. He clutched his phone to his chest and moved as fast as he could toward the elevator. The roof was only on the next floor, but the stairs weren't an option for a man who could barely walk.

He reached the rooftop, panting, his leg throbbing with pain. He looked to the sky, expecting his rescue helicopter. They wouldn't be so stupid as to leave him there. He was a valuable asset to the government. They needed him.

Engines roared in the distance, and Faulkner smiled despite it all.

They did come for me.

But it wasn't a helicopter that showed up between the clouds — it was a plane. Several planes.

Military ones.

Faulkner fell to his knees as he watched in horror, as the plane's hatches opened up, and the bombs were dropped, wiping away the entire city.

ABOUT THE AUTHOR

Viola Tempest is a dystopian fantasy and paranormal romance author who yearns to expose the truth of those in the modern world: the good, the bad, and the ugly. Her inspiration primarily stems from life experiences, those who annoy her, ex-boyfriends, and the crazy dreams that pop into her head every once in a while.

Stalk her below!

Website: https://www.violatempest.com/

Facebook Page: https://www.facebook.com/authorviolatempest

Instagram: https://www.instagram.com/author_violatempest/

Goodreads: https://www.goodreads.com/author/show/21693342.Viola_Tempest

Bookbub: https://www.bookbub.com/authors/viola-tempest